Angel
Of Light

Clash of the Kingdom Realms

D1291004

Patricia Carroll

ISBN 978-1-63630-461-8 (Paperback)
ISBN 978-1-63630-462-5 (Digital)

Covenant Books, Inc.
11661 Hwy 707
Murrells Inlet, SC 29576
www.covenantbooks.com

Second Corinthians 11:14–15

Acknowledgement

I want to thank those people who were instrumental on my author's journey. Jim Wilson for being a great teacher, Kathy Mincer for her constant support and editing expertise, Connie Wolfe for her attention to detail and my wonderful husband Dave for his unconditional love.

chapter 1

June 1998

A dream is a wish your heart makes when you're fast asleep. That's what Cinderella said. She wasn't talking about *my* dreams, especially the one I had just before my world changed.

I was staring into a void until a whisper of mist began forming into a cloud. The cloud descended and hovered in front me. I was fascinated. I felt the presence of a being before I was actually able to see that the cloud was the outline of a man in a long white robe. The bearing of the man was regal. As his face came into focus, I was attracted by the perfectly balanced features. The eyes were intense and communicated a message of wisdom and superiority. The man reached out his hand as if to bestow a gift. I looked at the open hand and saw a key. It was ornate and beautiful. I reached out to grasp the key and my hand closed around it. It seared my palm and the pain was indescribable, but I couldn't let go. In my panic, I looked up to plead with the man for help. No longer was I looking into the beautiful face of the white robed man. The face that now appeared before me was contorted into a mask of malevolence. I began to scream. The sound of my voice hung in the air like an alarm.

The alarm echoed until it bounced back and then changed into a familiar ring. As the source of that noise dawned on me, I also became aware of the fact that my hand was wedged under my pillow with persistent pins and needles. As soon as my hand was free, the sound from my bed side table demanded my attention. I grabbed the phone with my good hand and managed to get out a not too irritated, "Yes?"

"Joy!" The voice on the other end of the line was familiar but strained.

"Claire. What's wrong?" Claire Cohen was a friend. Not just an ordinary friend. We had history. We lived in our own separate states now, but we kept in close contact and managed to get together at least twice a year. She was the kind of friend that when you see them, it's like no time has elapsed since the last time you were in each other's company.

"I, I can't. I just can't do this alone." Claire's voice was halting and racked with pain.

"Claire, what is it? Tell me what's happening." I fought to stay calm even though fear was rising in me.

"It's Jacob. He's missing." The tears were flowing through the phone. "No one has seen him or heard from him in two weeks. He always calls me at least once a week."

"Maybe he just went on a trip or fell in love." I tried to keep my words positive.

"No, his roommate found his suitcases in his closet and his phone was under his bed smashed to pieces. A detective called me this morning asking questions and said that they have put out an APB on his car. I have been so busy with the Sausalito Art Show planning that time got away from me, and I just feel so guilty for not checking on him sooner."

"He's a big boy and has his own life now. Don't blame yourself. I'm sure we will get to the bottom of this. I'm on my way, Claire. Please hold on. I can be there by tonight, and I will be praying all the way."

After reassuring Claire the best I could, I hung up and launched into action. Fortunately, the summer break was just three days away. The fifth graders at Valley View School were going to have to say goodbye to their last elementary year without me. I called all the numbers and secured a sub and a flight. As I packed my bags, I began to see the historical patterns of our lives emerge from the past to the traumatic present.

Claire and I shared a history that reflected the turmoil of our generation. There was a cultural shift that occurred in the 1960s and '70s that broke boundaries and opened doors. Not all those doors led to good places. There was a succession of doors, a chain of events that lead to a destination much farther than intended.

I distinctly remember the first door I opened. It was a warm spring evening in Pasadena, California. It was my sophomore year of college. A welcomed breeze was moving through the eucalyptus trees, an especially clear night for the foothills of the San Gabriels. The LA smog had blown out of the valley and I could even smell freshness in the air. But the breeze could not blow away the tension and frustration I was feeling. I was becoming aware of so many possibilities, and yet I had always been sheltered from them. I was standing behind a plate glass window. I couldn't reach out to touch and taste for myself. I looked up to the clock tower on the campus chapel. I remember saying, "God, I have tried it your way and I just don't see any direction. I want what I have never had, the forbidden fruits. They look so juicy from here." That was it. A point in time, a simple thought, a decision made, and WHAM! The door flew open.

With God tucked into my back pocket, I stepped through the candy store door. The first thing I sampled was a marriage to a young agnostic. He was the first link in the chain that began to form. And it was through my husband that I met Claire. His best friend was married to my soon-to-be best friend. Ah, Claire. She was everything I wanted to be: artistic, outspoken, uninhibited, and a world traveler. She did not suffer from any of the guilt hang-ups of religion. Claire was beautiful and confident. She had an exotic mix of ethnic influences; Italian from her mother and Jewish from her father. Her thick, dark hair and creamy beige complexion made her attractive to all who met her. She became a perfect companion as we began a four-year crash course on how to liberate ourselves. Those were exciting times. The four of us spent a lot of time together. We partied, played, and explored the ever opening world of alternatives. Some of our tools were drugs and alcohol. This was the early seventies. A lot of research had already been done by our generation, and we were going to cash in on all that new ground that others had broken.

"All passengers, please return to your seats and fasten your seat belts. We are making our descent into San Francisco." The pilot's voice brought me back to the present.

Claire had agreed to meet me at the airport even though I assured her I could get a cab to her home in Corte Madera. She was anxious to see me and didn't want to wait. She needed to *do* something. Our greeting was bittersweet. She clung to me and fought her tears. As we let go and our eyes met, I felt all her fear and confusion. I determined to give her as much comfort as I could.

"I am so glad you're here." Claire broke the silence and got us moving toward the baggage claim. I was at a loss for words. I didn't want to cheapen the moment with small talk.

We made it out of the terminal and into her car. As we headed out to Highway 101 north and on to the Golden Gate Bridge, even the beauty of the bay could not change the atmosphere in the car. I had a million questions but wanted to wait for Claire to open the conversation that I knew would evolve as we settled into the familiar surroundings of her home. Claire lived in a "village" in Marin County, just north of Sausalito. She had inherited the home and with support from her ex-husband and proceeds from her artistic endeavors; she lived comfortably in one of the most beautiful areas in California. The bayside shops and restaurants were a blur as we made our way north. We pulled into her driveway and silently went about the business of unloading my luggage and settling into the evening. After a light dinner, we made tea and camped out on the comfy, overstuffed couch in her cozy living room.

"Tell me the whole story," I finally said. I tried to create a safe space for her to let go of her worries as I could see that she was fighting to maintain her emotional balance.

"I was awoken early this morning by a door bell," she began. "A Marin County police officer was at the door and asked if he could come in and speak to me. He said he needed to ask me some questions about Jacob. A missing person's report had been filed by his roommate, Alex." Tears started to flow as she then looked at me with wild eyes. "Why didn't Alex call *me*?"

Claire dried her eyes and blew her nose on the handful of tissues I gave her. "I can't believe it! He was doing so well in his new job. The last we talked, he said he had something important to tell me and would be coming home soon to visit." Her eyes met mine, and I was broken by the pain I saw. "I have to go to Berkley tomorrow to talk to a detective. You have to come with me! I can't face all of this alone. And I am sure Tom will be there. You know how he is in times of crisis. He will be looking to lay blame everywhere but on himself. I mean, I don't *blame* him." She said. "I just don't know what is happening." Claire broke down again and I decided that I would not probe any more tonight. She needed rest, and I hoped the chamomile tea would sooth her enough to allow for some sleep.

I walked with her to her room and sat on her bed as she got ready for the night. I lay in bed with her for a time. Just the comfort of another person near was enough to bring on the sleep she needed. I quietly left the room and headed to the guest room. So many questions were swirling in my head; I knew it would be a fitful night. As I lay awake, I thought about the influences of our early years together and how they may have laid the foundation for Claire's troubles.

Claire and Tom introduced Bruce and me to the "wonders" of marijuana. We went on a hike into the San Gabriel Mountains. We had day packs and enough food and water for the day. Tom had also brought along some very strong pot. We hiked for a while and did not see anyone so we stopped and sat on some rocks and proceeded to learn how to smoke weed.

"Hold it in," Tom said. "You have to get the full effect."

And did we! The disorienting feelings of that first trip were disturbing. I really couldn't enjoy it. I became excruciatingly aware of the centrifugal forces of a revolving planet. I suppose it would have been pretty comical to see me clinging on to rocks and trees to keep from being flung into outer space. That sensation was overtaken by a dramatic realization that I might never return to my normal state of awareness. Since it was my first time, I had no way of knowing that it would indeed wear off. Claire kept reassuring me that I would be just fine. She was my devoted companion through this initiation rite. I don't know why I ever tried it again after this unnerving first experience, but it became an integral part of our social life. How else would I ever expand my consciousness without some means of being propelled over that threshold of normal reality?

We collected a group of friends from all over the LA area and spent many evenings and weekends exploring these alternatives. One of our early "trips" was to Death Valley. We were a family of fellow travelers drawn together by a fabric of our times. We were dedicated to a common cause, to answer the age-old questions: who are we? And what are we doing here? We did arrive at one definite conclusion on this particular camping trip. We were collectively experiencing the timeless nature of the California desert. We felt the inescapable unity of all things. The golden sun poured over us as we basked like lizards on the giant boulders near our camp. Everything seemed so simple. Life was a hilarious joke. It was on that momentous camping trip we all came to the astounding revelation that: IT DOESN'T MATTER, AND IT DOESN'T MATTER THAT IT DOESN'T MATTER. As I thought about that statement now, it seems very silly. But back then, it was of immense importance. It was a license to deviate from trodden paths, to break the rules.

I finally dozed off and dreamt: *I was standing on the banks of a river. I thought it was peaceful until I started to see people in the current. They were desperately trying to swim to shore. I waded out as far as I dared and reached out to grab a woman as she rushed by me. I couldn't connect. Then I heard a voice behind me say, "Here, let me help." I looked back and saw a man coming into the river. I could not really see him well as the sun was shining behind him. As he got closer, I saw his eyes. They were dark brown and held an intensity that both gave me reassurance and concern. Together we began to reach out and pull the people out of the river.*

When I awoke, I was shivering. Not from the cold river, but from the fact that I had kicked my covers off and the cool morning breeze was blowing in from the open window.

Claire and I went about our morning routines and then met in the kitchen for coffee and toast. We knew we would face challenges on this day and reassured each other that we could handle them.

It was a short trip from Marin to Berkley, back over the Golden Gate, and then on to the Bay Bridge. We both wished it had been longer as we dreaded what lie ahead.

I had offered to drive, but Claire needed to be busy, and she knew the roads and the features of her new Lexus RX. We had an appointment with David Kramer, a detective in the Berkeley Police Department. We arrived early and were shown into a waiting room that looked like a holdover from the '70s, nothing fancy. After a few minutes, Detective Kramer entered the room.

"Claire Cohen?" He looked at us and waited for Claire to respond. Claire stood and extended her hand and he nodded and shook *her* hand. "And you are?" He looked at me, and for a moment, I couldn't speak. I felt something shift in the atmosphere. Something about his eyes was so familiar. After an awkward pause, Claire said, "She's my best friend, Joy Morgan from Boise, Idaho."

I couldn't move. I felt like a heavy weight was pressing me into the chair.

Finally the detective just smiled at me and asked us to please step into his office. Something broke and I was able to stand and follow them down a dim hallway and into a small office.

"Your son, Jacob Cohen, was reported missing yesterday morning, although it seems that his roommate last saw him two weeks ago. Do you have regular contact with your son?"

Claire looked down to the hands in her lap, and I felt a stab of pain as I saw her struggling with her guilt. "Yes, although he did miss our regular weekly calls the last couple of weeks. He just started a new job, and I thought he was so busy he just forgot to call."

"His roommate, Alex Turner, said that he thought he was with you. He had talked about a visit." Detective Kramer looked at us both with an intensity that made me feel like I had done something wrong.

Claire responded with a quiver in her voice. "Yes, we talked about a visit, but I have been very busy with a new art exhibit and with his new job, time just flew by."

"I see. I would like you to go to his apartment and see if you can find anything that might lead us to his whereabouts. Do you have access to his room?"

"Yes," Claire replied. "He gave me a key to his apartment and his room, for emergencies. We have a very trusting relationship. I love my son so very much." Claire almost lost her composure as she tried to explain the depths of her feelings for her son.

"LIKE HELL YOU WILL!" a booming voice exploded from the hallway. The detective jumped to his feet and moved quickly to the door. We turned and saw Tom Cohen coming around the corner. Detective Kramer met Tom with equal force and said, "What is this about!"

"I want to know what happened to my son and what you are doing about it." Tom's face was flushed, his dark hair disheveled, and his tie crooked.

"I tried to stop him, sir. I'm sorry." A female sergeant in uniform said as she followed Tom into the office.

"That's okay, Delano. I can take it from here." Detective Kramer assumed command of the situation, and Tom started to settle down. Tom finally noticed Claire and me sitting at the desk and looked surprised to see us.

"Why wasn't I invited to this party?" Tom said as he realized we had taken the only two chairs in front of the desk.

"Mr. Cohen, I assume? We tried to reach you this morning but were only able to leave a voice mail."

"I got it," Tom answered with impatience. He awkwardly stood by the door and radiated his dominance and self-assurance.

"Now that we are all here." Detective Kramer assumed his position of authority. "Let's see if we can recreate Jacob's last few weeks. Tell me about your last communication with your son."

Claire looked at Tom to see who would start. Just to fill the void, Claire began to relay her last conversation with Jacob. "He sounded really upbeat. He had a new job and was excited about the opportunities ahead. He said that he had made some big changes in his life and couldn't wait to tell me about it. I tried to get details, but he said he wanted to talk to me in person. That was the last I heard, and I assumed that he got busy with his new job and would be calling me back to set up a visit home any day. The time just slipped by." The weight of guilt was apparent in her face.

We all looked at Tom, and he hesitated. "Well, I think I talked to him last month some time. He was applying for a new job and wanted to know if I knew anything about the company."

"Is that all? No other contact?" Detective Kramer said, turning his piercing gaze on Tom.

Tom just shrugged and said, "I didn't really know anything about the company and I asked around but everyone in my office came up blank." Tom was a lawyer in a San Francisco firm that employed at least one hundred associates.

"Okay, not much to go on. I have been doing some checking and found that Jacob had just started working for Global Awareness. It's a nonprofit organization that does research on large corporations and their impact on local economies and vulnerable populations. He was a research analyst. He worked for the organization for only two weeks before he just stopped coming in. They tried to reach him with no results." Detective Kramer looked at all of us to see if any of this was ringing any bells.

"Why didn't that Global group call us to see if we knew where he was? We could have had a two-week head start on this fiasco." Tom's face was heating up again. His temper could boil over at any minute.

"I asked that question myself and they said that he only listed his roommate as a contact, and they couldn't get him on his phone either."

We let that sink in, and Claire asked, "Have you talked to Alex, Jacob's roommate?"

"Yes," the detective answered. "But he had been out of the country on a mission trip and only found out about Jacob's absence when he returned yesterday. He called us as soon as he realized that Jacob had been missing for most of the time he was gone."

"This is so crazy! What are you doing to find my son?" Tom's impatience was creating a hostile atmosphere in the small office.

"I assure you, Mr. Cohen, that we are following all the leads we have. Unfortunately, there is not that much to go on."

Tom looked at his watch for the fourth time and said that he had to go but wanted to be kept up to date on all developments.

None of us were sad to see him leave the doorway. I took a deep breath and asked for peace to return to my mind and heart.

"There is one more piece of information that I would like to share with you." Detective Kramer hesitated and then said, "I have met Jacob Cohen. Just recently he began to attend my church."

Claire and I looked at each other with surprise and disbelief. Jacob had never been interested in formal religion and made a point to play down his Jewish ancestry. "I am a member of a Messianic Christian congregation. About a month ago, Jacob was invited by a friend to one of our evangelistic meetings and"—the detective paused to be sure he communicated his next statement carefully—"Jacob gave his life and his heart to Jesus. One week later, he was baptized."

It took some time for this to sink in. Claire was conflicted. She was not raised in a religious family, and though she tolerated my Christian beliefs, we tiptoed around the subjects of salvation and eternal destinations. I, on the other hand, was exploding with excitement and praise inside. I wanted to jump up and dance, shout, and wave my hands in gratitude to God. This was a miracle!

Claire was too shocked to respond. I looked at David Kramer and our eyes communicated everything we could not say at that moment. Eternity interrupted time and we felt the connection that our shared beliefs could only create. Claire's sobs brought us back to the moment and I moved to comfort her.

"Why didn't he tell me? I feel like an outsider to my own son's life. This is too much to take in." Claire's foundations were shaken. She had built her life on shifting sands, and there was nothing to hang onto in times like these. I was reminded of some of the paths we had followed that always seemed to come to a dead end.

In the early days of our friendship, we had experimented with more than marijuana. We explored the world of spiritual alternatives. One of them was self-hypnosis. I wasn't sure what to expect as Claire, Tom, and Bruce and I crowded into their VW bug. We wove in and out of LA traffic and followed the freeway across town to an obscure office building in an industrial part of the city. The teacher looked more like a real estate salesman than a guide to cosmic truth. But we had paid our money and were on the bus. He started out by giving us a good dose of positive thinking straight form Norman Vincent Peal. But we didn't know that at the time and it all was so new to us that we soaked it up like thirsty sponges. Our teacher lured us with promises of wealth and possessions we would gain through the exercise of his techniques. On subsequent visits, we learned the practices of relaxation, guided imagery, and then plunged into the unknown depths of our subconscious minds. To me, it was pretty scary territory. I couldn't help but feel that a person could get lost in there. It may have been this fear or perhaps the protection from above, but there was a barrier beyond which I was not able to go. I found this foray into the supernatural to be frustrating and unsuccessful. I guess that I would never get my Cadillac because I just couldn't master the art of self-hypnosis.

Detective Kramer expressed his concern and then began to lay out some practical steps we could take to aid the investigation. He said that a forensic team had gone through Jacob's room but that he would like Claire and I to inspect it one more time to see if we could find something that would open up more leads. We agreed to meet back at his office around five to compare notes. He escorted us back to the station lobby.

"Okay, I will do some more research," he told us. "You and Joy see if you can find anything in Jacob's apartment. We will meet back here around five," Detective Kramer repeated his plan. Just before we left the front door, he extended his hand to Claire, and he shook it with care and concern. Then his hand came my way, and I slowly reached out; the first touch was electric. I think we clasped hands a little longer than necessary, but we both were caught up in the moment. I flushed and said an abrupt and embarrassed "goodbye." Then Claire and I were on the street headed to her car. Claire looked at me and said, "What was that all about?"

I looked at the ground and didn't know what to say. I was struggling to make sense of it myself.

"Nothing!" I said a bit too strongly, and Claire backed off and let me regain my composure. I had not felt this kind of attraction to a man for quite some time, and I really didn't think it was appropriate under the circumstances. I hadn't had a relationship since I was liberated from my sojourn in the New Age movement. I had given my heart to Jesus, and that had filled my life so completely, I wasn't looking for fulfillment anywhere else. I had only been married once, to Bruce, but my journey in the realm of alternatives opened a door to many relationships. With self as god, it was a simple thing to discard a husband and set out to discover the world of open relationships. After all the song said it all, *Love the one you're with*. I didn't realize that door would lead me into a maze of confusing love and loss. I gained a transcendental attitude toward romances. Marriage was certainly antiquated, and as far as men in my life, more is better. Men became merely companions for trips, playmates, and stepping stones on the path to enlightenment. Of course, I became emotionally attached to some, but even those feelings could be overcome for the higher good...*self*. These thoughts always brought feelings of regret. So I tried not to dwell on my past life. It was behind me for good.

"Let's stop for a bite to eat and some more coffee," I said as we got into the car.

"I am not really hungry." Claire was staring ahead and seemed to be in another world. It was my job to keep her going in a positive direction, and at that moment, it was feeling like a big weight was on us both.

"You have to stay on top of your emotions and sometimes a little food and caffeine can boost your mood," I told Claire. "Let's stop at that little café we like over on the square."

We drove west and found a parking spot right near our destination. I could see Claire relax a little as we entered the comfort of the cafe with its familiar aromas and surroundings. We had spent many pleasant times here sharing our hearts and ideas.

As we sipped our coffee and shared our rice and chicken, I began to build a positive picture of what was an overwhelming task ahead. "We will find something in his apartment that will direct us to the right person to help us unlock this mystery," I told her. "Tell me what Jacob was into these days."

"He was part of an activist group," replied Claire, "called One Humanity. He said that they were working on projects to bring people into a new way of seeing the world. I know that sounds really vague, but that's all I know about it. He had worked with the group for about a year and was being groomed for a leadership position. It was the head of the group that got him his new job. It all sounded so positive and uplifting. He invited me to one of their meetings," she told me. "But I haven't been able to find a time that worked out for both of us."

"One Humanity? I don't think I have heard of them. Who is the leader?"

"His name is Rallen Mandu."

"That's a strange name. Where is he from?"

"He is an American, I think a Californian as well. He spent many years in India studying under many of the spiritual masters. Jacob said he was really powerful and was given a mandate to bring peace to our country. He wrote a book, I think I have it at home somewhere. I haven't had time to look into it myself. In fact every time I have tried to pick it up, something gets in the way."

The sensors of my discernment were screaming! CAUTION! A cold chill went down my spine as I absorbed the information about this group that Jacob had been sucked into. It brought back memories of another time that Claire and I were enticed by darker spirits and then protected from entering that gaping door. I feared that Jacob had stepped too close to the source of deception. His involvement in One Humanity may have cost him his freedom.

chapter 2

In those early days, Claire and I took a course in Hatha yoga. This was my first exposure to Indian mysticism. Taking yoga in LA put you in the mainstream of the guru guild. My sister Shari, Claire, and I just happened to go to a yoga class one night. It was not our usual class, but one that had been recommended by a friend. When we arrived, there was excitement in the air. The class had been canceled in honor of the arrival of a yoga master from the East. We found ourselves swept up in the rush to join the delegation of devotees in a large hillside home. There were refreshments on a long table. I could not recognize anything but the rice, but even it had a reddish color and a biting taste. These were obviously Indian delicacies in keeping with the theme. The expansive living room was crowded with people. Some were in saris and turbans. There was an upper balcony to the room, and from the tension in the air, and the way people kept looking up, I knew that any minute I would be looking at the object of adoration of all in attendance; then he came out in a flowing robe. His hair and long, full beard were salt and pepper. The look in his liquid eyes said everything to the upturned faces of his worshipful followers. So this was Swami Sachedenanda. I can't remember if he said anything or not. But he certainly knew how to make an entrance.

The study of Eastern religions was a basic for all who would attain a degree in cosmic consciousness. I remember the life-altering day that I locked myself in my room with a copy of *Be Here Now.* It was a mega-dose of all the distilled wisdom of Eastern religion and the hard earned revelations of the drug culture. It was like a birthing.

I came out of my room a bona fide member of the "me generation." That's what it was really, an outrageous excuse for self-absorption. But this information was so fresh, so exhilarating. How was I to know that it was as old as Babylon and the Garden of Eden? It all boiled down to the same old lie. YOU CAN BE AS GOD. That was the selling point. That was the reason for all my excitement. I had come to believe this age-old lie from the beginning of time. It sucked me in and drew me deeper into error.

We pulled into a parking space at the apartment complex where Jacob had been living. Claire had a key, and we let ourselves into the living room. We were both pleasantly surprised by the appearance of the room. It was colorful and neat. Even the air was sweet with the aroma of lemon grass from an air freshener in the corner. We made our way to Jacob's room. We both felt a pang of sorrow as we opened the door. We could tell that it had been searched but was in reasonable order.

"You take the closet, I'll take the desk," said Claire.

We systematically worked our way through the room for a few minutes when Claire held up a notebook and said, "I think this is his journal." We sat on his bed and looked at the notebook deciding whether it was permissible to open up his secrets. The decision made, we started to read entries that had begun about a year ago and contained sporadic dates.

"I recognize the handwriting, but the way he expresses his thoughts sounds so different than the Jacob I know." Claire shook her head and looked at me with confusion all over her face. "He was such a happy boy and so loving and open. I know that we have been more distant as he struck out on his own, but this is making me wonder if I should have kept closer tabs on his emotional state."

The journal was a roller coaster ride of joy and depression as he searched for his identity. Then the tone changed to one of hope and curiosity as he told about his encounters with the One Humanity group. He made connections and was awed by the wisdom of its leader, Rallen Mandu. We skipped a few of the rambling pages of exploration of the mystical concepts he was learning. As the dates grew closer to the present, the tone changed again from acceptance to skepticism.

"*I will not allow the leadership to restrict my actions and expressions like this. I thought we were a free and open community,*" Jacob said in his entry dated about three months ago. "*I know they want me to take the leap into the next level but at what cost? Rallen says that I am special and can do a lot of good, but I am beginning to see some of the motives behind that smiling face.*"

Red flags were beginning to show in Jacob's experiences with the OH group. Claire and I looked at each other after reading a few more entries that questioned the foundations of the group. We both said OH? Which got a giggle out of us, but we knew we were treading on serious ground.

"Look at this entry!" Claire got excited and pointed to a page with all caps. "*THIS IS IT! IT ALL MAKES SENSE NOW. I SEE EVERYTHING SO CLEARLY.*" Under this line was a rapidly scribbled paragraph. "*Collin took me to the Rock tonight and I was not really eager to go, but since he was so happy about it, I decided to go to just get him off my back. It was so different! I knew it was a church, but it sure didn't feel like any church I ever heard about before. The music was great. A whole rock band, and then some. The people were really friendly. There must have been a couple hundred kids dancing and singing. I didn't know you could dance at a church! Anyway this guy got up and said some stuff about Jesus. I never really thought about him as a real person. But when he finished, I felt this tingling and I knew that I needed to meet Jesus for real. I went up front and something happened. I fell down on my knees and got overwhelmed by the load of mistakes and wrong things I ever said or did. Then I saw HIM! It WAS Jesus! He held his arms out to me and all I could say was 'I want you.' Then I felt his arms around me and all the love I could ever dream of came all around me. My friend Collin says that I am saved now. What? I didn't even know I needed saving, but I feel so good! I want to keep this going. I want to find out everything about Jesus and this salvation thing. And now looking from this vantage point, I see right through Rallen and the OH. I know what I have to do!*"

We both sat and soaked it in. I felt tears streaming down my face and was so full of gratitude and praise I almost jumped up and shouted, but then I looked at Claire and saw the pain and confusion and quickly corralled my emotions. "I can't believe this!" Claire said. "He was raised to be open minded and a free thinker. He knew all about alternative religions. Why would he fall for this Jesus cult? I mean, I know you go to a regular church, Joy, and I respect your decision to follow your faith." She was backpedaling and trying to cover up her prejudices against Christianity. She had rejected her Jewish roots and had never left the continuous quest for "enlightenment." Religious affiliation was one subject we always tread lightly on when we were together.

"I believe he found something authentic and real, and personally I am thrilled for him." I hoped that she would at least entertain the reality of Jacob's conversion.

We turned the page and found it blank. That was his last entry almost a month ago. The ominous last sentence hung over us: "I know what I have to do."

What was it he had to do and did it lead to his disappearance? We needed to know more about this One Humanity group and their leader. Could they have anything to do with Jacob's absence for the last two weeks? We also needed to talk to this Collin person to see if he knew anything. We began to search the room again and Claire found a few phone numbers on a scrap of paper in his desk. We took the numbers and the journal with us as we left the apartment. It was about three thirty, and we needed to be back at the police station at five.

We drove to the station and just sat in her car for a while. We were both reeling from all the information of the last few hours. Our friendship had been through so many momentous events that we did not feel the need to analyze the present. The night that Claire and I left our husbands was one of those events that stood out. We both had begun to be disenchanted with marriage. We needed space to explore.

One night, and this is ironic, we were shopping for a wedding gift for a friend. We had walked into town from Bruce and my little bungalow in Monrovia. My sister, Shari, who was a seven-month veteran of divorce, lived just a block off the street of shops we were looking through. We casually stopped in for a visit. We smoked a little and began talking of liberation and Shari's newfound freedom became infectious. The pep rally grew in intensity till we were making a rousing pact of sisterhood. I can't remember if we actually did the blood mingling ceremony or not, but the effect was the same. Claire and I, with great resolve, decided that we would tell our husbands that very night. Well, in the meantime, Tom and Bruce came looking for us and found us at Shari's place. The air was electric as they entered the room. They knew something was up. Claire and I took them back to my house to break the news. We packed a bag and crashed at Shari's that night. The next day, we were house shopping. We found a three-bedroom in Altadena that fit our artistic needs perfectly. That was it. We were single without a glance back. I thought of that story now with an ache in my heart. How could we have been so cold? Practice makes perfect. Though Claire eventually returned to her marriage, I never looked back.

Claire and I entered the station with Jacob's journal in hand. We were quickly led into the back offices by Sgt. Delano. Detective Kramer stood from his desk as we entered, his eyes focusing on the journal Claire was holding.

"What do you have there?"

"It's Jacob's journal. I'm not sure how much help it will be, but it does have another contact that we could explore. The friend that brought him to your church may know something. His name is Collin. Do you know him?" Claire reluctantly held out the journal.

"Yes, I know him. I knew that he was friends with Jacob and I have talked to him already. He has been wondering where Jacob has been since he was so involved with the Rock youth group and then just stopped coming. He and the group have been praying for Jacob."

"Is that all you have?" Claire sounded on the verge of tears.

"No, I've done some digging and discovered some interesting information about the One Humanity group. They were founded by Rallen Mandu in 1985 in Malibu, California. Rallen had inherited a large sum of money from his father and used some of it to travel to India to study under several so called masters of Eastern religious practices. He says that he had an encounter with a spirit being who recruited him to take the "truth" to the states and set up an organization that would transform the American culture. He used his large ocean side home to recruit his followers with weekend seminars. For the last two decades, he has managed to grow his organization to about twenty thousand members. He has pockets of devotees all over the US: Ashland, Oregon, Shasta, California, and Sedona, Arizona, so called hot spots for new-age activity. He travels extensively speaking at various conferences and gatherings. You can see many of his presentations on the internet. He has a rather hypnotizing effect on people."

Claire jumped to her feet and said. "I knew it! He used some kind of hypnotic power on my son. I don't think that Jacob would join a group like that of his own free will."

I took her hand and eased her back into the chair in front of the detective's desk. "Claire, we need to stay focused and calm. We will take this one step at a time with the detective's help and find out if the OH had anything to do with Jacob's disappearance."

"We have tried to contact Rallen," Detective Kramer pressed on as he gave Claire a nod, "but he is well insulated by his core group. They said he is out of town at the moment and won't be back for a week. I asked if I could set up an interview with him and they were very evasive. However, I will make a visit to his headquarters when he returns and demand that he sees me to answer questions about his relationship with Jacob."

"A WEEK!" Claire's eyes got big and she was about to explode. "We can't wait another week to get information from the OH."

"You met Sgt. Delano. She will be visiting the Berkeley center and posing as a seeker. She will go undercover for a few days and see if she can identify someone who would talk about Jacob."

"You can't be more aggressive? I mean, get a warrant and bust in there!" Claire was ready for action.

"Mrs. Cohen, we have to approach this carefully. We don't have any evidence linking the OH to your son's disappearance. I feel a more subtle approach is best. We may be able to shake something loose that will lead to some hard evidence. And please do not visit the center yourself. We do not want to alert anyone to our investigation." Detective Kramer gave Claire one of his serious stare's.

chapter 3

We wrapped up our session with the detective and headed out to the car and then out of Berkeley. When we were back in Claire's home, we collapsed on her couch and discussed our progress or lack thereof. We focused on the OH group and decided to look it up on the internet. We went to Claire's office and booted up her PC. It didn't take long to pull up a slick video on the virtues of Rallen Mandu and his enlightened vision of a transformed society. There was a link to one of his "channelings." He said that these concepts were not from him but from the ascended masters who were guiding him.

My defenses were heightening as I recognized the ear marks of error that I knew all too well. After Claire and I had left our husbands and spent six months partying in Altadena, we took a summer trip to Europe. We backpacked and toured with our Eur-rail passes for three months. We returned to California and decided to ditch our old lives and move north to Arcata. We had friends who had moved there recently, rented a large house, and said we could come up and share. This was the same group that we had "shared" with at our party pad. So Claire and I moved to Northern California. We just happened to have a couple of friends that wanted to be more than friends, and we moved into their rooms and experienced the joys and sorrows of communal living. It didn't take long to burn out as Claire and I became chief cooks and bottle washers to a bunch of pot heads.

I recall how Claire was getting regular calls from Tom. He wanted her to come back to him. This was amazing, since most male egos would not tolerate the wayward nature of his wife. She was conflicted. She finally decided to go back to LA and stay with Tom for a while to see if this is what she really wanted. She talked me into going with her. She packed up her belongings in her little yellow bug and we set off for So Cal. About two hundred miles later, she stopped abruptly by the side of the road and said, "NO! I can't go back. What was I thinking?"

She turned the car around and headed back north. We only got about twenty miles before she stopped again and sat behind the wheel, frozen with fear. She had ended things with Steven and just couldn't go back to him. So she turned the car back around and we headed south again. We stopped at a cheap motel to spend the night, and for about two hours, Claire paced the floor going back and forth on whether she should return to Tom or beg Steven to take her back. Thinking about it now, I wonder, were those the only two options? Anyway, she was caught in this dualistic dilemma. I don't think I was much help. I was experiencing my own feelings of not knowing where I belonged in the world.

We started out the next morning, and I was not sure if Claire would turn south or north. She only hesitated a few moments and then she turned south and resumed her life with Tom, and eventually Jacob came along and fulfilled many of her longings.

That turning point in Claire's life coincided with my own departure from my life path. After visiting friends in Los Angeles, I called my sister in Berkeley and said I wanted to visit on my way back north. I borrowed a car and drove north. Shari had joined a group that was housed in two former fraternity houses in the hills above the Berkeley Campus. I was not prepared for the impact of this very organized, yet free expression of communal living. It was nothing like the Arcata house. These people were joyfully following the teachings of their founder Michael Gabriel. They called themselves a family, and there were a few children running around to prove it.

Michael had published a book, *The New Gospel*. It contained the automatic writings of a man who claimed to have been beamed aboard a flying saucer and given the plan for humanity to take the quantum leap into the fourth dimension. He was chosen to be the messenger for the New Age covenant.

The Universal Mind, Michaels's idea of God, was bringing mankind to a great turning point in which we all would gain the cosmic consciousness necessary to become citizens of the universe. This may sound infinitely absurd, but to me at that time, it all made perfect sense. Michael's writings were laced with all the right buzz words and sprinkled with enough well-chosen scriptures to give it credibility to a person coming out of a Christian background, such as myself. It seemed to tie all the strands together and provided a missionary zeal that hooked me right off the bat. I had always felt mission oriented, and this new age family spoke to that need in me. We had to tell the world about our space brothers and sisters who were just waiting around out in our outer atmosphere to show us the way to bring peace on Earth. They offered an end to all poverty and disease. They had all the technology to transform this world into a Garden of Eden. We just had to inform the world of their existence and teach them how to transcend into that level of consciousness that would allow them to communicate with us directly. We had to preach the brotherhood of man and bring an end to nationalistic boundaries. All my training had prepared me for this ultimate calling. I was going to be a big shot in the new world government. I was getting in on the ground floor with Michael and the comrades of the Cosmic Earth Collective. Yes, this group had something for everyone. Marxism was a part of the founding principles that would bring about a world that shared everything.

Claire and I spent a tension-filled three days at her home. We did venture out for groceries and to have a light lunch in one of her favorite restaurants. We both jumped when the phone rang on Sunday, the evening of the third day. It was Detective Kramer and he said he had some good news. That got us pretty excited, until he explained that the undercover work was fruitful and that he had managed to schedule an appointment with Rallen Mandu the next day. Rallen was back in the area, and according to his assistant, was eager to clear things up and assure us that the OH had no idea where Jacob could be. Detective Kramer wanted us to come to the station and accompany him to the interview. He asked us to arrive a couple of hours before we went to the OH headquarters, so he could share all his information and prepare us for the confrontation with Rallen Mandu. Claire and I spent the evening on edge, anticipating the day ahead.

It was a restless night. Toward morning, I awoke with a start. My dream was very vivid and I remembered it in detail: *I was walking down a road in the country side. The air was warm, and as I looked around, I saw a few people walking toward me. They were dressed in saris and loose tunics. They looked at me as they passed by but did not acknowledge my presence. Their blank stares were unnerving. I walked by a high wall and felt a presence emanating from the space it surrounded. I came to an archway and was drawn into the entrance, even though I was fearful of what lie inside. I followed a path to a building that was brightly painted and had strange symbols and paintings of animals on it. I recognized some of them as Indian deities. The door to the building was open, and I knew I had to enter, even though I really wanted to run the other way. Once inside, it was a maze of corridors and rooms. Thick clouds of incense were floating through the passageways. I heard voices and followed the sound to its source. A man was standing over a person curled up on the floor. "You will renounce your false god and surrender to my will!"*

The person on the floor was moaning and saying, "No, no, no," over and over. Suddenly, the man turned and saw me in the doorway. "You again," he said in a harsh voice.

I wanted to scream, but could not make a sound, for that man was the same "key" man I had seen in my dream before I got Claire's call; that seemed like weeks ago. Then I looked at the person on the floor and saw who it was. It was Jacob! I was so shocked that it woke me and I lay in bed for some time, trying to make sense of the dream.

I didn't tell Claire about the dream. I was still troubled by its meaning. We busied ourselves with preparations for the day ahead. The drive to Berkeley was a silent interlude before the looming events we knew would come. We made it to the police station with plenty of time to meet with Detective Kramer. He told us about Sgt. Delano's visit to One Humanity. She went as a curious young seeker open to alternative religious ideas. A woman named Naomi befriended her and explained the basics of their beliefs. They were founded on a compilation of Eastern religions and a "synthesis" of Western faiths. The distilled truths were affirmed by Rallen Mandu's connection with several ascended masters who communicated with him as he moved into a high level of consciousness. It was all wrapped in love and peace, of course. All of this sounded far too familiar to me and warning bells continued to go off.

"Sergeant Delano is not through with her investigation but picked up some hints that all was not really so peaceful in the center. While she was there, she said that a man stormed out of one of the offices and confronted Naomi about some missing documents and the fact that he knew that she was responsible for their disappearance. Naomi reassured Delano that it was a misunderstanding. However, they had lunch in the dining room, and as they entered, a young woman was sitting in a corner by herself with tears running down her face. When Delano asked about it, her guide just dismissed it as growing pains."

"That all sounds interesting, but what does it have to do with Jacob?" Claire was impatient and wanted to see some real progress toward finding her son.

"I am just laying some foundation for what you may encounter today," he explained. "We have also done some background checks on the leadership of the group and there are some shady characters involved. Not the least is Mandu, himself. His real name is Milo Ripley, and he was indicted years ago on fraud charges but never convicted due to some very expensive legal representation. It was some kind of pyramid scheme. Some of the leadership team also has questionable pasts. Actually, the FBI has had their eye on the OH for some time, and I will be meeting with one of their agents to get some more background."

"Shall we meet you at the center?" I asked to get things moving.

"I would like you both to ride with me for safety purposes."

Claire and I exchanged a look and decided that we would take Detective Kramer's recommendation since we did not feel comfortable approaching the OH center on our own. We followed him to the parking lot and loaded into his unmarked Toyota. It was a quick trip to the foothills and the looming three story Victorian style home. We climbed some stairs and entered the front offices. A receptionist took our names and asked us to wait a few moments for our interview with Rallen Mandu. Apprehension was increasing as we did not know what to expect from our meeting with the head of One Humanity. The receptionist returned and asked us to follow her through a maze of corridors and into a large office that was colorful and decorated with many diverse religious symbols. There was a cross on one wall and a yin/yang symbol on another. The carpet was patterned after a Buddhist sand painting.

Behind a large desk sat a man with thick dark hair that framed his tanned face with curls and waves. As he stood, I saw that he wore a robe with full sleeves, belted at the waste. He spoke, and *then* I saw his eyes. Those eyes! They were the same ones that had haunted my dreams for the past few days—the eyes that could communicate such benevolence and then flash the essence of evil. I was stunned. I stopped in my tracks and could not move until the sound of Claire's voice penetrated my consciousness.

"Joy? Joy, are you okay?"

I finally regained my composure and managed to nod to Rallen as he gave me a look of recognition and suspicion. The smile returned to his face as soon as the attention was back on him, and he continued to welcome us and steer us to a sitting area with a couch and two velvet chairs. He, of course, took the larger chair and sat with an air of command.

"What can I do to help you?" Rallen opened the conversation and conveyed his complete cooperation with our inquiry.

"We are trying to piece together the last two weeks of one of your members. Jacob Cohen has been missing, and we are following every lead to discover his whereabouts." Detective Kramer took the lead. "Claire is his mother and has regular contact with her son and that contact stopped abruptly. Do you have any information on his activities here at the Center? Could he have gone on a mission trip for your group?"

"I was alerted to your investigation by my secretary. I have checked with some of Jacob's contacts here, and they also noticed he just stopped all communication about two weeks ago. They did not have any relevant information as to why."

"Would it be possible to question one of his close associates?"

"Let me call Naomi and see if she is available. She is in charge of all of our newer members," he told us.

Rallen went to his desk and made a call, and in his absence, Claire and I exchanged looks. Hers said, "What's going on with you?"

Mine just said, "I am reeling and will have to tell you about it later."

We both looked at Detective Kramer, and his face read, "Something is not right here."

"Naomi will be here in just a few minutes. I want to assure you that we take this matter very seriously. Jacob was an integral part of our Center, even though he was relatively new. He embraced our message and mission with his whole being. We were grooming him for leadership."

"What is your mission?" Detective Cohen asked.

"In a nutshell, it is to spread love and healing across the planet. We embrace all faiths and want to see humanity make the leap to the next stage of evolution and become one."

"That's pretty vague. What do you *do* to complete your mission?"

"We have Centers all over the West and we spread our message and invite enlightened individuals to join us in our quest for peace."

It was clear that this answer did not satisfy the detective and he was about to probe more deeply when the door opened and a woman walked in. She had long blond hair that cascaded around her lovely face. She wore flowing pants and a tunic that hung perfectly on her tall frame.

"Ah, Naomi!" Rallen greeted her with apparent relief. "This is Detective Kramer and Jacob Cohen's mother and…her friend. They want to ask you about your interaction with Jacob here at the center, and if you have seen him in the last few days."

"Jacob was really special," she said. "We all saw great potential for him in the Community. He embraced the principles of One Humanity with such passion. He was a regular here until a couple of weeks ago, and then just stopped coming. I called him and even stopped by his apartment but could not make contact. I assumed that he had gone on a trip or was taking some time to decide his level of involvement here as we were offering him a path to leadership."

"Did he tell anyone here what his plans were?" Detective Kramer asked.

"Not that I could discover. I am sure he will return when he is ready."

The conversation stalled and the detective gave his card to both Rallen and Naomi and asked them to please contact him if they found any new information about Jacob.

We were ushered out of the building and returned to the car. We all sat for a while and thought about our encounter with the OH. I was in turmoil. I wanted to tell Claire and Detective Kramer about my dream, and the recognition that passed between me and Rallen Mandu, but I didn't know if they would take it seriously. I didn't want to damage my credibility with the detective.

We started out into the early afternoon traffic and headed back to the station. As we made a turn west, a large black SUV headed full speed right toward the driver's side of our vehicle. Time stood still as we all saw there was no way we could avoid a collision. Then the strangest thing happened. It was like we were in a bubble of air, and it gently floated us to the shoulder of the street. We sat for a few minutes and tried to understand what had just happened. I looked at Detective Kramer and saw an expression of awe and amazement. I couldn't help but believe that he knew exactly what or who had sheltered us from sure disaster. When we had all regained our composure, Claire said, "What just happened?"

"I believe that there are forces of good and evil that we cannot see with our human eyes," Detective Kramer said. "We just witnessed a triumph of good. There is something going on with the OH that is beyond Jacob's disappearance. Someone does not want us to continue our investigation. We must be very vigilant now because this threat is *not* over." Detective Kramer's voice assumed a calm and command that was reassuring despite the obvious peril we were facing.

We continued to our destination and when we arrived at the police station, we were asked to come into the office to give a statement about our visit to the OH. By tacit agreement, we all left out the near collision—even though we knew that it was an added layer to the facts of the case.

When Claire and I finally made it home that evening, we were exhausted. We had a light dinner and then retired to the cozy couches and sipped our tea. We knew we wanted to talk about the day, but were not looking forward to delving into all the ramifications of our experiences.

Claire broke the ice by asking, "What did Kramer mean by 'forces of good and evil'? He seemed to know more than he was telling."

"I think he has some special insight into the nature of people that only someone who deals with good-and-bad, life-and-death situations would have. He sees things that we would dismiss as coincidental. But what happened with the near accident goes beyond your everyday experience. I know that even he was overwhelmed with the way we were protected. You could say that it was *supernatural*."

"Supernatural? Even in all my studies of spiritual disciplines, I have not heard of that level of intervention. I felt like we were transported on a wave of air. What could possibly do that?" Claire was seeking answers that I hoped she would accept—the answers that were based on the truth of God's Kingdom Realm.

"Do you really want to know?" I was opening a door that we had avoided for years. I felt that she might just be ready to hear what I had to say.

"Yes! I have to understand what is happening so I can find Jacob."

"When Detective Kramer said that there are forces of good and evil, he was declaring the reality of the unseen realm. We are in a battle between good, which is God's will and influence in our lives, and evil, which is the demonic realm. There are three heavens. The sky we see is the first heaven. The domain of God and his Heavenly Hosts is the third heaven. And in between is the realm of Satan and his host of ministers of evil. Planet Earth is the battleground and *we* are the prize. You probably think that this sounds like a fairy tale, Claire. But to ignore this fact is to jeopardize your eternal destiny.

What happened today was a physical manifestation of God's protection and we are on a very important mission or else we would not have been spared in such a dramatic way."

"You know that this is very hard for me to believe. But I cannot deny that I felt a tingling sensation when we were lifted out of the path of that SUV. It felt like we crossed into another dimension for a moment, long enough for us to be swept to safety."

I was praising God under my breath as I saw the opening of Claire's mind to the possibility of that truth. If she could recognize God's hand in her life, she may be able to see how Jesus has been perusing her all along.

"I need to tell you about the dreams that I have had since I started on this journey with you," I finally said. I heard a whisper from God that gave me a release to tell Claire about the gift of dreams that I was beginning to see as a calling in my life.

We spent the next hour exploring the meaning of my dreams about the man with the evil eyes. I finally said, "I believe that man is Rallen Mandu and he is behind Jacob's disappearance. He is a master of disguise and can appear as a minister of peace when he is really orchestrating plans for evil behind the scenes. Remember what Jacob said in his journal? He knew something was wrong at the OH and he was going to expose it. What if Rallen stopped him and has hidden him somewhere so that he cannot act on the knowledge he has? It all makes sense if you put the pieces together."

A look of revelation grew on Clair's face as she absorbed all the implications.

"We have to call Kramer right now and tell him!"

"Not so fast," I cautioned. "Let's get a plan together first. If we go ahead with these accusations and our evidence is a set of dreams and supernatural experiences, we could cause more harm than good. I think the detective is open to our input, but we have to get something credible that he can present to his superiors that will allow him to follow the Mandu lead."

We both agreed that we would sleep on it, hoping that we would be able to sleep. I asked Claire if I could pray with her before we went to bed. She said yes, and I took this as a sign that she was softening toward the Lord.

"Father, I thank you for your protection today and for Detective Kramer who is helping us to find Jacob. I ask for further protection as we pursue the path that you are preparing before us. Let your angelic hosts stand over Jacob and ourselves. We put our trust in you and know that you will provide and protect us on this journey. I ask these things in Jesus's name. Amen."

Claire thanked me for the prayer and we headed off to our rooms.

It took some time for me to calm my mind. I used my declaration, "release and relax" a few times before I felt the tension and trauma of the day start to ease away. I did not know what the next day would hold, but I knew who held that day in His hand.

chapter 4

*M*y world was on fire. I was running on a path that was barely passable between the flames. I came to a cliff and knew that if I could just scale down the steep precipice, I would be safe from the menacing inferno. I looked, and it was a frightening height. I could see no way down. Suddenly a presence surrounded me with peace and confidence. A ladder appeared before me and I began to climb down the cliff face. As I descended, I could feel gentle hands supporting me as I took each rung, one by one. When I reached the bottom of the cliff, I was in a green garden and all traces of fire were gone. A sweet aroma filled my senses.

I opened my eyes and could still feel the comfort I had experienced in my dream. And I could smell freshly baked sweet bread coming from Claire's kitchen. I pulled myself from the bed and wandered out to see what was happening.

"Good morning, sleepyhead. I thought you would be in bed all morning." Claire was standing over a loaf of banana bread that she had just turned out on the wooden top of the island in her kitchen. "I just had an urge to bake when I woke up this morning. It calms me."

"I'm not complaining. I love your baked goods. You were always the best baker back in our communal days. I'm going to get a bath before breakfast. Save some of that gorgeous bread for me." The smells and feelings of the moment led me to consider the past again as I drew a bath and settled in for a soak.

After Claire returned to LA and to her home with Tom, and I made that fateful visit to my sister Shari in Berkley, Claire came to visit me at the commune. She was feeling restless again, and her visit turned into a six-month stay. Our first assignment at the Andromeda house, one of the residences for the commune, was on the breakfast detail. It was like KP in the army. Definitely boot camp. When Claire came, she shared my room and we worked the morning shift together. The first order of the day was to clean up all the messes from the midnight munchers. Considering that the communal members were serious pot smokers, there were always signs of their nocturnal exploits in the kitchen. After cleaning up, we had to fix a hearty, wholesome meal for twenty to thirty people. It was a thankless job since most of the people who came in for breakfast were either busy with kids, or too hung over to notice anything.

There were two big houses right next door to each other that formed the living quarters of the commune. Your status in the commune was exhibited by the location and size of your room and your function in the group. It soon became evident that the highest-ranking positions around had to do with the "music school." All the jobs in the commune were called schools. They were schools of experience where we were learning the ways and means of organizing society into a new order for the Aquarian Age. That gave us all a sense of importance, but the real power went to the people who were involved with the communication of the message to the world. Since rock music was so much a part our cultural experience, it took first place in the hierarchy. We had a band called Pulsar. One married couple formed the core of the band, and John was the leader and one of the song writers. We had a natural foods restaurant, bakery, and music venue right on Haight Street.

One Saturday night, we had a visit from Tom Cohen. He came to the Andromeda house and found Claire and me hanging out in the living room. We were both surprised to see him although he had been calling often, begging Claire to come home. They left the house and were gone for some time. Tom was not comfortable with the communal vibe. When they came back, Claire found me in our room and her eyes were red. She said she had to get back to reality and was leaving with Tom. I tried to reason with her, but it was not working. I hugged her and said I would miss my breakfast buddy.

I followed her out. I watched as Tom drove her away. One thing you could say about Tom, he never gave up loving Claire and would always take her back no matter what, but Claire's independent streak would finally win out.

After my bath, I entered the kitchen to find Claire talking to Tom on the phone. I was surprised—*just as I had been thinking about him*. "No, Tom, I don't want outside influences in this. We have to give the police a chance to follow the leads. You could make things worse or even get him killed!" Claire listened for a while and then just said goodbye.

"What was that about?" I asked.

"Tom wants to hire a private company to find Jacob, another typical Tom solution, just throw money at the problem. But I can't blame him for seeking help. I just don't want someone getting in the way of the police investigation. I trust Detective Kramer to get some answers soon."

"Speaking of Detective Kramer," I said, "we should call him this morning and find out what the next move might be. We have to keep the pressure on so Jacob stays a top priority." I was also feeling the need for action.

"Could you call him? I have to get a shower and get ready for whatever this day holds."

I picked up the phone and dialed a number I knew by heart. Detective Kramer picked up on the third ring. He said he had a plan to dig deeper into Jacob's background and had set up a meeting with Alex, Jacob's roommate, later that day. He asked if we could meet him at the station at one.

After a brunch of eggs and banana bread, Claire and I headed out to Berkeley. We were a little early for our meeting with the detective, so we stopped and got a coffee at our favorite spot. I noticed a familiar face sitting at a corner table. I started to smile but was stopped dead when I saw her look of judgment and hate. It was Naomi, the woman from OH that we had questioned on our visit. She quickly broke eye contact and began studying the book in front of her. A cold chill coursed through my veins. What did that look mean? She seemed so helpful when we saw her at the center. As we left the café, I asked Claire if she had seen Naomi. She said, "Who?"

"Naomi from the center, she was in the corner, by the window."

"No, I was too distracted thinking about our meeting today. Was there something about her?" Claire asked as she saw the look of concern on my face.

"She just looked really mean."

"Mean? Like, how?"

"Oh, I don't know. Let's just get going to the station. We don't want to be late."

We made it to the police station with a few minutes to spare and were ushered right into David Kramer's office. He said they had not made much progress at the One Humanity center because Sgt. Delano felt that her cover had been blown. Her next task would be to track down some former members and see if she could dig up some dirt on the group. Kramer said that he wanted to follow up on some more loose ends, and that is why he had set up the meeting with Alex. He asked us to ride with him again, and Claire and I looked at each other to confirm that this would be a good idea considering what had happened last time. After some reassuring words from Detective Kramer, we decided to take him up on his offer.

We arrived at the second-story apartment safely and were welcomed in by Alex. We sat with him in the living room for a few minutes and asked him some questions about Jacob's routines and habits. Detective Kramer took notes and asked some important questions about the last time Alex and Jacob were together. As we were winding up our inquiry, we started to smell smoke. We all looked at each other with questions and fear. The smoke alarm in the kitchen started to blare, and Alex ran there to check the stove. The smoke was not coming from the kitchen. He started to go to the door to the hallway when Detective Kramer jumped up and ran to the door and put his hand on the surface.

"It's HOT! Alex, is there another exit?"

Alex was frozen with fear and started to look around wildly. "No, the fire escape was taken down a month ago."

We all moved to the back of the apartment to Jacob's room and looked out the window. It was a good twenty feet to the paved alley below. David Kramer closed the bedroom door and opened the window. He then went directly to the closet and grabbed a bundle. He threw the rolled end of a rope ladder out the window and hooked the upper end to the sill.

"Alex, you go down first and hold the end of the ladder." The smell of smoke was stronger now, and Alex focused quickly on the importance of his task. Out the window, he went and called up when he was in place. Claire went next, and I waited for her to make it to the ground. I scrambled down behind and took each rung carefully, but my foot slipped, and I felt like I would fall. I frantically looked up and saw David leaning out the window, and the look of confidence gave me hope. I also felt an unseen hand steady me as I regained my balance and continued down the ladder. We all made it safely to the alley and heard the sirens grow louder as help was on the way.

"I made a quick call to 911. Let's get away from this building, and let the fire department do their job," Detective Kramer said as he led us out to a safe distance on the street. Luckily, he had parked away from the building and we gathered around his car.

"How did you know where the ladder was?" Claire asked in amazement.

"I had a feeling that Jacob was the careful type and would not let his and Alex's safety be jeopardized."

"But you went right to it," Alex said.

"That is not important right now. We need to find out how the fire got started and I can't help but feel it is connected to Jacob's disappearance and his connection to the OH. I believe someone is trying to scare us away from this investigation. But they do not know these close calls just make me more determined to find the source."

After making sure Alex had a place to stay, Detective Kramer drove Claire and I back to the station and would not return to his office until he was sure that we were okay and could make it back to Marin. We assured him we would be fine. We sat in Claire's SUV for a while, just to collect ourselves before we started for home. Claire's anxiety over Jacob's safety was growing with each threatening experience we faced. In my spirit, I knew that Jacob was still alive and we would find him. I did my best to relay that confidence to Claire. As soon as we were back at Claire's home, she called Tom to tell him what had happened and, of course, there was a heated discussion. Tom was more convinced than ever of the need for some outside help. Claire was hard-pressed to keep him from acting after the two close calls we had. She agreed to his demand for a private investigation.

I cautiously agreed with the decision and said to Claire, "We should call Alex and make sure he is settled at his friend's house. Maybe he has some information about the fire and how much damage was done to their apartment. I really hope there was no destruction to any clues to Jacob's situation." I felt giving Claire a task might just help relieve some of the stress of the day, and of her discussion with Tom.

As she dialed Alex's number, I went to my room and closed the door. I needed some time to myself and with the Lord. "What is going on, Father?" I prayed. "I'm scared! I know that you have protected us from harm, but the event today really tested my faith." I sat quietly on the bed and listened to see if He had anything to say that would ease my fears. I felt led to open my Bible and my eyes fell to Isaiah 41:10. *"Fear not, for I am with you; be not dismayed for I am your God; I will strengthen you, I will help you, I will uphold you with my righteous right hand."* And it was at that moment that I remembered the feeling of a hand holding me as I slipped on the rope ladder earlier that day. I could not contain my gratitude and love for my Heavenly Father as I realized the truth of His word. He really was holding me! The tears flowed, and with them, much of the stress of all that was happening flowed out of me, and God's peace descended like a blanket. I fell back on the pillows of the bed and rested in His presence. The next thing I knew, Claire was knocking on my door.

"I made some veggie soup. You've been asleep for two hours. Are you hungry? Our last meal was this morning."

"I'll be right out. Thanks!" I was refreshed. My faith and confidence were renewed.

I knew that God was with me, and in Him, I could face whatever the next day might bring.

After dinner there was a knock on the front door and Claire and I stopped our kitchen cleaning duties to look at each other. *Who could it be?*

"Are you expecting anyone?" I asked with a rising tension in my voice.

"No." The knocking grew louder.

"I guess I had better see who it is," Claire said as she moved to the front of the house and peeked through the side lights of the door and saw Tom Cohen. We were both relieved but also not really happy to see him.

"It's about time!" Tom came through the door with his usual brash manner. "I came over to give you an update on the progress of the private search for Jacob."

"Already? I thought you just hired them," Claire replied.

"Well, they have been at it for a few days now." Tom looked down at the floor and braced himself for Claire's response.

"Tom! We were supposed to be making that decision together."

"Somebody had to do something about Jacob. I couldn't wait around for a bunch of incompetent police types to do it."

Claire just dropped her complaints and resigned herself to accepting Tom's tactics. We all moved to the kitchen table, and Claire started a pot of coffee.

"My sources have dug up some dirt on this guy Mandu. He's a real winner. He's a college dropout, been arrested three times, and is currently under investigation for sexual harassment." Tom reached into the pocket of his suit coat. "Seems that part of his little operation is based on some kind of hokey eastern sex practice, and not all of his followers are going along with it. My guys found a couple of former members who had a lot to say about Mandu's exploits with his female devotees. He liked to encourage them to be devoted to his *personal* needs."

"I could have told you that he was slimy. What do the PIs know about Jacob?" Claire wanted to steer the conversation in a more productive direction.

"They have reconstructed his last day before he went missing. He was definitely at the OH Center and did not show up at a meeting he had planned with his minister later that day. The pastor said that Jacob had some important information to share with him and needed guidance on what to do next."

"Claire and I went to the Center today and talked to Rallen Mandu," I spoke up for the first time. "He says he doesn't know anything about his disappearance."

"Like you could believe anything that guy says. We have got to get him in an interrogation room with the police. He is dirty and knows exactly where Jacob is." Tom's face was getting red, and he looked like he would explode any minute.

Claire put a hand on Tom's shoulder and spoke in a calm voice, "We need to share this information with Detective Kramer. He has the authority to bring him in for questioning."

"Yeah, sure, that's why I brought the report from the investigators. Give it to Kramer and make *him* follow through. You'll have more luck with him than I will."

"I will get this to him tomorrow," Claire assured him. "Thanks, Tom, you are a big help. Please try to be calm and let's do this carefully so that we don't scare Mandu into doing something we will regret." Claire gave Tom a look that was both loving and stern.

Tom left. Claire and I took our places on the couches in the living room. I decided to share with her some parallels I could see between the One Humanity group and the communal experience of our younger days. Claire had left the Berkeley commune before the advent of some disturbing events had occurred.

"You know, Rallen isn't the only one that has used his position of power to gain access to women for sexual favors," I began the conversation, and Claire settled in for my recollection. "You knew Michael Gabriel, the leader of the CEC. He was in his fifties in those days. He was wiry and full of energy. He wasn't one of those pampered gurus who sits on a pillow and rides in a Rolls. He worked right along with us to build the new world community. But I'm sure he got a big grin on his face the day his 'space guides' gave him the plan for sexual bliss in the new age. Michael received all his *inspired* messages by automatic writing. What was channeled to him was as much a surprise to him as anyone. I believe that this is true, but also knew that those writings did not come from the source he attributed them. They came straight from the master mind, Belial."

"Belial? Who in the heck is that?" Claire was tracking the story but got hung up on this name.

"It's another name for the devil," I answered.

"You don't mean to tell me that Michael was demon-possessed! Like in the exorcist or something?"

"Yes, I believe he was being used by the devil to preach his false doctrine." I hoped my tone would convey the seriousness of this revelation.

"But he was such a cool guy. He was friendly; easy to relate to." Claire was struggling to make sense of my characterization of Michael Gabriel.

"Just like the devil, Michael was a master of disguise." I could see that Claire was considering the possibility of deception in the ranks of the commune.

"Michael claimed to be in communication with 'space beings,'" I explained. "They relayed to him the trouble with the human race in regards to sex was that they were too possessive. No one man or woman can fulfill all the many-faceted desires of any one person. We needed to expand our concept of marriage to include multiple partners. We could have one mate, but also be open to sharing with other couples in a ritualistic practice that would free our bodies to express all our myriad of selves. This process was couched in the guise of a tantric circle. Somehow giving it a pseudo-religious title made it plausible. Just because it had rules and structure did not make it right. These meetings were called *natural selection* events. In years to come Michael would reap a bitter harvest as his own wife 'naturally selected' his best friend, John, to be her mate. Leaving John's wife without a partner to live with and raise their children. It was all very messy and confusing for everyone, and it was the little children who suffered the most."

The next day started with hope. We had a task to complete and some more answers to share with Detective Kramer. Claire called the police station early and set up another meeting with him. We quickly performed our morning rituals and ate some yogurt and fruit before heading off on the well-worn route between Claire's home and Kramer's office.

"Here is a report from the private investigators that my husband Tom has hired." Claire handed the papers to Detective Kramer and steeled herself for the reaction she knew would come.

Kramer just held the pages. He was weighing his words. "You know that involving a private company could jeopardize the police investigation. I am not comfortable with this."

"Yes, but they did uncover some important background on Mandu," Claire stated with all the grace she could muster.

I was ready to jump into the conversation to bring the two sides together. We needed all hands on deck if we were to be successful in our hunt for Jacob, but I could see that the detective was softening and working out the possible advantages of having help in the search.

"I have some new information as well," Detective Kramer said. "Sergeant Delano has befriended a member of the OH. Her name is Ashley, and she has been a fringe member for some time. She also has experienced some of the darker sides of the organization. She witnessed one member being pressured to *donate* his recent inheritance to One Humanity. He was shamed into giving a substantial sum to Rallen to further the mission. He was rewarded with a position on the core assembly. The assembly guides major decisions with Rallen's approval, of course," Detective Kramer referenced a growing file on the OH and its leader.

"The clock is ticking, Detective. When are we going to have enough proof that Rallen Mandu is involved in Jacob's disappearance? You need to bring him in for questioning under oath," Claire countered.

"We are close. We are running our information through legal as we speak. With this background you just delivered, we will be able to tip the balance, I'm sure," Detective Kramer reassured us and walked us out of the building. We drove away with a lighter spirit.

On our way back to Marin, we rode in silence as we each sorted through the hopes and fears of our present situation. It was then that I remembered a song from the old days of my time in the Cosmic Earth Collective. This was one of the hymns of the new age religion.

We sang it with reverence at many group functions. We sang it in rooms with guitars and just two or three gathered around. It embodied all that I dreamed the commune would be. It was sung to a lilting melody, and was a favorite as long as I was in the CEC.

> This is the Kingdom, right here on Earth.
> And all the Joy in your heart gives it its worth.
> Come all you children, play, dance and sing.
> Creating's divine, so come on, do your thing.
> Do it here in the Kingdom.
> Take your place in the sun
> Our gifts will be shared.
> The Kingdom of God will come.
> Beautiful scents filling the air,
> As the wind gently blows through your hair.
> So come all you children, play, dance and sing.
> Creating's divine, so come on, do your thing.
> For this is the Kingdom.

Creating's divine. There it is, disguised in one more inventive setting. It is the LIE. The one that Satan used at the very beginning, "You shall be as God." He tripped the first man and woman up on that one and has used it successfully all throughout human history. You would think that it would become a bit shabby and shop worn by now. But he never tires of coming up with new packaging for this trap that is the premier of all his cavalcade of sins. It is the one that got him thrown out of the high ranks of God's armies of angels. It must be a personal challenge to see how many vain humans he can dupe with that one. It is straight from the lips of the "angel of light" himself, Lucifer. He can wrap himself in a cloak of righteous rhetoric. It all sounds so good on the surface. It lures impressionable people like Jacob and Ashley. But when they step out on to that surface, it turns to quick-sand, and they are sinking before they are aware of the danger they are in. Sex, drugs, and rock 'n' roll were the real foundations of the CEC. All the high sounding propaganda was a smoke screen, an elaborate rationalization for our selfish indulgence and dreams of godhood.

I awoke the next morning with a feeling of foreboding. I had just come out of the bathroom when a call came through from Detective Kramer. Claire put the call on speaker, and we listened as he said he had some important information and would like to share it with us right away. Instead of coming into the station, he could to come to us and be there within the hour. Claire agreed and we quickly dressed. Coffee and toast were consumed with anticipation.

"We got a search warrant and a subpoena for the OH and Rallen Mandu. We arrived early this morning and conducted a thorough search of the center. We did not find Rallen or Jacob; however we were able to confiscate some files that are being reviewed right now by Sgt. Delano and a team of clerical staff. We believe that Rallen has fled to his residence in Ashland, Oregon, along with his core group. We still do not have enough evidence of Jacob's kidnapping to involve the FBI. I would like to go to Ashland. If I find Mandu, I can bring him back and interrogate him. A search warrant for the Ashland property is being processed with the local police department, and it should be ready soon." Detective Kramer was energized by the prospect of tracking down Rallen Mandu and possibly uncovering the location of Jacob's captivity.

"This is great news," Claire exclaimed. "I hope you can get Rallen to come clean about his involvement with Jacob's disappearance. He seems pretty slippery though. How did he know that you would be after him this morning?" Claire questioned the detective.

"He seems to have some sources that we can't pin down," Kramer said. He looked at me with an unspoken acknowledgment.

The phone rang, and Claire said she should probably see who it was. She went to the kitchen and began a conversation with Tom Cohen. I knew that it could be a lengthy call. I looked at Detective Kramer. Without words, we exchanged volumes.

"You know, I lived in Ashland for a few months back in the '80s," I said. It has always been a hot spot for alternative religions and practices. I am not surprised that Rallen has a base there. I was involved with a group that had a small enterprise in Ashland. It was called the Cosmic Earth Collective. I know, It sounds pretty silly, but I was very involved with them for a number of years and learned a lot about the new age movement. That was before I turned my life over to the Lord." I hoped I had not lost Kramer's respect by divulging my past.

"We all have things in our past that we may not want to brag about, but are the things that have led us to compassion and insights that inform our present," the detective smiled, and I was reassured.

"Certainly you don't have any skeletons in your closet," I replied.

"Well, I wasn't always the dignified detective. I had some wild years back in college. Fortunately, nothing that would have disqualified me for service in law enforcement."

There was a pause in the conversation and we both found some area in the room that needed inspection. There was tension in the air that we could not acknowledge. I felt a strong attraction to David, and I could tell that there were similar feelings on his part. David… that was the first time that I had thought of him as anything other than a detective. I wanted to ask him more questions about his background but was not sure it would be appropriate.

"Your knowledge of the new age and Ashland could make a difference to our investigation. Perhaps we could meet to compare notes." At those words, my heart raced. I wanted to spend more time with him.

"That was Tom," Claire said as she returned from her phone call. "He said he has a man in Ashland looking into the OH. They have a center on the main street of town and Rallen has a residence on a hill overlooking Lithia Park." Claire interrupted my moment with David. I was both relieved and disappointed. I needed to get a handle on my feelings.

"Looks like our investigation may be moving to Oregon. I will check with my supervisor to see if this is when we need to involve the FBI. Of course, we still don't have concrete evidence that Rallen is complicit in Jacob's disappearance, but we also have the legal right to question Mandu and his associates. Our sources say that he is in Ashland," David gave us the assurance that he was still invested in the search for Jacob.

David Kramer left us with hope that our answers could be in Oregon, and he would pursue them as quickly as possible. After David left, Claire and I went to the kitchen and started to put together a salad for lunch. I loved the way she made her salads. I always thought it must be Italian. She didn't cut the lettuce; she tore the pieces and tossed them in the bowl with bell peppers, onions, cucumber slices, and celery. A light drizzle to oil and vinegar made the perfect balance. We added some chicken breast and were ready for a healthy lunch. I admired Claire for her dedication to maintaining her body. She made exercise a routine and her diet was usually excellent. She loved sweets as much as anyone but consumed them in moderation.

As we sat down to eat, Claire looked at me and asked if I wanted to say a prayer. I was surprised, but also elated to see that she was open to my practices of honoring the Lord.

"Father, thank you for this food and all your blessings. We know that you love us and are working things out for our good. Thank you for Detective Kramer and all his help. I ask that the search for Jacob will end soon, and he will come back to us unharmed. Guide us as we take every step that you give us on this journey of discovery. Amen."

"Thanks, Joy, that was a good one. Now, I want the skinny on what is going on between you and the detective." Claire gave me one of her impish looks.

"What...what are you talking about?" I was stumbling over my words and we both knew that it was a dead giveaway.

"I peeked into the living room while I was talking to Tom, and the atmosphere in there was so thick, you could cut it with a knife."

"Come on, Claire, we were just talking about the investigation. I told him I had some experience with the new age and had lived in Ashland. That's all." I tried to cover my tracks.

"I can see that Kramer is attracted to you," Claire shot back.

"Nonsense. He is too professional for all that. And besides I don't think that I could turn his head." I was losing ground.

"You turn a lot of heads, Joy. You, with your wavy, golden brown hair and sparkling blue eyes. I have always envied your peaches-and-cream complexion."

"I've always thought *you* were the beauty of the bunch. Men are always checking you out," I tossed the ball right back to her.

"Admit it. You like Detective Kramer." Claire was not to be denied her observation.

"Okay, he is attractive and his air of authority is reassuring." I finally admitted the obvious.

It was good to banter with Claire. It reminded us of old times and the fun we had over many years of friendship. It also signaled our belief that Jacob would be found unharmed.

We were relaxing on the patio with some iced tea when the phone rang. Claire jumped up to answer it. It was Detective Kramer. He asked to speak to me. Claire handed me the phone with an arched eyebrow. We both knew what she was thinking.

"Joy, I have an idea I would like to run by you. Could you come to the station later today?"

"What about Claire?" I was surprised that he did not ask Claire first.

"This has to do with One Humanity and the background that you had revealed to me earlier today. I think that collaboration would be fruitful." David's tone was tentative.

"Can I check with Claire?"

"Of course, and Sgt. Delano is prepared to pick you up if you are available. I can hold if you want to check with Claire right now."

I took one look at Claire and knew that she was jumping out of her skin to know what the call was about. I explained the request, and she was curious but said it would be fine and that she had some work to do anyway.

"Okay, I can be ready anytime. Is there anything you need me to bring?" I was hoping I would get a clue about the nature of this "collaboration."

"No, I just want to bounce an idea around with you and see if it would be feasible. Delano can be at Claire's house in about an hour." David was holding his cards close.

We finished the call. I looked at Claire and I could see that same impish smile as she let me know that she knew exactly what was going on. I assured her that this was strictly business, but it was a hard sell.

My heart was jumping as I waited for the sergeant to arrive. I changed clothes three times before I settled on the blue top that would accent my eyes. I freshened my make up, but as I looked in the mirror I said to myself, "What are you doing! This isn't a date."

"You wanna bet!" Claire's voice came in from the hall. She had been passing by just as I made my statement.

"CLAIRE! Stop it!" I was so embarrassed that she had found me out.

ch**5**ter

Susan Delano, the officer from the Berkley Police Station, picked me up just as Detective Kramer had said she would. As we rode along, she shared some of the experiences she had while investigating the OH center. Her impression of the members was one of dependence and fear. There was a permeating sense of paranoia that overshadowed the proposed message of love and light. She felt that Rallen ran a tight ship and expected unquestioning loyalty from all of his followers. I shared with her my reaction to meeting Mandu for the first time. She had not met him personally but got a good sense of his nature from pictures and propaganda she saw at the center. It was her opinion that following Mandu's trail could very well lead to Jacob.

"Thank you for coming. I really appreciate your willingness to share your expertise on alternative religions," Detective Kramer warmly greeted me as we arrived at the station. He was dressed casually, and his demeanor was relaxed. We spent a good hour going over some of the printed material that Delano had gathered from the center. I gave him my take on the group and shared more information about the commune that I had been involved with. We could see some very strong similarities.

"Let's go back to the center and take a reading on the mood there," David suggested. "I think that we could learn something about how they are coping with the invasion from the police and Rallen's departure." He was energized by the prospect of catching the members at a vulnerable moment.

On our way to the center, we stopped at the coffee shop and got some drinks to go.

I needed to use the bathroom and excused myself as he was ordering. In the hall on the way to the ladies' room, a woman who looked vaguely familiar approached me and pushed something into my hand. I started to ask her what she was doing, but she was gone as quickly as she had appeared. I looked at the object and saw a velvet pouch with drawstrings at the top. I put it in the pocket of my jacket as I entered the bathroom. I decided to wait until I was with David before I opened it.

"A woman, I think from the OH center approached me in the hallway to the bathroom," I announced as I took my coffee from David's hand.

"What did she want? Was she threatening you?" David was asking with concern in his voice.

"No, she gave me this." I held out the deep purple pouch.

"That could be anything—poison, an explosive, who knows." David's eyes widened as he looked at the pouch.

"I don't think so. I can feel something heavy, perhaps metal. The woman had a pleading look on her face and didn't seem threatening at all," I said calmly.

We both were ready to satisfy our curiosity. David held my coffee while I carefully pulled the strings on the mouth of the pouch and looked inside. It was metal and golden in color. I pulled out a key. My heart stopped. It was the key from my dream, the one that seared my hand and was given to me by the "angel of light." I knew that it was time to tell David about my dreams. This key was a clue to finding Jacob. My whole being was resonating with the importance of this moment.

I asked David if we could sit for a few minutes while we drank our coffee. We found a table in a quiet corner, and I proceeded to tell him about the dreams that I had been having since Claire's call a week ago. I couldn't believe that it had been only a few days; it seemed like a month since I got the call from Claire with the news that Jacob was missing.

"Joy, you are being directed by God. This key proves that there is more to this search for Jacob than meets the eye. There is a spiritual connection. I believe we are involved in a moment in eternity when the forces of light and dark are battling for very high stakes. I have a similar confession to make. I hope we can keep this between us. As a law enforcement officer, I deal in cold hard facts, but the experiences we have had do not fit into the normal scheme of things. I saw angelic assistance during both of our recent life-threatening events. There was a very large angel in the street when we had the near miss with the SUV. He moved us out of the way, and when you slipped on the rope ladder, a smaller angelic being reached out and held you so you would not fall."

I did not know what to say and we sat in silence for a moment thinking about the significance of our supernatural encounters. I finally broke the spell. "We have to pursue Rallen. I just know that it's our mission to expose him. In doing so, we will find Jacob. God has assured me that he is being protected even though he's held in the enemies' camp."

"I am not sure how I will convince my boss, but I need you in Ashland. You have the KEY! Literally. Would you be willing to go with me?" David conveyed his conviction and his concern.

"Yes. I have to, for Jacob's sake and to fulfill the destiny that I know God has prepared for me." We both felt the weight of the Spirit and the importance of the moment. God was preparing us for the journey ahead.

We left the coffee shop and headed to the OH center. As we approached the building, it looked strange. We walked up to the entrance and saw a sign. "Closed for renovation." We looked through the glass doors and saw no one. It seemed to be abandoned. "Wow, that was fast. I think we must have struck a nerve. All it took was a search warrant, and they scattered. Let's go to the station and see if the team has found anything more in the documents that we took from the center." David led us back to the car and back to the Berkeley Police Station.

"The clerical team found some serious inconsistencies in the financial records of One Humanity," Delano reported. "We will put together a recommendation for subpoena of bank records. There have been some large donations that don't show up anywhere. They may have been diverted to off shore accounts."

"Good work. Keep digging. I will be heading to Ashland, Oregon, soon, and I could use all the ammunition I can get." David gave Delano a verbal pat on the back. "I will take Joy back to Marin. Thanks for all your help."

Delano gave me a smile and as soon as David turned to go, she gave me a wink. I blushed and hurried out the door behind the detective.

"Tell me more about your background," David asked as soon as we were in his car and on our way back to Marin.

"I was raised in church and went to a Christian college. But I rebelled during my senior year and married a nonbeliever. I taught school in Monrovia, California for four years before I divorced, dropped out, and eventually joined the Cosmic Earth Collective. I lived and worked with them for nine years. Then one Christmas, I went to church with my parents. It was a candle light service. I felt the presence of God so strongly. My heart melted. I surrendered my heart to Jesus and then had to tell the people I had lived with for all those years, that we had bet our lives on a lie. That went over real well! They turned their backs on me. I tried to tell them about my return to Christ, but they were deaf to my words. In the CEC all faiths were respected except the truth of Christianity. I had to pack up my things and leave. Even after working tirelessly for nine years, I had very little to show for my efforts. I went to Idaho with two suitcases. I had to start from scratch, but luckily, I had my teaching degree and was able to find a good job in my field."

"That is an amazing story of redemption. I'm impressed that you had the courage to face your former commune members with the truth." David shot me a look of reassurance that I needed after exposing my past to him.

We spent the last few minutes of our journey with some light discussion of the beauty of the bay and the light on the water. We were both working on our presentation as we made our way back to see Claire. We needed to have her blessing over our plans to go to Ashland together.

David jumped right into the heart of the matter as soon as we were seated in the living room. "Claire, I want to ask you if you could spare Joy for a few days."

"What do you mean?" Claire looked from David to me and back again.

"I've received the go ahead to investigate the Ashland center. I don't want to delay, so I will be leaving tomorrow. I want to verify that Rallen is there and possibly find evidence of Jacob's location. I feel that Joy would be a valuable asset in dealing with the group up there. She has insights into their modes of operation that could prove valuable," David stated his case with professional detachment.

"Joy, do you want to go? What about the danger in dealing with the OH?" Claire searched my face for signs of fear.

"I want to find Jacob. If I have to go into the thick of it to do that, I am all in!" My answer was a definite yes.

"We could use your help here, Claire, working with Sgt. Delano," David explained. "There are still a lot of loose ends with the fire. We are also looking into Jacob's connections at the Rock church. You know he had just started attending there. I would like you to go with Delano to interview pastor Ben." David assured Claire she was very much in the loop.

We spent the next hour discussing the details of the trip to Ashland. David also let Claire know that Delano would be contacting her tomorrow to set up the meeting with the Pastor at Rock Church. David gave us both his assurances that the search for Jacob was on a fast track. We were making good progress.

Claire and I were tired. We said good night early. When I got to my room, I began to intercede in prayer for Jacob. I felt that God was leading me into the enemy's camp, not only for Jacob's sake, but for a greater cause. I felt a calling to expose Rallen Mandu. My life had come full circle as I used my past to inform my present challenge.

I lay down to sleep and a story from the Bible came to me, one that had special meaning. When I came back to the Lord, my mother said that if I had been the only person on Earth, Jesus would have died for me. The story that Jesus told of the one lost lamb said it best. He was willing to leave the ninety-nine other sheep to search and rescue the one. It was even more meaningful as I saw how it related to our search for Jacob. I felt that in the process of rescuing Jacob, we would cause a ripple effect that could impact more than just the one.

I drifted off to sleep with an even stronger conviction of my destiny. God's plans were unfolding, and I was to be in the center of it all.

chapter 6

Morning came too quickly, and I woke with excitement, but I also felt the weight of the task ahead. I packed quickly and made sure that the purple pouch was in with my belongings. I ate a light breakfast with Claire. We did not have a lot to say. We were both preparing ourselves for the job ahead. When we heard David's car drive up to the house, we clung to each other as if it would be the last time.

"We are going to find Jacob," I said to Claire as we parted. Her eyes were teary.

"I believe you. I am so glad you are on my side, along with your God." Claire gave me a brave smile.

I grabbed my bags and was out the door before David could ring the bell. We needed to get an early start. He took my bags and put them in the trunk of his car. I settled into the passenger's seat. There was an awkward few moments when we realized we would be confined to this small space for a few hours. I broke the ice by asking if there was any new information on the Ashland center. I wanted to keep the conversation away from more personal topics.

"I made a call to the police chief in Ashland. I let him know that I would be investigating a case that involved the One Humanity Center. He appreciated the courtesy call but didn't have much information on the group. He had not been aware of any illegal activities. The group kept a low profile as far as he could tell. He said he would help in my investigation in any way possible." David assumed his professional tone as he answered my question.

"I know that Ashland has a variety of alternative groups. You would be surprised at how many ways people can find to express their individualism." I was opening the conversation up to more exploration into my background. I was cautious about revealing too much but still wanted David to know more about my experiences with the new age movement.

"Tell me about your involvement in Southern California with communal living," David inquired.

"It's a long story, but I could give you one piece that may tell you a lot about it. Please don't judge me. I am a completely different person now. In fact, when I look back on my life, it seems like I am watching a movie.

"A branch of the commune opened up in San Diego. A small group of the members from Berkeley moved down. San Diego was a hot bed of the holistic health movement. Our emphasis on vegetarianism fit right in. We opened a small crafts shop and all lived together in a home in the El Cajon hills. We befriended some people who lived out in the desert just north of the Mexico border. They called themselves the monks of Madre Grande Monastery. Now when you think of a monk, you usually imagine a little bald guy in a robe off in some corner of the world lost in meditation and prayer. These monks definitely defied that definition. They hailed from some obscure monastic order. The one tenant of their brotherhood was, 'Every man finds his own way to God.' But somewhere in their hidden agenda was the old adage 'If it feels good, do it.' Most of these 'monks' held down regular jobs in the city, but the weekends would find them in the desert hills on this communally owned piece of property that was once a ranch. It was nestled back in a remote dead end canyon. The hills were strewn with huge white boulders, teepees and dome shelters. It was another experiment in living based on the back to nature theme. There was a large communal garden, a rambling ranch house, and the old barn had been converted into a meeting place and dining hall called the Sun Center. It had a striking mandala of an orange and yellow sun painted on the side." I paused to read David's reaction to my tale.

"Go on, this is fascinating. I've lived in California all my life and know about many of the quirky groups in our state, but my life has always run in conservative lanes." David encouraged me to continue.

"Our group was invited to join the monks one weekend. I was attracted to the natural beauty of the place and to the unusual mix of people. Though there was diversity in the members of the monastery, they all held one thing in common. They liked to get naked. Yeah, to our surprise, Madre Grande Monastery was actually a nudist colony. When the sun came out, the clothes came off." I peeked at David to see if he could tell that I was blushing. I didn't know how to tell the story without revealing this important fact.

"So did you join them?" David asked.

"Yes, you have to realize that we were dedicated to throwing off old conventions. This was a challenge to our liberation. We had to meet it," I explained.

"Did you ever go back?" he asked with a curious smile.

"As a matter of fact, I moved there a few months later."

"That's a bold move. How did it happen?" David was not shying away from the more controversial details of my past.

"We were forced to leave our El Cajon home because of a fire. It was on the night of my thirtieth birthday. Some members from our Maui branch—"

"Whoa! The CEC had a group in Hawaii?" David interrupted my narrative.

"Yes. There were a few members with ties there and they had the funds to make things happen. But that's another story," I replied.

"Okay, let's stick to the San Diego story for now. By the way, your excellent story telling is making the miles fly by," David encouraged me and gave me confidence.

"Some members from Maui came to the mainland for a visit. The two women had a couple of their children and one boyfriend along. We were all one big family as they planned to spend a few days with us at the El Cajon house. We all had our share of alcohol and fine Maui buds, when I looked out the back door and saw a wall of flames. Rex, appropriately named for his uncanny ability to destroy things, was living with us for a while. He was another refugee from the Berkeley center. One of our members had set up a candle factory in the garage. Rex took a joint in there for some private toking. He threw down the smoldering roach and it landed in a pool of dried wax. The garage, office, sewing school and half the house went up in smoke. But even in our disobedience, God sent his angels to protect us. All of us escaped unharmed, even though two of the children were fast asleep in a room right next to where the fire broke out."

"How frightening!" David looked at me with wide eyes.

"When I saw the flames, I grabbed the phone in the kitchen, but the line was dead. I yelled for someone to come, and then I ran across the yard, vaulted a six-foot chain-link fence, ripped past a wall of rose bushes, and made it to the neighbor's door in record time. They called the fire department. When I made it back to the house, I found everyone standing on the front lawn in horrible fascination as they watched the flames leap thirty feet in the air. That was the event that scattered our little group. A few of us landed at the monastery."

"Were you giving up on the Cosmic Earth Collective?" David asked.

"No, it was just a detour that lasted about six months. It was an exhilarating experience to live close to nature with simple needs and a simple day-by-day existence. It only cost sixty dollars a month, per person, to stay on the land and that included the food, and it was wonderful. It was like checking into a health resort. Everyone took turns preparing the meals. They were wholesome and natural. No meat, no dairy, no eggs, no sugar, and no wheat products. That may sound very restrictive, but you would be surprised at how much variety you can find in the vegetable kingdom. Fresh handmade tortillas from the nearby town of Tecate, Mexico, were a staple. Much of the vegetables were grown in the communal garden. There were lots of local avocados, seed milk and seed yogurt, beans and rice. I came away from Madre Grande slimmer and healthier than ever in my life."

"If it was so great, why did you stay for only six months?" David the detective was digging for the deeper currents to my story.

"As idyllic as it may have been, there are always the political aspects of a group. There was definitely a hierarchy to be reckoned with. Factions and interest groups were constantly playing tug of war over the direction of the monastery. There were the 'monks' who were into a spiritual trip and just wanted a place to express their strange brew of asceticism and hedonistic-nature religion. There was the entrepreneurial contingent that had great plans for the land to be developed into a slick health Mecca. There was the back to naturists who wanted to keep things simple and just live there undisturbed. Then, of course, there were the party people who didn't much care what happened as long as there was enough sex, drugs, and rock 'n' roll to go around. Try making a cohesive body out of all that—a task that I'm sure is beyond any human capability to this day."

"There are many examples of failed cultural experiments mirroring this one," David interjected.

"Exactly, the monastery had numerous meetings to try and hash out their differences, but a clear direction never seemed to emerge. I'm sure much of our clarity was undermined by the liberal use of drugs. It seems very strange to me now that cigarettes and alcohol were expressly discouraged while the use of all types of psychotropic drugs was an integral part of the lifestyle, but you see this throughout the new-age movement. There is a double standard of substance abuse. It must have to do with the fact that most of the new agers, and certainly the leadership, are veterans of the sixties dazzling drug culture, where the psychedelic experience was put on a pedestal as the open door to ultimate spiritual awareness. However, it is my experience that the great revelations of drug induced states never really translate well to the condition of human existence."

"Your insights into the new-age movement are invaluable. You have me seeing a different side to the foundations of groups like One Humanity. I am not sure about their involvement in the drug culture, but the motivations are similar." David's observation gave me a feeling that I really did have an important part to play in the journey ahead.

We grew quiet for a few minutes as the car sped north on I-5. I finally broke the silence. "I am telling you a lot about myself. Tell me something about your past that has shaped you."

"Nothing as dramatic as yours, and you know I have to keep a professional front for the sake of my position." David gave me a sly smile.

"I certainly wouldn't want to blow your cover!" I tossed him a matching smile.

"Okay, point taken. I'm a native Californian. I grew up in a small town in Northern California. Weaverville is a few miles west of Redding. It's in the hills on the edge of the Trinity National Forest. Lots of trees, old buildings, history, a pretty idyllic place to grow up, I guess. It is a typical small town. It's a tourist attraction, and my folks ran a small motel there. My dad was also a back woods guide. I have two brothers. I am the middle son. I was always the peacekeeper in the family and also the scapegoat at times. I was a pretty good student and played a little baseball. When it was time to go to college, I left my sheltered life there and moved to Southern California. I got a scholarship to go to California State at Hayward. It's in the East Bay area. I managed to get my criminal justice degree, and then went on to the police academy in Oakland. I got a job in the Berkeley department right away and worked my way up to detective. Now, doesn't that sound really exciting?"

"I have a feeling you left out the colorful bits." I hoped I could get him to open up about his personal life.

"Well, Ms. Morgan, I'm afraid that would require a higher security clearance." He had a hard time keeping a straight face with that reply. We both started laughing. Layers of tension were relieved. There was a softening in our connection.

"Any time you need a break, just let me know. Redding will be coming up soon. We could stop for gas and lunch. I know the area pretty well. There are some good restaurants. What kind of food do you like?" David asked.

"Anything, really, I do like fresh veggies and local foods. I was a vegetarian for a few years, so I learned to love natural foods. I eat meat now, but in moderation." I hoped we could agree on a place that would accommodate both of our tastes.

"Sounds good to me. I know just the place."

We stopped for gas first, and I ducked into the bathroom to freshen up. It felt good to get out and stretch my legs after almost four hours in the car. Although I couldn't believe it had been that long. The time just flew by. My heart fluttered a little when I thought about sitting so close to David and sharing my darkest secrets with him. I know he was keeping a professional distance on the surface, but the under currents were rising like the tide. I met him in the convenience store as he paid for the gas and I bought a couple of bottles of water for the car. We drove a short distance through town to a small bistro in a quaint building. The lunch crowd had not arrived yet, and we got a cozy table in the corner of the main room. The menu lived up to my expectations as I saw a number of signature salads and vegetarian entrees. I ordered a salad with local greens and grilled tofu. David ordered fish tacos. We filled the time waiting for our meal with small talk.

"You know this area because Weaverville is just a few miles from here. Do you visit often?" I hoped he wouldn't realize that I was fishing for more details.

"Yes, I still have some family and friends here. Weaverville is a small town, and we would come to Redding for shopping and to see movies." David's tone did not invite further discussion.

"Do you see that woman across the dining room with the purple blouse?" David said in a quiet voice.

"If you mean the one who has been staring at us since we sat down? Yes," I replied with matching confidentiality. "Do you know her?"

"That's just the thing. I have no idea who she is or why she is so interested in us." David's detective sixth sense was kicking in.

"Here we are. Do you need anything else?" The waitress presented our plates with a flourish.

We were distracted by the food and overdue for a meal. The food not only looked good but tasted even better. About halfway through, the woman in purple was suddenly at our table. She had a radiant look that put us at ease. She was not threatening at all even as she hovered over us.

"I have a message for you. The Lord God wants you to know that you are on a mission for Him. There is a great prize awaiting you on your journey. The battle will not only be in the flesh, but in the spirit. Stick together. You are stronger as a team. Oh, and by the way, there are two huge angels standing behind you." She finished her message and was gone before we could react.

"What? What was that?" David asked with a look of complete surprise.

"I think we just received a prophetic word. That woman was moved by the Holy Spirit to give us a word of encouragement." I felt a tingle. Something of eternal importance had just happened.

"I am not used to receiving messages like that. It kind of gave me goose bumps," David was struggling to make sense of his reaction.

"I feel the same way. That is what happens when Heaven collides with Earth. There is a spiritual current running through this area. I have heard that a local church has had a visitation from God that has awakened a number of people. Perhaps she is one of them. She certainly was bold. I believe that God used her to give us a glimpse into the importance of this job we have, not only to find Jacob, but to uncover the sinister workings of One Humanity." I felt led to help David understand the meaning of the message.

"That certainly puts a much bigger responsibility on our shoulders." He took a deep breath and slowly let it out.

"You know we are less than two years away from the millennial change. This is a time when a lot of forces will be clashing. Will we react with fear or faith? Is it a time to retreat or advance; some even think that time will end at the stroke of midnight 2000. So many theories running around. I choose to trust in God and let Him have His way. 'Thy Kingdom come, Thy will be done.' Perhaps what we are doing today will make a difference for the uncertain times ahead." The tingling was only increasing as I expressed my awareness of a larger stage that we could be playing on.

Now the delicious meals were forgotten. The leftovers were abandoned as we paid the bill and left the bistro. We both felt like our consciousness had shifted. I expected to see angles hovering over our car as we got in. The atmosphere was so full of questions as we drove out of Redding; we could not even speak. We headed north again toward Ashland.

chapter 7

The miles from Redding to Ashland seemed to evaporate as David and I sat in silence. The message we received had such weight, it lingered like a heavy blanket. I was curious. What could the "prize" be? Surely it was the discovery of Jacob's location, and yet it felt like it was of even greater importance. I came back to the present just as we exited I-5 and drove into the town of Ashland. It was early afternoon, and the streets were filled with tourists and residents going about their business. The Shakespeare festival was in full swing.

"This town is full of tourists. I hope we can find a hotel room." I looked at David to see if he had the same misgivings.

"Not to worry. I had Delano book two rooms at the Stafford Inn. It is very close to downtown. We can actually walk to Lithia Park. Remember that Rallen has a home overlooking the park. Let's check in and get situated, and then we can spy out the lay of the land and get some dinner. I would love to get a walk in after spending the day in the car," David reassured me with his efficiency.

I was comforted by the cozy, clean room as I wheeled my suitcase into number 17. David was in number 19, same side of the hallway one door down. I took a few minutes to freshen up and hang a couple of items from my bag. I even took time to brush my teeth. It always felt more secure when you knew you had a place to land in a new environment.

"Ready?" David met me in the lobby.

"Let's go. It's been awhile since I've been in Ashland. I lived here for a few months back in the eighties. It looks like the tourist trade has really picked up. You know, besides the festival, this town is a Mecca for new-age groups and leftover hippies," I said, as I felt the heaviness falling away with each step we took toward Main Street and the center of town.

"While I was in the lobby, I asked the guy at the desk about a good restaurant. He recommended Greenleaf on the square. It has the local, fresh foods you like," David said in a relaxed manner that let me know he, too, was feeling lighter.

"That sounds great. One thing about a town like Ashland, they have a variety of good places to eat," I replied.

We chatted about the scenery and the anticipation of dinner. We had been interrupted at lunch and were both feeling the growls in our stomachs. We found the Greenleaf without any trouble. It was early for most tourists' dinner hour, so we were shown to a table right away. I ordered a stir fry and David settled on a pasta dish that the waiter said was a specialty.

"Tell me about how you came to live in Ashland," David asked as we waited for our food to arrive.

"After the fire in El Cajon and the stint at Madre Grande, I was not sure where to go. I could have gone right back to the main communal group. They had moved from Berkeley to Stockton, California." I began my story.

"Really! Stockton isn't exactly known for its liberal atmosphere. I've been there a time or two, and the favorite restaurant in town is the Ground Cow." David was surprised by this turn of events for the CEC.

"I think they were just looking for a cheaper place to live. They found a large, old house in Stockton called the Wong Mansion. It was built in the 1920s by a Chinese immigrant who made his fortune in gambling houses. The property also had an apartment complex and a pool. I did finally move there, but that was after my adventure in Ashland." I took a break from my story to appreciate the sight and smells of our entrees. We both went quiet for a few minutes as we savored the food. It was delicious, and as they say, hunger is the best sauce.

"You moved around a lot during your commune days," David observed.

"That was part of the lifestyle. Putting down roots was looked at as an antiquated concept. We owned the world. We were world citizens who did not like being defined by old ways of being and thinking. Just another way the enemy robbed us of our roots. It's hard to build a solid foundation when you have no ties to the land or people."

"But you had your 'family' within the commune," David countered.

"It would seem that way on the surface, but those ties were tenuous at best. You can see that by the way the group morphed and splintered. There was a couple from the house in El Cajon who moved to Ashland to start their own branch of the Cosmic Earth Collective. Denny and Suzanne had two children together. They were trying to make a go of it by gardening and sewing. Suzanne had been a productive member of the sewing school. She was creating items and selling them to local shops in town. Denny saw himself as a new age farmer. He produced some vegetables for restaurants in town. His main crop, however, was cannabis. They invited me to stay with them to help Suzanne in her business. We wanted to set up an airbrush studio to add to the variety of her inventory."

As we finished our meal and our conversation lulled, I looked everywhere except at David. I couldn't shake the feeling that we were on a date. I didn't want to add to that feeling by looking too long into those eyes. But when I did look up, he was staring at me with an intensity that made me catch my breath. Our eyes locked. Time stood still. The connection was deepening despite our attempts to keep a professional distance.

"Do you want desert or coffee?" The waitress interrupted the moment with her question.

"No, just the check please," David finally answered.

We busied ourselves with the tasks of gathering our things and paying the bill. We left the restaurant and stopped to take in the scene on the street.

David laughed and said, "I see what you mean about the left-over hippies. They add a colorful element to the town. Let's walk up to the park. I am sure we will see even more sights up there. We can also get a look at Rallen's house from below."

We strolled up the street and entered Lithia Park. "The park got its name from the water," I told David. "You may have seen that fountain in the square. The spring has mineral water that is supposed to have curative powers, if you can get past the taste." I wanted to keep the conversation on the light side. Acting as tour guide gave me a safe distance from the feelings that were swirling around inside me, but as we walked along, David stepped aside suddenly to avoid colliding with a little girl who was running ahead of her mother to get to the playground. As he bumped into me, I lost my footing and stumbled. David reached out to keep me from falling and held me at my waist. I was not expecting the electric shock that ripped through my body. I looked at David. I could tell by the look on his face that he felt it too. I gained my balance, but he kept his arm around me. It was one of those moments when there should have been a kiss involved. We parted though and resumed our walk along the pathway. David cleared his throat and pointed to a large three story house on the edge of the cliff overlooking the park.

"That is Mandu's place. Looks kind of sinister, but maybe that is just me reading into it since I know who lives there."

"When do you plan to confront him? That is, if he is there," I responded.

"I have good intel that says he is home. I have to check in with the local PD tomorrow. We'll come up with a plan to take him into custody and search the premises. If Jacob is being held there, this could all be over tomorrow." David assumed his detective voice. The reality of our reason for being in Ashland brought us both back to a sobering frame of mind.

"Let's go back to the park entrance and walk up Fork Street. That's the one the CEC house is on," David suggested.

"Wow, have you memorized the map of Ashland?"

"I like to know the layout. I spent a little time last night checking out the map of the town and area."

We were enjoying the walk along Lithia Creek. Heading out of the park was not as pleasant as we turned back up the hill and started walking toward Rallen's home. It was getting dark by the time we reached the location. We crossed the street and stood under a tree to get a good look at the house. It was imposing. There were lights on every floor. Its river rock foundation created a fortress-like impression. Suddenly I felt a pressure in my head. It was increasing. I looked at David. He was grimacing in pain.

"What is that?!" David managed to whisper.

I could not answer, but I knew that it was coming from across the street. I grabbed David's arm. We turned and hurried down the street back toward the center of town. As we got further from the house, the pressure began to subside. When we finally reached the square, the pain was completely gone. We stopped on the side walk. As we looked at each other, we were overcome with determination to find the source of the pain we had felt as we stood outside Rallen Mandu's house. It was not only sinister-looking, but radiated a malevolence that threatened our very being.

"I refuse to succumb to fear!" David declared with conviction that was contagious. "I know we will find a way to penetrate Rallen's defenses. Tomorrow is a new day. We will bring our own show of force to deal with the threat. I will be Rallen's worse headache." We started our walk back to the hotel with little conversation as we both steeled ourselves for the day ahead.

David and I parted in the hall with unspoken acknowledgment that we needed time to assimilate our recent brush with Rallen's influences. I got ready for bed. Reading was out of the question, even though it was a bedtime ritual in my "normal" life. My mind was racing with possibilities for the intensity of our experience outside the One Humanity house. This was another effort of the enemy to discourage our investigation. That is the thing about Satan's tactics, he often comes on too heavy, and then the intended results backfire. I could see by David's determination right after the incident, that he was more vested than ever in our search for Jacob. He also wanted to find the truth behind Rallen and the OH. All our contacts with them had been steeped in deception. Their intentions were not good but meant to spread fear.

I finally relaxed enough to drift off to sleep. Sometime during the night, I awoke suddenly with a start. I turned on a light because I felt a lingering presence in the room. I searched the bathroom and closet to be sure that I was still alone. I went back to bed and sat with the covers pulled up to my neck. Slowly the dream that had awoken me came floating back.

I was in a dark dungeon-like room. It was like a scene from a fright movie I saw as a teenager. Wall sconces held flickering flames. Shadows bounced across the stone floor and walls. I looked across the room to a passageway. I was drawn to it and walked into a hall that seemed to go on forever. I wanted to find the way out, but there was no way to tell which direction would lead to an exit. As I walked along the corridor, I noticed openings, doors to small rooms at irregular intervals. I stopped at one. Within the recessed opening a wooden door appeared. I tried the door thinking it might lead to the outside. It was locked. It was then I remembered the key. I reached in my jacket pocket and took out the purple pouch. I removed the key and tried the lock. It didn't fit. Determined to find my way out of the depressing maze of rooms, I went to each door and tried the key. Finally I had found a lock that accepted the key. As I started to turn it, I looked down and it was glowing. It became quite warm in my hand. It was heating rapidly. I knew I had to get the door open quickly. I pushed the door open. The room was flooded with light. My eyes took a minute to adjust to the brightness. There in the middle of the room at an old wooden table sat Jacob. He looked up at me. His eyes were searching mine for answers to why I was there. I wanted to tell him all about our search and how much his mother missed him. I started to approach him. Each step I took caused him to move further away. Then a dark robed man appeared behind him. He threw his robe over Jacob and they both disappeared.

That's when I woke up. I tried to focus on the last scene of the dream. I wanted to remember the face of the man in the robe. I thought it would be Rallen Mandu. It was not. It was a man, but no one I had seen before.

chapter 8

Morning came too quickly. I had managed to go back to sleep for a couple of hours after my dream. I still could see the face of the robed man as I got ready for the day. David and I had agreed to meet in the breakfast room at eight o'clock. I hurried down and was glad to see him already sitting at a table.

"Are you all right? You look a little pale," David observed.

"Another dream," I answered.

"Let me hear it. These dreams of yours have proven to have a bearing on our search." David encouraged me to relate my latest revelation.

I told him about the dark corridor and the doors. I told him about the importance of the key.

"Perhaps you should bring the key with you today," David interrupted my retelling of the dream. "I hope we will be able to gain access to the Fork Street house. It may be useful."

I pulled the purple pouch out of my pocket and showed it to him. I finished the story with the dramatic appearance of the dark robed man who whisked Jacob away.

"I have to check in with the local PD this morning. I thought you could rest up and wait for me here. It shouldn't take long." David gave me an apologetic look.

"No problem. But I think I would like to get some walking in. Go ahead and let's meet at that coffee shop we saw last night at the entrance to the park," I suggested.

"Okay, are you sure you feel comfortable on your own? We had a significant scare last night." David searched my face for any traces of fear.

"I'll be all right. I know that I have some unseen protectors with me all the time."

I gave David a smile and a wink.

"Angelic assistance is comforting, but you still need to be on guard. Stay aware of your surroundings at all times," David cautioned.

"I will." I gave David my most confident expression. We finished our breakfast. David took off and I sat for a few minutes, finishing my orange juice.

I went back to my room and reapplied my lipstick, combed my hair, and gathered up my purse and scarf. As I left the safety of my room, I had a brief jolt of apprehension. I said out loud, "God did not give me a spirit of fear, but of power, and love, and a sound mind." Speaking this Scripture into my atmosphere brought a new strength and resolve. I marched down the hallway and out the door of the hotel.

It was a beautiful late spring day. The air was fresh, and the sun was warm. I stopped to admire the flowers along the way. The exercise was doing wonders for my mood. I felt hopeful. It was a new day. I knew we would find answers that would lead us to Jacob. We would find truths that would expose the One Humanity cult.

I entered the downtown square and saw a crowd of people gathered just inside the park. I couldn't see what they were watching. I walked up to the fringes of the group hoping I would get a glimpse of the action. It was a street performer. He was dressed in a jester's costume. A small dog was jumping through a hoop. The dog's antics and the jesters exaggerated encouragement sent ripples of laughter through the crowd. I joined into the happy mood of the crowd until I saw a face across the circle of people. I knew that face! I had studied it last night. I had memorized those features. It was the black robed man from my dream. He was dressed in black, but the robe was missing. He was looking right at me. The evil intent in his gaze was unmistakable. Suddenly the bright and happy day turned dark. I did not know whether to confront him or run for my life. I remembered David's words from earlier, "Be aware of your surroundings." I scanned the area for further threats and ways of escape. When I looked back to the man in black, he was gone. Frantically I looked around the area. Had he moved to sneak up behind me? I couldn't see him anywhere. I quickly retreated to the coffee shop where I was to meet David. I found a table against the wall and took a seat that gave me the best view of the door. I was reeling. The man in black was not just a dream. He was real!

Within a few minutes, David came in the door of the coffee shop. He found my table and approached. "You haven't gotten your coffee yet?" he said as he saw the empty table top. "What's wrong? You look like you've seen a ghost."

"You don't know how right you are," I answered. "Can you get our coffee, and then I will tell you all about it."

"Okay, shoot," David said as he set our cups on the table.

I started by reminding him about my dream I had early that morning.

"Then just now, I saw the black robed man from my dream," I said with all the drama I could muster.

"What? Where?" David returned.

"I was watching a street performer with the crowd outside. I looked across the crowd and he was looking right at me. The message he was sending was not good," I explained.

"What happened then?" David encouraged me to expand on the story.

"He disappeared, just like in the dream."

"He can't just disappear. He must have gone somewhere. Did you look for him?" David's police training was kicking in again.

"I looked around but didn't see him anywhere. I just came to the coffee shop as quick as I could. I really didn't want to meet up with him. You didn't see the look on his face," I explained.

We sat in silence for a few minutes drinking our coffee. We were trying to make sense of this new twist.

"With all the excitement, I forgot to tell you about the call to Delano. While I was at the Ashland PD, I checked in with her. She and Claire met with Jacob's friend Collin and Pastor Ben at Rock

Church. They were concerned about his disappearance but did not have any ideas about his current location. They were confident in God's ability to protect him. The youth group has been praying for him every time they get together." David relayed the information from his call.

"The search warrant for Mandu's home is still in process. I think we should stop by the OH center and pay a friendly visit. It's just across the square." David was steering us toward action.

"What if the man is there?" I asked apprehensively.

"That would be great. Then I could find out what his intensions are," David said with confidence.

"I guess we can't just sit here wondering. We've finished our coffee. Let's go." I was ready to break the mood I was in and do something productive.

We left the coffee shop. I slowly stepped out onto the side walk and looked around. I didn't expect to see the man in black, but I was still being cautious.

"Don't worry. I'm not going to let anything happen to you," David declared.

I felt a flush rise to my face as I absorbed the words and the protective strength behind them.

"Thank you," I said. Even in that simple exchange, a deepening connection was formed.

The One Humanity Center was open. We walked inside and were greeted by a lovely young lady with long dark hair and a flowing sari. She even had a red spot on her forehead that symbolized the third eye of Eastern religions.

"My name is Amaya. Welcome to One Humanity. How can I help you?"

"We are interested in your programs. Do you have any meetings planned with your leader Rallen Mandu speaking?" David enquired.

"Not at the present time. We do have group meetings with our members and anyone interested in our work. They are held every Tuesday and Thursday evenings at seven. You are welcome to register for the next meeting," Amaya replied. She turned and gathered a brochure and registration forms from a desk behind her.

"You can sit at that table over there and fill out these forms." She pointed to a small table with two chairs in the corner of the foyer.

"Can we take them with us? I don't think we are ready to fill them out right now," David said. He glanced at the closed door at the other end of the room. "Who else is here today? Anyone who could set up a meeting with Rallen Mandu?" David pressed.

Amaya narrowed her eyes. Her suspicions were rising. "I think you should attend one of the scheduled meetings first. Then we could see about getting an audience with our honored leader."

"Thank you for the information." I jumped into the conversation and took the brochures from Amaya's hand. "We will consider the opportunities you have mentioned." I gave David a look that said it was time to go.

We walked out of the center. "She was a gate keeper," David said as soon as we were a few feet from the entrance. "I wanted to know what was behind door number 1."

"I could see that she was beginning to get suspicious. We don't want them to know that they are being watched. The same thing could happen here that happened in Berkeley." I hoped to pull the reins back a little.

We stood on the sidewalk for a while and contemplated our next move. I could see that David was ready for action. He was used to making things happen; being in Ashland meant that he had to wait for the local authorities to give the green light.

"Let's go to the Ashland PD and see if they have gotten the search warrant for the Fork Street house," David suggested.

"Sure, do you want me to go with you?" I asked, not sure of my roll when interfacing with the local authorities.

"I think it'll be fine," he assured me. "They seem to be pretty open to our help. Of course they don't have the same urgency that we do. We really don't have any concrete evidence that Jacob could be at the OH house. I don't think they would consider dreams and angel visitations are the usual basis for an investigation either." David gave me his signature smile.

We walked back to the coffee shop and found David's car. It only took a few minutes to drive to the police station. We parked on the street and entered the building. David asked for the detective that he had met with earlier. We were ushered back to his office.

"I wasn't expecting you back so soon," Detective Connor said as we entered his office. He seemed a little annoyed by our intrusion.

"This is my associate, Joy Morgan," David introduced me. "She is advising on our investigation. We just tried to get some information from the One Humanity Center in town. They were very protective, especially about any meetings with their leader, Rallen Mandu, or should I say Milo Rippley." David tossed out Mandu's legal name to see if he would get a reaction.

"Who is Milo Rippley?" Connor asked.

"That is Mandu's legal name. He has quite a back story if you care to look into it," David answered.

"I want to be cooperative, Detective Kramer, but there is only so much time I can spend on this little fishing expedition of yours." Detective Connor was throwing up his defenses.

"It is more than an expedition. There is a missing person involved. The clock is ticking, Detective Connor." David matched Connor's tone. I was afraid they would get into a macho contest any minute.

"Detective Connor," I jumped into the fray. "We do have legitimate facts that support our suspicions. A young man's life is in jeopardy. Can you tell us when you would be able to assist us in a search of the One Humanity house on Fork Street?"

"I am afraid we have run into a bit of a snag," Detective Connor informed us. "It seems that Rallen Mandu has some friends in high places. Our request for a search warrant has been denied."

"What?!" David reacted with shock to this revelation. "You can't just let that stand."

"I'm afraid my hands are tied. You will have to find another way to gain access to the property, a legal way, of course," Detective Connor said with finality.

We were dismissed by a phone call that Conner said he had to take. I'm sure he was thinking, "Saved by the bell." He didn't want to continue to escalate the conversation with David.

We both left the station in a state of shock. This was a blow to our whole reason for being in Ashland. Without legal backing, a proper search of the Fork Street house was impossible. We felt shut out. The protective walls around Rallen were looking impenetrable. Mandu was smart to retreat to Ashland. He knew that he had allies here not only legal, but spiritual.

"We need to regroup and find a new strategy. Let's get some take out and head back to the hotel," David suggested.

"Okay. That Thai place on the square looks like a good bet.," I made my own suggestion.

We stopped off and bought some curry and chicken satay. Once back in David's room, we sat at the small table. It was quiet as we ate our meal.

David finally broke the somber mood, "I can't believe that local PD would not cooperate with us. So much for interagency coordination. They must have ties to the One Humanity group."

"That is very likely. At least the judge must be a fan. From the looks of the OH house, there is a lot of money flowing into the local coffers from Rallen's businesses," I added. "Maybe they don't want to rock the boat. Or the spiritual darkness we have felt here is a strong ruling power over the town and its government."

"We need some irrefutable evidence that links Rallen to Jacob's disappearance. Let me call Sgt. Delano and see if she has come up with anything." David clearly wanted to do something to break the mood of disappointment we were feeling.

David left me to finish my lunch while he walked out into the lobby to make his call. I understood that he had to set some boundaries in our relationship. He was a professional, and certain protocols had to be observed. During his absence, I began to look back on our time together. I was drawn to David more so than any other man in my life. The physical attraction was definitely there, but the added spiritual dimension made for a compelling mix. I had not been able to share my deep relationship with the Lord with any of my past loves. They were all intertwined with my rebellious years. We talked a good game of acceptance and "higher love," but the sin nature had not been dealt with and kept raising its ugly head. All the pitfalls of romance were evident: jealousy, power struggles, guilt, the blame game, past hurts, and obsessions were just a few of the spoilers.

When I came back to the Lord, I had an experience that started my healing process. I realized that I had given away pieces of my soul to each man that I had sexual relations with. God wanted me to release the pieces of their souls and take back what I had unwittingly given. One whole day, I sat in His presence and wept. I repented of my foolish squandering of my most precious possession, my purity. God helped me make that divine exchange. After nearly emptying a whole box of tissues, I emerged a new woman. I felt like a virgin, clean and spotless. It was a miracle. And now my purity was not something I took lightly. It was a precious gift from the Lord. I had not put it at risk in the years since I left the CEC. I would never surrender it until the day He allowed me to marry the man *He* had appointed for me. Was David that man? I couldn't help but wonder.

"Good news!" David declared as he walked through the door. "Delano had another contact with Ashley. Remember she was the woman from the OH Center in Berkeley. They cleaned out the offices at the center just after they closed the doors. They needed all hands on deck to get everything packed up quickly. They asked Ashley to help. She was emptying some drawers in Naomi's office. There was a box of video cassettes in her bottom drawer. One of the labels read "Jacob C. interview." She said that it was like a bell went off, and she knew she had to get that tape out of the building. She did manage to smuggle it out. When she watched it at home, she was shocked. It had proof that Jacob was not interviewed but interrogated by Naomi. At the end of the tape, two of Rallen's bodyguards overpowered Jacob. They put a cloth over his mouth and nose and he went limp."

"Oh no!" I gasped. "That's how they got him out of the center. Poor Jacob. What a nightmare! I cannot believe that they would have documented their crime."

"But this is just the evidence we need to compel the local authorities to investigate the One Humanity house and center here in Ashland. I have asked Delano to make copies of the tape and send us one via overnight mail." David had his smoking gun and was determined to make it count.

chapter 9

Our momentum was at a standstill in Ashland until we
received the videotape from Berkeley. We agreed to take
some rest time until dinner. Perhaps with reflection we
could come at the situation with new energy. I retired to my room.
David said he had some calls to make to the home office.

I took the opportunity to read a few passages from Psalms. I
knew I would find comfort and confidence in the words of King
David. He knew what it was like to have the enemy block you at
every turn. He faced many unthinkable challenges by strengthening
himself in the Lord. Being in God's presence was his way of recharging his batteries. That is what I needed. I wanted to see the situation
we were in from God's perspective. After filling my mind with the
Word, I stretched out on the bed. I focused on the goodness of God.
I silently praised Him. I relaxed and enjoyed the feeling of being
lifted out of the problem. I ascended into the way maker's realm, and
my confidence in the Lord's guidance was renewed.

The faces of friends from years ago came to my mind. Julian
and Sarah were part of the group that coalesced around the Cosmic
Earth Collective message in Ashland during my time there. They
ran a small shop on Main Street. Suzanne and I had sold some of
our air brushed clothing to them for resale in their shop. Were they
still in Ashland? I felt compelled to connect with them. Taking out
the phone book, I remembered their last name. Edgers, there was a
listing. I picked up the phone and called the number. To my surprise,
Sarah answered after three rings. Explaining that I was in town, I
asked her if she and Julian still had their shop. She said they did and

that it was more than just a gift shop now. They had moved and expanded to a coffee shop and bookstore as well. She would love to meet me there and catch up. I asked if she was available that afternoon and she said she could get away for a short visit. She gave me the address and the time to meet.

I phoned David's room and told him that I wanted to check in with an old friend. He asked if I wanted him to go along. I told him no. I could tell that he was relieved because he still had work to do. David and I planned to meet at the Greenleaf café for dinner later.

"Sarah! You look great!" I greeted my friend with a hug. "I am so happy that we could get together. Thank you for meeting with me on such short notice."

"You look pretty good yourself. I know it's been a while, but friendship proves to be timeless. Don't you think?" she replied.

Sarah settled me down in a cozy booth and then ordered some coffee from the bar. "I hope you like flavored latte, we have a new machine and it makes the best espresso ever."

After we were settled with our drinks, I asked, "Tell me what you have been up to since I last saw you."

"We've had our ups and downs like any small business. But we stuck with it and now we are doing great. I pretty much manage the shop and coffee bar. Julian has a job with One Humanity." With these words from Sarah, my spirit jumped. I tried not to react too overtly. My mind was racing. I prayed, "Lord is this why you had me connect with these old friends?" Of course it was. I saw the pattern of His direction. Some doors had been slammed in our faces, but God was opening a window. I asked for His peace as I continued my conversation with Sarah.

"Oh, One Humanity, what is that?" I asked as calmly as I could muster.

"Ever since the CEC folded here, we had been looking for a group to partner with. We feel we have a calling to bring about the elevation of man's consciousness. Three years ago, One Humanity, we call it OH, opened a center, and we were some of the first people to be led into their mission here in Ashland and around the world. Its leader is amazing and so full of wisdom. He brought us right in and gave us a purpose that we had not felt in a long time. Julian eventually gained favor and was brought on the organizational team. He loves it. It is everything that he has been working toward for so many years." Sarah expressed her devotion to the OH and Rallen Mandu. Her beaming face sent shivers down my spine. How could she be so vested in a lie? The Angel of Light had hypnotized another vulnerable soul.

"Rallen Mandu is our leader and he is having an open house tomorrow night at his home. It is just for the closest associates. I believe we can bring a friend. Would you like to go? I am sure that your experience with the Cosmic Earth Collective would be of interest to Rallen." Sarah was eager to introduce me to her new obsession.

"Could I bring a friend?" I asked. "I am in town with my traveling companion from the Bay Area. He would love to find out more about the One Humanity mission."

"Companion? That sounds exciting." Sarah gave me a look that said volumes. "Sure, I would like to meet this mysterious *traveling companion*."

"Great, give me the address and we will be there. About what time?" I asked.

Suzanne went to the coffee bar and jotted down the address and came back to the table. "Here you go. This will be really fun. I can't wait for you to meet Rallen and the people from the center. Now, tell me what you have been doing since we last met."

I gave her a thumbnail sketch of my life in Boise. I centered my narrative around my teaching assignment. I did not mention that I had switched sides; that I had learned the truth about the new age movement and given my heart to the God of Abraham, Isaac, and Jacob.

I realized that it was almost time to meet David for dinner. I excused myself and hugged my old friend, telling her it was good to see her again. She repeated her invitation to the open house. As I walked around the square toward the Greenleaf restaurant, I began to question my acceptance of Sarah's invitation. Yes, it was a way to access Rallen's lair, but how would we avoid meeting him face to face? He knew us. One look at David and I could cause the Ashland group to follow the reaction they had in Berkeley. We could lose them again. How many safe houses did Rallen have?

When I entered the restaurant, David was already seated at our favorite table. He greeted me warmly and immediately noticed my troubled mood.

"What happened at the meeting with your friend?" David asked.

"It was great seeing her again. She revealed something that really shook me up."

"I can tell, what happened?" David's concern gave me confidence to share my impulsive decision to attend the meeting at the OH house.

"She and her husband are members of the One Humanity group here in Ashland." I waited for David's reaction.

"No way!" David's surprise was immediately followed by a look of calculation. I knew he was considering how we could turn this to our advantage.

"I know what you are thinking. I had the same thoughts. I may have overstepped. She invited us to a gathering at the OH house, and I accepted." I took just a beat before continuing. "I have already run through the pros and cons. It would give us access to the house, but we would have to find a way to avoid contact with Rallen Mandu. If there is enough of a crowd, we could hide out long enough to get our bearings. I know from the dream messages I have received that Jacob is being held in a basement. We have to find a way to access the lower floor of the house."

"Woah! You are way ahead of me. Let's take a few minutes to sort this out." David put on the brakes.

"Are you ready to order?" the waitress interrupted our intense conversation.

"I think we need a little more time," David said with a forced smile.

We took just a couple of minutes to decide on the special for the day. The description on the card inserted in the menu sounded excellent—grilled sea bass with a side of local greens and roasted potatoes. The waitress returned and took our order. She reassured us that we had made a good choice.

I was hungry but was having trouble focusing on the task at hand. My mind was racing. Could we really pull this off?

"You know, if we get the evidence of Jacob's abduction by the OH group tomorrow, we will be able to gain access legally. There would be no need for the cloak and dagger move," David started the conversation again.

"You're right, I just couldn't pass up the invitation. It may still be a viable option," I countered.

"Okay, let's leave it on the table for now, and let's focus on what is on the table right in front of us." David picked up the basket of crusty rolls and passed it to me.

We managed to have a pleasant meal after all. We chatted about our current careers. David shared a couple of stories from past investigations. I told some amusing tales of the ups and downs of teaching elementary school children. I had the joy of dealing with fifth graders, the ones who were the big cheeses on campus about to be brought down to Earth by their entrance into the world of middle school angst.

We rode back to the hotel in a tense silence. We were both playing out the many scenarios that could greet us the next day. We said our good nights in the lobby of the hotel. David said he had to check with the clerk to see if he had received a fax that afternoon. He was trying to wrap up some paperwork on another investigation. As I headed toward my room, I noticed a woman sitting in the corner of the lobby. She was watching David as he approached the hotel desk. When she saw that I was watching her, she quickly turned and looked toward the front door as if she were waiting for someone. There was something about her actions that alerted me. Were we being watched? Perhaps Rallen already knew that we were in town.

I tried to forget the woman in the lobby as I entered my room. I changed into my night gown and robe. As I washed my face and brushed my teeth, I thought about Claire and decided to give her a call.

"Claire, its Joy." She answered her phone right away. "Are you expecting a call?"

"Just yours, I had a feeling you would contact me tonight," Claire replied.

"Do you have any updates for me?" I asked. It had been a couple of days since we last spoke. The way events were progressing that seemed like a lifetime.

"Not since we got the videotape from Ashley. You should receive it by tomorrow morning," she explained.

"Things are at a halt here until we get that tape. We need leverage to get the local authorities to help us. There is one development that is promising. I met with Sarah Edgers. I don't think you knew her from the CEC. I met her through the couple I stayed with here after I left San Diego. You won't believe it, they are part of the One Humanity group now."

"Wow, what a coincidence," Claire responded with enthusiasm.

"I guess you could call it that. I prefer to think that it is a divine appointment." I hoped that Claire would accept my explanation.

"I am not sure I get that reference. You think that God had something to do with it?" Claire countered.

"Yes, I do. This whole journey to find Jacob has been divinely appointed. There is a lot more going on here than meets the eye. We are in a battle between good and evil." I was treading on thin ice with Claire by bringing up my beliefs.

"Come on, you don't really think the One Humanity group is *evil*. I mean Rallen Mandu is a crook, for sure, and I do believe he is involved with Jacob's disappearance, but you can't just paint them all black." Claire was putting up defenses.

I whispered a quick prayer for wisdom and direction for my next words. "Claire, I know that your study of Eastern religions has brought you to a belief that there are many ways to God. You have accepted the popular notion of situational ethics, that everyone has a right to find their own truth. I have to tell you that there is only one truth. Life really is black or white. There is no gray area. You either accept God on His terms, or you are playing in the devil's arena." I waited for Claire's response, knowing that this was the first time I had ever challenged her belief system. I knew it was a defining moment. I could lose a friend, but the time for tiptoeing around the truth was over.

"I don't know what to say." Claire's usual air of confidence was gone. I sensed confusion. I expected her to throw up a wall, but the Holy Spirit was urging me to press into the moment.

"Claire, you know I love you. You are my oldest and dearest friend. I would never do or say anything that would hurt you. What I am saying now is in your best interest. I only want you to know the kind of eternal love that I have found in the arms of my Savior, Jesus Christ. He is real! You could reach out and touch Him right now. He loves you so much and wants you to find fulfillment in a life with Him. This doesn't have anything to do with religion, Eastern or otherwise. It is about a relationship with the God who created you to love Him back. All you have to do is say 'yes' to that love. He will reveal Himself to you and show you the way to build that relationship. It is as easy as that. Just say yes." I had poured my heart into those words. Now it was up to the Holy Spirit to make them come alive to Claire.

It was quiet on the other end of the line. Then I heard a sniffle. Claire was crying. *Oh, God, please, please let this be the moment of revelation.*

"You make it sound so simple," Claire said through her tears.

"It is! I wish I was there with you right now. I want to hug you. You are facing the moment of truth. It is a turning point. Just reach out and take His hand."

"But I feel like my whole life has been a lie. I have been so blind to God's true love for me. I always wanted it to be on my terms. I wanted to create a god that I could control. Can He ever forgive me for shutting Him out all these years?" Claire continued to pour out her heart over the phone.

"YES! That is what He does. Jesus gave His life for you. His blood was given to cleanse you of all your mistakes and false beliefs. Now believe that He died for your salvation. Accept Him as your personal savior. He will make everything new. You can do this," I urged her on.

"What do I say? There has to be some ceremony or something, doesn't there?" Claire returned.

"Not really. Just tell Him what is in your heart right now and ask Him to take you into *His* heart. He is in love with you. He's been waiting so long to embrace you. Just surrender to His love." I was overwhelmed with the importance of the moment. I was feeling goose bumps all over.

"Okay, I am going to pray and you tell me if I am doing it right. Jesus, I am sorry that I have ignored you all my life. Even though I had a friend that knows you so well, but I want you to have my heart now. I want to feel your love. I need you! I don't want to go one more day believing a lie. Please show me the truth." Claire's prayer was perfect.

I waited for the impact of Claire's prayer to mark the moment. She began to sob and then to laugh. I was crying now too. There was no time, no distance, as the fulfillment of so many of my prayers for Claire became real.

I managed to speak through my emotions. "Claire, that was perfect! I can tell even over this phone that you have turned a page in your life and it will never be the same. God will lead you into the truth. You will experience Him in ways you never could have imagined. He will fill up your life. A hunger for His Word will consume you. Do you remember that Living Bible I gave you a couple of Christmases ago? Just open it up and God will begin to speak to you. Those words will dance off the page. They will become alive. They are food for your soul."

"I feel so different. It's like time has just stood still. I can't believe that I have resisted this for so long. I had no idea. I always knew that there was something so real about your relationship with God. Now I can see it. Thank you for being so patient with me." Even Claire's voice sounded softer.

"Will you be all right?" I asked. "I've got to get some rest. It's a big day tomorrow."

"Sure, but I really want to see you. Do you think I could come up there?" Claire asked.

"I'll have to check with David. I want to see you too. Let's check in tomorrow, and if you have any big questions about what just happened tonight you have Pastor Ben's phone number. Perhaps you could go see him and let him know that you have followed Jacob into the Kingdom of God," I recommended.

"I don't think I can come down off this cloud and sleep tonight. I am going to go and find that Bible right now. I want to see what God has to say about all this," Claire exclaimed.

"Sounds like a plan. I am so happy for you. You can count on walking on that cloud for quite a while. Good night. I love you," I signed off.

"Good night, I love you too." Claire hung up her phone.

I was energized. I wanted to share Claire's amazing transformation with David. I called his room. There was no answer. I thought that was odd since we were both looking forward to some quiet time in our rooms after a busy day. I quickly dressed and went to his door and knocked—no answer there either. I walked down the hall to the lobby. It was empty. Even the suspicious-looking woman was gone. I asked the clerk if David Kramer had picked up his fax; he said he had some time ago and then left the hotel. My concern was growing. I didn't think that David would leave without telling me. Of course, I had been on the phone for a long time with Claire. I went out to the parking lot to see if David's car was there. It was gone. The sky was dark. There was a caution in the air, and I felt like I was still being watched. A chill went up my spine, as I retreated into the lobby. What could I do? David was a detective. He knew what he was up to, even if I didn't. He must have gone out to check up on a lead.

Back in my room, I called David's room phone and left a message. I was disappointed that I could not share with him the joy of Claire's salvation. I began to get ready for bed. As I crawled under the covers, I prayed for David's protection.

chapter 10

I awoke with a jumble of emotions—excitement over Claire and worry for David. I called his room. There was still no answer. I dressed quickly and went to the breakfast room. To my relief, David was sitting at our favorite table drinking his morning coffee.

"I was worried about you!" I said as I sat down opposite him.

"I got your message, but I thought it would be too late to return it when I came back to the hotel."

"Where were you?" I tried to keep any annoyance out of my voice.

"When I picked up my fax last night, I noticed a woman in the lobby. She was staring at you as you left to go to your room. Something didn't seem right to me. I walked over to her and asked her if she was waiting for someone," David explained.

"That was pretty bold!" I said with a small smile.

"She thought so too. She said it was none of my business and got up to leave. I followed her out and pretended to be getting something out of the trunk of my car. She got in a fancy sedan and a driver took her away. My curiosity got the best of me. I jumped in my car and followed them as close as I dared. Just as I predicted they drove straight to the OH house on Fork Street." David's story was getting good.

"Very mysterious. I saw that woman staring at me in the hotel lobby too. She gave me the willies," I added.

We both took a few minutes to get some toast and eggs from the buffet table. I couldn't wait to hear the rest of David's story.

"I drove past the house and doubled back. I parked across the street and waited to see if I would feel that intense head pain again. Maybe because I was in the car, I felt nothing. The car, the driver, and the woman drove into an underground garage. There were lots of lights on in the house. I could see some people moving around inside. Nothing else happened for a while, and then the front door opened. A man, hard to see because he was dressed in black, walked out into the yard with a flashlight. He aimed it right into my face. That's when I got the message to leave. I drove back through town, past the One Humanity center. It was all closed up for the night. I came back to the hotel, saw your message, and decided to just hit the hay." David completed his story with an expression that told me how unsatisfying the whole incident was.

"I wonder if that man on the lawn was the man in black from the park." It seemed to me more than a coincidence.

"It very well could be. I don't think we've seen the last of him. Now tell me what you called about last night. You sounded really excited." David opened the door for me to relate the miraculous conversion of Claire Cohen.

I told him all about the way the Holy Spirit guided my words. He brought Claire to that point of decision and eased her over the great divide, from darkness to the marvelous light of the gospel invitation to eternal life. Tears flowed as I relayed the timeless encounter. David blinked back a few tears himself. This story of salvation brought back the experience of our own entrance into the Kingdom.

"That is wonderful. Now mother and son can rejoice together. I can see that God has used Jacob's trial to bring his mother to the Lord. What does the Word say? All things work together for good, to those who are called. Now we just have to make the reunion between Jacob and Claire a reality. Let's go see if that videotape has arrived. Delano assured me it would be here this morning." David was anxious for action.

We entered the hotel lobby and approached the desk. "Do you have a package for me? David Kramer, it should have come in this morning by overnight courier."

"Yes, I signed for it myself." The clerk turned to retrieve the package. He looked on the shelf behind the desk and then started searching the drawers and counters. "That's strange. It was right here. Let me check with the secretary." He stepped into an office to the side of the registration area. When he returned, he looked mystified.

"I am so sorry, sir. Your package has seemed to just disappear. I had it right here."

He looked around frantically.

"Did you leave the desk area at all after it arrived?" David asked.

"Only for a couple of minutes to use the bathroom. I am so sorry. I have never had this happen before. What can I do to make up for this terrible mistake?" The clerk was obviously concerned for his job.

"I don't think this was your fault. There are people who would do anything to get their hands on that package. It looks like they found a way to do just that. I am not going to file a complaint, but if you could just keep your eyes open for any suspicious looking people hanging around." David was giving the man a way to save face.

"Certainly, I will call you if I see anything. Thank you for your understanding." The relief on the clerk's face was evident.

David and I exchanged a look of frustration. Another door had been slammed in our faces. "Back to square one, there are too many indications of a coordinated attempt to block our investigation of Rallen and the OH. It is no secret that we are in town. Our every move is being anticipated. It looks like the open house tonight may be our best bet to get close to the inside track. Can you call your friends and set up a meeting place so we can make sure we are allowed into the open house. Perhaps we could meet them for dinner," David suggested.

"I will call them right away. Let's go to your room. I'll call from there and we can also check in with Delano to see if there is another way to get that videotape," I said as I led the way down the hall.

I was able to reach Sarah and arrange to meet her and Julian for dinner. She suggested the Thai restaurant on the square. We would meet them at five thirty. That would give us plenty of time to make it to the open house by seven. I told her that I was bringing my friend.

She was excited to meet David. I conveniently left out the fact that he was a detective from the Berkeley Police Department. We had plenty of time to come up with a cover story.

"It's all set. What are we going to do today? I thought we would be watching that video and then working with the local police to set up the search warrants for the OH center and house," I asked David who was sitting at the table and looking rather glum. He was used to making things happen. Sitting around all day was not a prospect he was looking forward to.

"I have some calls to make. Do you want to meet me in the lobby in about an hour? I may have some direction by then." David was not being rude by dismissing me. I knew that he was just keeping the lines between work and our personal connection tight. He gave me an apologetic look as I left the room.

I didn't want to go back to my room and mope around. I decided to go to the lobby and sit for a while. I found an overstuffed chair in a quiet corner and grabbed a local newspaper off the table nearby. I was wrestling with my emotions. I loved to be with David. His presence was reassuring, but the boundaries of our relationship were hazy. There were wild swings between attraction and distance. It was confusing. Part of me just wanted to come right out and tell him how I felt about him. Then the reality of what we were doing would set in and override my personal feelings. This was not the time or place to start a romantic relationship. I knew that we both felt the connection between us, but there were greater forces at play. We had to keep our distance for Jacob's sake.

As I was browsing through the paper, I came upon an ad; it read, "Lonely? Lost? Looking for purpose? Come to the One Humanity Center. We have answers and people who will embrace you with all the love you deserve. Open meetings every Tuesday and Thursday evenings a seven. Come as you are; you will be accepted." There was an eye catching graphic of a pyramid holding an eye. It was the same image that appears on our very own dollar bill. I knew it was also an image from Freemasonry. How did that symbol relate to Rallen Mandu and the OH philosophy? Perhaps it was just a way to get attention or there could be a deeper connection. I wouldn't put it past Rallen to use any symbolism to give his message credibility.

My contemplation was interrupted by a commotion at the check-in counter. "Can you wait right here, miss? I want to check with my supervisor before I release any information on current guests." The same clerk that we had spoken to that morning was speaking to a woman standing with her back to me. As the clerk left the counter and entered the office, she turned and looked down the hallway. I saw her profile. I recognized her immediately. It was the mystery woman who had been spying on us the night before. My first reaction was to approach her and ask what she wanted, but there was something about her that caused me to think twice. I felt a check in my spirit. Just then, David came walking rapidly down the hall.

"My name is David Kramer. I believe you have something that belongs to me." His authority and aggression were intimidating.

"I…I don't know what you are talking about. I have never met you and I certainly don't have anything of *yours*." She faltered but regained her balance quickly.

"I received a package here this morning. You were in the lobby when it disappeared," David pressed.

"You are out of line, Mr. Kramer. You have no proof of my involvement in your disappearing package. I am leaving now." She turned and walked out of the hotel.

It was true. David had no proof. His tactic of surprise had not yielded any evidence of her involvement with the coordinated effort to block his investigation. The clerk peeked out of the office. He saw that the woman was gone.

"I am so sorry, Mr. Kramer. I called you when I saw her, but I couldn't really say she was the one who stole your package. She was asking about your friend, Ms. Morgan. She wanted to know how many days she was booked in the hotel. Of course, I can't give out that information, but it gave me a chance to go to the office and give you a call." The clerk was apologizing again.

"That's all right." David paused and read the name tag on the clerk's jacket. "Samuel, you did a good job. It is up to me to prove her involvement. Your vigilance is much appreciated. I don't need to tell you that there are some people in this town that would like to see Ms. Morgan and I disappear. Just keep a look out for us, if you will. Let us know if you see anything else that looks suspicious."

"I sure will. No problem that is part of my job," Samuel replied with a growing sense of purpose.

David looked around the lobby. When he saw me in the corner, he headed for the seating area there. "I am sure you saw all that. I am really frustrated. It is so difficult to deal with these people. They are really slippery."

Making himself comfortable in one of the chairs next to mine, he gave me a look of resignation.

"Don't let it get you down," I said. "We are going to get a break here soon."

"Do you know something I don't?" David asked.

"Not really, I just know who's on our side. God did not bring us here to fail." My effort to bolster David's mood started to take effect.

"My call to Delano was productive," David began. "She was surprised by the stolen tape. She said she would send another one to the Ashland Post Office by registered mail. We could have it as soon as tomorrow afternoon. She has continued her search into the OH financials. It looks like the house and center are not the only properties they have in this area. They also own a farm a couple of miles outside of Jacksonville. It's a town north of here."

"What do they do there?" I asked.

"I'm not sure, maybe it is a retreat of some sort. It could be another convenient spot to stash unwanted guests." David gave me a knowing look that said volumes.

"We don't have a lot to do today, let's take a ride up there and just get the lay of the land, literally," I suggested.

"Good idea, I have the address. It shouldn't be too hard to find." David was visibly relieved to have a destination and direction for the day.

chapter 11

I remembered I had a phone call to make. I had promised Claire that I would call her this morning. Before David and I went to our rooms and prepared for our drive to the farm, I told him about Claire's request to come to Ashland. He didn't like the idea. I agreed that we had to keep a sharp focus on our mission. Finding Jacob needed to be our number 1 priority. Claire's presence could cause a distraction. Perhaps when we found Jacob her help would be needed.

"Claire," I said when she answered her phone. "It's Joy. We have hit a bit of a snag here. The videotape has disappeared. It was delivered this morning, but someone took it right off the counter at the hotel desk. There is no doubt that the One Humanity group knows that we are in town. They are blocking our investigation anyway they can. David has ordered another copy to be sent to the Ashland post office. It won't be here until tomorrow. I talked to David about your request to come to Ashland. We both feel that it is premature. Just hang in a little longer."

"I understand," Claire grudgingly agreed. "I will call Sgt. Delano and see if there is anything I can do on this end of things."

"That's a good idea. How is the Bible study coming?" I asked.

"Amazing, I never knew how interesting the Bible could be. I started at the beginning of the New Testament. I am getting to know Jesus. He is so wonderful! I am falling more in love with Him every day." Claire declared her newfound relationship with her Savior.

"I'm excited to see how quickly you are grasping the importance of the Word of God. You are on the journey of a lifetime. Now I have to go, but I will be in touch every step of the way. I love you."

"Love you too, stay safe," Claire signed off.

David and I started out on our trip to the One Humanity farm. It was a short drive up I-5 and a jog west to Jacksonville. The drive gave us a few minutes to share information.

"Claire was fine with the suggestion that she stay in Berkeley for now," I opened up the conversation.

"Good, I am glad she is being reasonable. I know it must be hard for her having to hear everything second hand."

"It's been difficult enough for us to deal with all the setbacks here. I can't imagine having to manage Claire's emotional roller coaster firsthand. We definitely made the right decision," I confirmed. "When I was waiting for you this morning, I picked up a local paper and saw an ad for the OH center. It had a graphic of the *All-Seeing Eye*. You know the one from the dollar bill."

"Interesting, what do you think they were trying to convey with that symbol?"

"The new-age movement has used all kinds of mysterious pagan symbols to hook people's curiosity. There are so many entry points to their maze of beliefs. Most Christians don't know that seemingly harmless pursuits like yoga, astrology, tarot cards, and Ouija boards can lead them into the realm of darkness. They are dangerous doors to deception."

"That is where spiritual discernment comes in," David replied. "We have to keep our eyes open to the many beckoning voices that would lead us off the path God has for us."

We entered the town of Jacksonville. It was picturesque. We could see by the many well-preserved old buildings that it was steeped in the history of the area. I knew that it had been a gold rush town in the 1880s, but now it was all about the wineries. The town now boasted about its boutique shops, wine tasting rooms, and atmospheric eateries.

"This place makes me feel like we are on vacation," David observed.

"Far from it, let's not get off mission. This town may look idyllic, but there are some darker forces at play nearby." I was trying to keep my focus.

"Take a look at the map. We are looking for Oregon Street. Then we take a left on Jonathan way," David instructed.

"Looks like Oregon is one of the main streets through town. There, that intersection up ahead. Turn right. Now it's just a short distance to Jonathan."

We kept our eyes glued to the road until we came to the left hand turn we were looking for. We had a street number, but all the places on this part of the road were large farms or ranches. We didn't see a lot of street addresses. Then our eyes were drawn to a wooden sign on a fence post near a long drive on the right side of the road. There were no address numbers on it, but it held a familiar pyramid symbol.

"That's got to be it," David said as he slowed and pulled to the side of the road.

"Now what?" I asked, keeping my sense of dread in check.

"Let's cruise the area. Maybe there is a less conspicuous way to access the property."

The fence that formed the boundary of the land continued for at least a quarter mile. It was a large property. There was a mix of trees, firs, maples and cotton woods, obscuring any view of the inner areas of the land. At the corner of the property, there was an access road that led back through trees and brush. It was more of a path really, but David was able to drive into the thicket and find a place to park that would hide the car from the road. We would have to walk the rest of the way to gain access.

"Are you good with this?" David asked.

"Sure, but how far do you want to go?" I was putting my bravest face forward.

"Let's just walk a ways and see if there is a place where we can get a view of any buildings." David's confidence was reassuring.

As we tramped along the pathway, we strained to see if there was an opening in the tree line. We eventually came to a small clearing. We couldn't see any buildings, but it looked like the best place to get through the trees.

David and I looked at each other and silently made the decision to climb the fence.

It was an old wooden structure that was easy to climb each rung and jump to the other side. We made our way through the brush. Suddenly we broke through into a pasture that was open ground. We could see all the way to a cluster of buildings. There was a large house and a number of smaller cabins. It certainly looked like a retreat center. We couldn't see any activity around the buildings, and we did not see any vehicles parked near them either. Without a word, we made the decision to approach the compound. Every step was made in caution. Halfway across the field we heard a bark. Dogs! Two large, black dogs came out from the big house. They started bounding in our direction. We turned and ran as fast as our feet and adrenaline would carry us. The dogs were getting closer. I knew we would not make it to the trees in time.

Let alone through the brush and over the fence. Just as the dogs were about to catch up with us, they suddenly stopped. I looked back and they were cowering on the ground. A mournful whimper was coming from them both. We didn't take the time to figure out what was happening. We were through the trees, over the fence, and down the path. When we were finally in the safety of the car, we took a few minutes to catch our breath.

"Did you see those dogs? They just stopped. I was sure we were going to get mauled." I looked at David to see his reaction to the puzzling event.

"I saw it. And I saw them. Two very large angels stood behind us. They had fiery swords. No way were those dogs going to mess with them," David explained.

I was speechless for a couple of moments as I assimilated this information. Had God sent His protectors to our rescue? It really was the only explanation for the dog's behavior.

"Thank you, Lord! You are so merciful and mighty." I felt like praising and dancing as I realized how God had protected us all along our journey.

"Let's get out of here. I don't want any of Rallen's men coming over here to check things out," David said as he started the car and drove back to the road.

Our trip back to Jacksonville was short, but nerve-wracking. David kept one eye on the rearview mirror the whole way. I worked hard to calm my nerves. We entered the center of town and it was just as we had left it. The normalcy of the shops and pedestrians was in sharp contrast to the supernatural experience we had just had.

"We might as well spend some time here. Let's get some coffee. I'd like to get a feel for the atmosphere. The fact that Rallen has his compound so close to town should be reflected here in some way." David was not ready to abandon his investigation of the area.

We found a coffee shop on the main street. We hoped it would live up to its name, Good Bean. From the aroma as we stepped into the shop, we knew we were on the right track. We ordered our coffee and found a table in the corner with a view of the door. Out of habit and experience David always sat with his back to a wall.

"I would have liked to get closer to the buildings at the farm, but at least we are familiar with the area now. If we have to make a quick trip here at some point in the future we will know exactly where to go and what to expect," David explained.

"Makes you wonder what they have going on there. Could they have other people being held against their will? Like you said, the farm would be a secluded place to hide anything you don't want exposed to the public and those dogs are a very effective deterrent to unwanted visitors."

"Exactly, if we have to go back there, we had better have some police back up." David was calculating his options.

"We have encountered so much resistance, there has to be something they are hiding. Delano has found some problems in their financial statements, hasn't she?"

"Yes, there are many inconsistencies pointing to hidden funds. There may even be off shore accounts and shell corporations involved. That is the typical route for people like Rallen Mandu." David was painting a picture of the OH group that made sense with all their layers of secrecy.

We finished our coffee and stepped out into the street. We decided to take a walk and check out the shops. There were the typical mix of gift, antique and specialty stores; one caught our attention. It was a gift shop that specialized in Eastern religious icons and crystals. It was the typical mix of New-Age paraphernalia, colorful, eye-catching and sparkly. We decided to go inside. I had to overcome a feeling of dread. The atmosphere was thick with incense and false spirituality. It took all my courage to stay in the shop and pretend to be looking for some rare treasure. I wanted out. David looked equally uncomfortable.

"Is there something I can help you find?" A clerk approached me. She was dressed in a tie-dyed dress that skimmed the floor. Her hair was long and braided in many strands that held jewels and silver charms. Three necklaces graced her neck, each one with a pendant representing some deity or religious symbol. "My name is Parvati. Are you visiting, or just passing through Jacksonville?"

It took me a minute to take in all of her adornments. "Just passing through, my friend and I were curious to see what kind of gifts you have here."

"We have everything you could want for spiritual enlightenment. These symbols hold great power to lift you into new levels of consciousness." She pointed to the pendants on her necklaces. She radiated a stunning sense of confidence. I knew that she was deeply committed to her beliefs.

"Do you know anything about the One Humanity group?" David asked.

"Oh yes, they are wonderful. I have a friend that holds meetings in her home to bring people into the ideals of One Humanity. They have a center in Ashland. You could go there and find out more about them," she gushed.

"They don't have a center here in Jacksonville?" David wanted to find out if the locals knew about the farm.

"I don't think so. It is more informal here. People meet and share ideas and then if they want to get more information they just go down to Ashland," Parvati explained.

"Do you ever see the leader, Rallen Mandu, here in the area?" David pressed.

Parvati looked at David with suspicion. "What are you trying to get at? One Humanity is a group that is doing an important work.

Your intensity is bringing the atmosphere down. Like I said, go to the center in Ashland."

David and I realized that our welcome had worn out. We managed to utter a thank-you as we left the shop. After we had walked a couple of blocks, I said, "Seems the veneer of peace and love is pretty thin. It didn't take much for that clerk to turn on us."

David stopped and said, "In 2 Corinthians chapter 2, there is a passage that talks about how we are an aroma of life to those who are being saved and a stench of death to those who are perishing. I think Parvati got a whiff of who we really are, but even all the incense wafting through her shop couldn't cover the deadly smell of what she was selling there."

"I was so uncomfortable in that atmosphere. I couldn't wait to get out of there."

"I could use a bite to eat. Shall we see if we can find a good restaurant here in town?" David was ready to move on to more positive ground.

"Sure, I just hope the whole town doesn't reflect that same atmosphere."

We walked back to the center of town and found an interesting eatery called Bella Union. It was in one of the historic buildings of the town. The interior was as inviting as we hoped. We found a booth and sat quietly as we took in the antique décor. A waitress brought menus and water. We decided on a light lunch since we would be having a dinner soon with my friends in Ashland. We ordered the soup of the day and a small salad each.

"I feel sorry for Parvati," I said as we waited for our food. "She has bet her life on a lie. She puts on a façade of beaming happiness, but you saw how easily she was moved into suspicion. I know from experience how the excitement of the New Age message can turn into a dead end. There are a lot of counterfeit promises. Satan has a counterfeit for every good work of the Lord. The only difference is that the false promises lead nowhere. I remember a day during my last month in the Maui commune. I had exhausted all the avenues of exploration into the illusory maze of new age religion. I was at the end of the road. I felt desolate as I wandered all day on the beach hoping that the sun and waves would lighten my mood, but I couldn't see the beauty around me. A dark cloud hung over me. All the promises of light and love just trickled through my fingers like the sand under my feet. It was just a few weeks later that I flew back to the mainland and gave my heart to Jesus. All these years later, the promises of God are still fresh and new. There is no end to my hunger for more of Him."

David looked intently into my eyes. "I can feel the truth of God in your words. The Truth *has* set you free."

I was speechless for a few moments as the intensity of our connection burned in his eyes. I didn't want that feeling to end, but the waitress brought our food and we turned to the mundane task of lunch. We ate in silence for a while. I had to work hard to ignore my conflicting emotions.

"We should get back to Ashland and get ready for our big night out with Julian and Sarah. This could very well be the end of our search as we may gain access to Rallen's lair. Be sure to bring the key," David announced at the end of our meal.

Back at the hotel, we went to our rooms to freshen up. I wanted to just rest for a few minutes to recharge my batteries. I took a quick shower to compensate for the sprint across the field at the farm. I wrapped up in my robe and fell asleep as soon as I stretched out on the bed. I awoke to the sound of the telephone on the nightstand. I grabbed it before I was fully aware of doing so. It was David. He said he would meet me in the lobby in twenty minutes. I was grateful for his call. As I fixed my hair and makeup, I remembered the dream that I had during my nap.

David and I were being chased across an airport tarmac. I knew that there was a group of men after us. As we neared the terminal, we saw a door that we knew led to safety. We tried the handle, but it was locked. I felt the weight of the key in my pocket and took it out. The men were getting closer. I fumbled with the lock. I dropped the key, and when I went to pick it up, it disappeared.

That is where the dream ended and the phone call from David interrupted my sleep. I shook off the feeling of disappointment and fear from the dream. I had to keep my thoughts fixed on a positive outcome for our visit to the OH house tonight. I dressed quickly and met David in the lobby with three minutes to spare.

We arrived at the Thai restaurant right on time. Julian and Sarah were already seated at a table near the front of the room. We greeted each other warmly, and I introduced David as a friend from San Francisco. I could tell by their expressions that they were waiting for more information. I quickly turned the conversation to questions about Julian's job with the OH. The fewer stories, the better. We had to keep our stories straight about who David was and how we knew each other.

Julian was more than happy to expound on his work with OH and Rallen Mandu. "I am so privileged to be working for this amazing man and his message. We are spreading the good news of a new age that is at hand. Mankind is transforming into its destiny as peace makers and creative beings. We are manifesting heaven on Earth."

It was difficult for me to keep my reaction from showing on my face. He was using words that were all too familiar. Satan was losing no time adapting to the moves of God in the Church. By using words and phrases familiar to Christians, he was hoping to snare them and draw them deeper into his web of deceit. It lined right up with Mark 13:22, "For false Christs and false prophets shall rise, and shall show signs and wonders, to seduce, if it were possible, even the elect."

"How do you get your message out to people?" David asked.

"We use all avenues: print, media, and internet. We hold informational meetings at all of our centers," Julian explained.

I was concerned that we would spark the same reaction that we had at the shop in Jacksonville. I quickly changed the subject and gave David a look that said, "No more questions."

I was relieved that the rest of our meal passed in pleasant conversation about how Ashland had grown along with Julian and Sarah's business and family. We followed Julian's car up the hill to the One Humanity house. Parking on the street was already limited. We had to hike up to the house and had no problem entering. The gathering was already in full swing. Pockets of people were in lively conversation all around the main room and even into the dining hall and library. Julian introduced us to a group of co-workers from the center. They welcomed us and luckily didn't ask too many questions about why we were attending the event. David and I accepted glasses of sparkling cider from a tray being circulated by a young lady dressed in a waiter's outfit.

"Ladies and gentlemen," a well-dressed man with silvery hair was drawing our attention to the front of the big room. "I am so pleased to see you all here tonight. You are all valuable members and friends of One Humanity. Your selfless service to our mission is much appreciated as well as your continuing financial support. We have called you all here this evening not only to celebrate our successes, but to identify our challenges. I know that Rallen will be able to lay some of your concerns to rest and paint a picture of our bright future. So now without further delay, here is our inspiring leader, Rallen Mandu!"

A strong and lengthy round of applause erupted from the crowd of adoring fans in the house. I hated to add to the din, but felt that I had to play along with the mood of the moment. I looked at David and saw similar conflicting emotions play across his face.

Rallen swept on to the raised platform with an angelic look of benevolence. He was dressed in his disguise as an Eastern Indian guru. Long, flowing robes of cream and white added to the drama of his appearance. He gazed at the hushed crowd, bestowing the blessing of his presence. I looked at some of the faces of the people around me. They were enraptured. My stomach turned as I watched his followers give him the adoration that should be going to the King of Kings, Jesus, but this crowd was ready to believe every word that would proceed from Mandu's lips.

"My beloved friends, welcome to my home. I am blessed to have every one of you here tonight. I know that we are at a turning point in our mission. I want all of us to experience the leap of faith that is drawing us upward to our calling. Some of you know about the interference we encountered in Berkeley. Governmental agencies conspired to block our efforts in the Bay Area. We must be gracious toward them. They are unenlightened. They are acting out of baser motives, and will soon come to the truth or the forces of Shiva will eliminate them. Mankind is on a path to ascension. It cannot be stopped."

The people surrounding the platform made sounds of affirmation. Some even bowed with hands together in worship to Rallen Mandu.

"We must redouble our efforts. Sacrifices must be made to assure our victorious expansion. Every day we are adding numbers to our cause. New centers are opening and I predict that the Berkeley center will open again. We are currently exploring new facilities that will make room for even more seekers there. I have invited you here tonight to present to you an opportunity to show your commitment to One Humanity. Every dollar you pledge will be multiplied to fulfill our mission. What is our mission? ONE HUMANITY!" The whole crowd shouted along with Rallen. This obviously was their rallying cry. It sent shivers down my spine with its combination of vehemence and determination. Mandu had these people right where he wanted them.

I then noticed that there were check writing stations set up around the room. People rushed to make out their offerings to Mandu and the OH. I looked at David and could tell that we were both struggling with our feelings of revulsion. What a masterful display of manipulation.

"How are we going to slip away to explore the house?" I whispered to David.

"Let's split up and ask to use the bathroom," he replied.

Before we could initiate our plan, Rallen Mandu approached us from the crowd.

"I was told that you were in town. I hope you are not going to try the tactics you used in Berkeley. I think you will find they will not be productive in this locale. I also know that you will not find what you are looking for here." Rallen's demeanor had changed. The gracious host now displayed menacing aggression. His true colors were showing.

"We are just following up on some loose ends. We won't be spoiling your little soirée," David countered with equal authority.

"You are welcome to enjoy my hospitality. Just keep your motives to yourself." Rallen dismissed us with a phony smile, but the eyes betrayed his contempt for David and all he stood for.

David and I split up and mingled with the crowd for a while. I stopped and talked to Julian and Sarah for a few minutes.

"Wasn't that amazing? Rallen is so beautiful. Every time I hear him speak, I get goose bumps. He knows how to convey the message we've all been waiting for." Sarah expressed her hero worship. "What did you think?"

"He certainly knows how to make an impression," I replied.

"You don't know all that he is doing for mankind. When you are working for him, you just know that you are on the cutting edge of a new age for humanity. Unity, that is the key, just as the name implies," Julian added with a look of dreamy devotion.

"Do you know where the bathrooms are?" I asked.

"Sure, I can show you," Sarah offered.

"No, I don't want to take you away from your friends. Just point me in the right direction." I quickly discouraged an escort.

As I headed down the hallway, I saw David in the shadows. I joined him and asked if he had any idea which way we could find an entrance to the basement. I was sure that was the most likely location to find a hiding place. He motioned for me to follow him.

We had only gone a short distance when we heard footsteps behind us. I looked back and saw the man in black. The light in the hallway was dim, and he was looking back as we slipped around a corner. We found a door, and David pulled me inside the room. We closed the door quietly and huddled in the corner of the room near the door. Seconds later, we heard the door knob to the room rattle as it was checked to see if it was locked by the man in the hall. The knob did not give. The door was locked. It had not been locked when we entered, and *we* had not locked it. Relief flooded my body as I realized that we had not been discovered by the man in black. I also realized that I was pressed up against David's chest and his arms were enfolding me. The emotions that raced through me were intense. I wanted to stay in his arms forever. I felt protected. The warmth of his body was so soothing.

We both became aware of our closeness at the same time, and we parted quickly. I was glad that the room was dark. I know my face was flushed as I grappled with my emotions. Trying to regain his composure, David found his flash light and snapped it on. It didn't do much to illuminate the large room. We entered the room further and moved the light around the area. It was a study. Book shelves lined the walls. There was a large desk in the middle of the room. David inspected some letters in an ornate wooden box on the desk. They were all addressed to Rallen Mandu. This was his home office.

"Let's look through his desk. We might find something useful." He turned on a desk lamp and bent it lower to the desk to keep the circle of light contained. "The drapes are closed but we can't risk anyone noticing a light up here," David explained.

We both carefully looked in the drawers and files of the desk. I didn't really know what we were looking for and hoped I would recognize something suspicious when I saw it. I kept looking up to the door. I felt that we could have visitors any minute. The tension was starting to jangle my nerves.

"Look at this!" David's whisper held controlled excitement. "It is a memo to Naomi with instructions for the transport of JC from Berkeley to Ashland. That has to be Jacob Cohen. It says to keep him sedated until arrival and to transfer him via the basement parking area at night. The room has been prepared. Interrogation will proceed when he has fully awakened. Coordinate with Damian." David and I exchanged a look of acknowledgment. The man in black very well could be the Damian mentioned in the memo. David folded the memo and filed it in the inside pocket of his jacket. He switched off the desk light. We moved cautiously to the door and listened. David clicked off his pen light and unlocked the door. Cracking it, he peeked out. He opened it wider and looked both ways. Seeing no one, we proceeded down the hallway.

Further down the hall and around a bend, we saw an opening for a stairwell. David approached the opening and flattened against the wall as he looked down the stairs. Seeing no one, he motioned for me to follow. We descended the stairs knowing that we were fully committed now to accessing the basement of Rallen's home. With the evidence in David's pocket, we were even more motivated to find the room where they were holding Jacob. Our quest could soon be over. We would trust God with the way to get him out of the house and back to his mother.

chapter 12

We made it down a few steps to a landing and the stairway made a turn to the left. David used the same maneuver to peek around the corner before proceeding. He looked back at me and nodded. I was grateful that the steps were made of stone. We only had to tread lightly to keep from making noise. At the bottom of the stairway, David looked both ways. The hall was empty for now. I was on edge. Any minute we might see Damian patrolling the halls. I was sure now that Damian and the man in black were one in the same. He seemed like the kind of man that could carry out Rallen's more sinister commands.

"There are three doorways just in this part of the basement. How do we know which one the key belongs to?" David whispered to me.

"I will know it when I see it. Let's check these doors anyway," I replied.

David quietly tested the knob on the first door. It was locked. I did not see any way my key would fit. We proceeded to the next door. It was locked. The third door was also locked. We would not satisfy our curiosity easily. The hallway we were in made a sharp turn ahead. Once again, David carefully peered around the corner. He took my hand and led me into the adjoining hallway. It was an unconscious act, but it sent goose bumps up my arm. His touch was gentle and yet dominant. I didn't want him to let go, but when he realized that we were holding hands, he quickly released me. I heard him take a deep breath and slowly let it out. He was refocusing. We had to stay sharp. We were in enemy territory.

At the end of the hall, the stone work of the walls changed in character. The stone slabs were replaced by river rock. The rocks were aged and worn. There was an alcove recessed into the walled end of the hallway. It was dark. David took out his pen light, and we crept into the alcove. At the end, we found a door. It was unlike any of the other doors in the basement. It was made of heavy wooden planks with rusted metal bars and rivets holding it together. It was arched at the top, and it had a heavy lock plate on its left side. I knew that this was the door that would open for us. We had the key.

Just as we were about to examine the lock, we heard heavy footsteps in the hall. David turned off his pen light. We pressed up against the wall of the alcove and prayed that the darkness would hide us. Even in the dim light of the hall, we could see that Damien was making his rounds. He was approaching our hiding place.

A woman's voice called out, "Damien, Rallen would like to speak to you. He is waiting in his office."

I recognized the voice of the woman. It was Naomi. The woman we had met in the Berkeley center. We watched as the man in black turned and headed back the way he had come. David and I both released our breath. I didn't even know that I had been holding mine.

"Angels?" I whispered to David.

"I didn't see any, but I am sure we received some divine assistance just now."

When we were sure that the footsteps were long gone, David took out his light again. We both inspected the lock on the old door. I took the key out of my pocket. My hand was shaking as I placed it in the lock. It glided right in. As I turned the key in the lock, it made a loud clanking sound. We both froze. When we did not hear anything from down the hall, we both started breathing again. Now, to open the door. Would it make a loud creaking noise? Could it be wired to a security system? We had come this far. We had to open the door. I was surprised that the door swung into the room beyond without a sound. David entered first. The room was a good size and with the small pen light it was hard to see all of it.

I closed the door behind us and called out in a soft voice. "Jacob? Jacob, its Joy, your mom sent me to find you." There was no reply. As I went further into the room, something slid across my face. I jumped and then realized it was a small chain. I reached up and pulled it. A weak lightbulb just barely illuminated the room. It was empty. Jacob was not there.

I fought off a wave of despair, and I breathed a prayer. *"Papa, please don't let this be in vain. I trust you to guide us."*

Even though we did not find Jacob, it was obvious that someone had recently been living in the room. A small cot in the corner was strewn with blankets. A side table held an empty bowl and cup. In a far corner was an RV potty, and from the aroma, it had been used recently.

David was inspecting the bed and table, looking for any clues as to whether Jacob had been the person confined to the room. There were no books or papers anywhere. I started to move the covers on the bed, when I saw something scratched on the wall just level with the mattress.

"David, come and look at this. I need your pen light." As we got closer, we saw some letters and numbers that had been scratched into the surface of one of the sandy river rocks. It looked like it had been etched with a nail or some other metal tool. "EPH 612."

"What is it?" David asked. It took just a moment for me to see that it was a Bible reference.

"Ephesians 6:12," I said. "I know that verse…just give me a minute. It's about the fact that we don't fight against people, but powers, evil spirits."

"Yes, I remember that too. This has to be a message from Jacob. He is telling us that he is being held captive by demonic forces."

"We know there is a sinister power behind the OH and Rallen Mandu. It is the well disguised Angel of Light. He comes robed in peace and benevolence, but his motives are pure evil."

"Jacob was here. They have moved him because of our presence in Ashland. I think that Rallen knew that we would be here tonight. Do you think your friends would have told him?" David asked.

"I don't know, but the OH group seems to be one step ahead of us all the way. They could have moved him to the farm." I wanted to explore our next step.

"That is a logical assumption. We will need a search warrant to get on to that property, which means we need that videotaped evidence. I don't think a scripture reference scratched on a wall is going to do it," David said with frustration.

"So that means we wait until tomorrow. I certainly hope that the post office doesn't conveniently misplace that second tape." My frustration was also showing.

"Okay, our next task is to get out of this basement without running into Damien. I don't think he would dare use force against us, but I don't want to put that theory to the test." David moved toward the door. He turned on his pen light and reached up to pull the chain on the overhead light. The gloom of the chamber where Jacob had been held closed in on me. I had to muster all my faith to keep a pall of depression from invading my spirit.

We slowly opened the door to the hall and peeked out. Seeing no one, we secured the door and quietly moved down the passageway. I was not sure where the exit was, but David was moving with confidence. As a detective, I was sure he had heightened senses of direction and observation. We made it to the stairwell without incident. Up the stairs and into the main house, we left the ominous basement behind. I told David that I really did need to use the restroom. He said he would meet me at the entrance to the main hall.

I lingered in the restroom a few minutes to get control of my nerves. I didn't want to go into the main hall and face the people there. I felt like a fish out of water. I felt like rushing up to the platform and announcing that they were all being deceived. I didn't want to let my frustration about missing Jacob spill over into my ability to deal with the OH members. I needed to remain loving. I said a quick prayer of forgiveness and asked for strength. As I left the restroom, I had a shock. The man in black, Damien, was standing just outside the door. He gave me an intense look of disapproval. "You spent quite a while in the lady's room. I hope you are all right." His words were dripping with sarcasm.

"I'm okay" was my weak and lame reply. I could not overcome the intimidation I felt oozing from his very presence. I left him standing in the hall, and I was relieved when I found David waiting for me as he had promised.

"Can we get out of here?" My request was more of a demand than a question.

"Are you all right? You look like you've seen a ghost."

"I'll tell you about it in the car." I led the way to the front door of the house.

"Leaving so soon? We have more very exciting information to relate. Rallen will be addressing us again soon," a female OH member said, stationed at the door.

"I'm so sorry, I just don't feel well." I was sure that my pallid complexion would validate my claim.

"Oh, I hope you feel better soon. Good evening." The phony smile did not match the words she had spoken.

When we were safely in the car and headed back to the hotel, I told David about my run in with Damien.

"It wasn't what he said, it was the way he said it," I explained. "If words could kill, I would not have made it out of that house."

"I am so sick of all their deception, intimidation, and manipulation. I am more committed than ever to exposing their vile schemes. Pinning Jacob's kidnapping on them will only be the beginning of our case against the One Humanity group." David's usual cool exterior was giving way to his deeper passionate nature.

As we entered the lobby of the hotel, David said good night. I heard him talking to the desk clerk as I started to my room. "Good evening, Sam, don't hesitate to call me if you see anything suspicious out here tonight."

I really needed some quiet time to assimilate all that had occurred on this eventful day. My mind was reeling with memories of dogs, gypsy shopkeepers, and the man in black one step behind us in the OH house basement. In the shower, I imagined the stress of the day being washed down the drain.

Wrapped in my cozy nightgown and robe, I settled onto the bed and took some time to entertain the Lord's presence. I listened for His voice. No distinct words came through, but a profound peace began to embrace me. It was good to remember who was directing my path, who held my life in His hands. I was going to ask for guidance, when I remembered the verse that we had found on the wall in the cell of the OH house basement. I had given a rough rendition, but now I wanted to read the whole thing in its proper setting. I took out my Living Bible. This translation meant a lot to me. Coming from a strict religious background, I enjoyed reading the Word in a language I could easily understand. I turned to Ephesians and found the passage I was looking for. Chapter 6, verse 12 read: *"For we are not fighting against people made of flesh and blood, but against persons without bodies—the evil rulers of the unseen world, those mighty satanic beings and great evil princes of darkness who rule this world; and against huge numbers of wicked spirits in the spirit world."*

That verse could send fear through me if I did not know that the angel armies of the Lord vastly outnumbered the forces of evil. It did, however, give me a perspective into the battle that we were in. This was the battle that Jacob was waging. I was amazed at his knowledge and ability to use the Word to overcome the enemy. He knew what he was up against, remarkable for a baby Christian. He was barely two months old in his relationship with Jesus. I took a few minutes to pray for his protection and asked the Lord to speed up our quest to find him.

chapter 13

I woke up around midnight with my Bible on my chest. I had fallen asleep while praying for Jacob. I put the Bible on the nightstand and crawled under the covers. The next thing I knew, it was morning. I had a vague recollection of a dream of being chased by big black dogs. I remembered that at some point in the chase they grew huge wings and flew over my head.

I shook off the dark visions of my dream and got ready for the day. I was to meet David at breakfast again. As usual he had beaten me to the table. I grabbed a cup of coffee on my way to greet him.

"How was your night?" David asked as soon as I had settled into a chair across from him.

"Pretty good, except for the creepy dream I had just before waking up this morning."

"Was it one of your prophetic dreams?" David gave me one of his intense looks that never failed to get my heart beating faster.

"No, I don't think so. I was just replaying our run in with the dogs yesterday. The only difference was that in the dream they sprouted wings and flew over me."

"That would be scary." David's eyes got round as he shared my vision of flying black dogs.

"That dream did seem to mirror the verse we found in Jacob's cell last night."

"How so?" he asked.

"Well, I looked up that verse on the wall, Ephesians 6:12. When we are through breakfast, I want to read it to you from my Living Bible."

We helped ourselves to the buffet breakfast. We had nearly finished our meal when we saw Julian walk into the room. David and I looked at each other with a question. Why was he here so early this morning? When we saw the look on his face, we began to get a clue to the nature of his visit.

"What do you think you are doing?!" Julian's voice was shrill and loud. The other hotel guest stopped and looked at us.

"Julian, please have a seat and calm down. You are making a scene." I quickly tried to keep the moment from escalating.

"Okay, but I need to know what went on last night." Julian lowered his voice but did not sit down at our table. "Rallen called me into his office first thing this morning and read me the riot act. He said that you two were at the party under false pretenses. He did not appreciate the fact that I had invited you, and that you had been sticking your noses into OH business. So what gives?"

David took command of the situation. "Julian, if you could just sit with us, we can discuss this quietly. We did not intend to put you in a difficult position."

Julian reluctantly took a seat between David and me. "Okay, this better be good."

David proceeded to tell Julian about Jacob's disappearance. He laid out all the clues that we had found that pointed to the One Humanity group's involvement. He did not mention the memo that he had taken from Rallen's office.

"We are expecting a package today that has video evidence. You can see it if you like. I am afraid that we will be requesting a search warrant for the OH house and the authority to interview the staff there." David delivered this last bit of information with care. It could send Julian into another fit of anger.

Julian's reaction was unexpected. He hung his head and sat quietly for a minute. When he looked up, we could see the moisture in his eyes. "I knew something wasn't right. Ever since the raid on the Berkeley center, the core group around Rallen has become extremely secretive. I hear whispered conversations, and when I ask what is happening, I get the cold shoulder. I'm beginning to feel like an outsider. Honestly, for me, the bloom is off the rose. I try to keep up a good front, but for quite some time, I have had my doubts about Rallen's motives and message."

I saw my chance to plant seeds of truth. "Rallen's message is shop worn. It has been packaged and repackaged many times throughout the ages. The only god that Rallen really believes in is himself. Is there any chance that David and I could meet with you and Sarah today to discuss what we are seeing in Rallen and the OH?"

"I think so. I'll have to check with Sarah. I'll call you in a couple of hours. We could meet at the shop, if it's all right with Sarah." Julian's countenance said volumes about his conflicted feelings.

We said our goodbyes and Julian left the hotel. David and I were excited about this turn of events. What started out as a problem had turned into a great opportunity. I let David know that I needed some time to call home and check in with my friend, Elaine, who looks after my apartment when I am gone. I also needed to call Claire. We agreed to meet up in the lobby in two hours, and by then, we would know if the meeting with Julian and Sarah was a go.

As we walked down the hall to our rooms, I remembered the Bible verse that I had promised to read to David. I grabbed my Bible and met David in his room. I read the scripture passage. We both sat and assimilated the depth of the meaning of the verse that Jacob had etched on the wall of his prison cell. We saw more clearly the battle between the kingdom realms. The war was waged for the prize of men's souls. Thankfully, we knew the outcome.

"God is telling us not to rely on our own strength in this search for Jacob. David proclaimed. Just as Rallen and his cohorts have unseen resources, we have even more at our disposal."

"Yes," I said, "we have the Word, the Blood, and the Anointing. And as you know so well, we have angelic hosts backing us up all the way."

I had met Elaine soon after I returned to Boise. She attended my church as well. We were both single and looked out for each other. We took little trips together to explore the state of Idaho. There were so many beautiful places to experience the wonders of nature. The little town of Stanley was one of our favorites. We had rented a cabin there a few times. Sitting on the slopes of the Sawtooth Mountains, the town was small, but so picturesque. We would take day trips to the surrounding lakes and even head south to Sun Valley to see how the other half lived. One of our favorite pastimes in Stanley was sitting on the deck of a local coffee shop that was situated right on the banks of the Salmon River. With the snow-capped peaks of the mountains in the background, the peace and quiet was a welcome change from our busy lives in Boise.

I caught Elaine at her desk at work. She was a loan officer at a local bank. She asked how things were going. I filled her in on the main events of the last week. She said she was praying for Jacob's safety and our success at finding him. She teased me about my working with Detective David Kramer, trying to find out if there was a budding romance. I changed the subject quickly and asked if I had anything important in the mail. She had been watering my plants and bringing my mail in for me. She said everything was pretty routine. I didn't want to keep her on the phone too long, so we said goodbye, and I thanked her for her faithful friendship.

My next call was to Claire. I was a little anxious about my report. We had come so close to finding Jacob. I hated to give her the disappointing news. So when I called and got her voice mail, I wasn't all that sorry to have missed her. I knew that I would connect with her soon, and perhaps by then, we would have a positive outcome. I left her a message that I hoped was encouraging, but short on details.

Just as I was putting the phone down, it rang. Julian was on the line. He said that he and Sarah would like to meet with David and me. He asked if we could be at the shop in about an hour. I said, of course, and immediately called David's room to let him know. He asked if I could come to his room. He wanted to pray for guidance as we shared with Sarah and Julian what we had learned about One Humanity. In the process of exposing the lies, we wanted to present the truth of God's perfect love and righteousness.

David and I entered Julian and Sarah's shop at the appointed time. Sarah led us back to a meeting room in the rear of the building. Julian was there and offered us coffee from a carafe on the table. They were both subdued. I could tell that they were deeply troubled by the subject of our impending discussion.

David broke the ice. "I don't think there is an easy way to get this started, so I will just jump right in. You know Claire Cohen, Joy's best friend, has a son named Jacob. He has been missing for a couple of weeks. Joy and I have been investigating his disappearance in Berkeley and here in Ashland, and all the evidence that we have found points to the involvement of the OH. You might know that Jacob was a member of the OH management team in Berkeley. He was privy to many of the financial dealings of the group. About a month ago, he had an encounter with Jesus and gave his life to *Him*. Jacob's whole perspective shifted. He felt he had a responsibility to expose illegal practices that were rampant within the upper management. We believe that when he confronted them with his decision to make them public, he was kidnapped and brought to Ashland. I have been tasked with the investigation into Jacob's disappearance. That is why the Berkeley center was searched and then closed. Joy and I have experienced misdirection, resistance and lies here as we have looked for Jacob. We are hoping that you may have information that will help us in the search."

There was an uncomfortable silence in the room until Julian finally spoke up. "I have only heard rumors about someone being held in the basement of the OH house here in Ashland. I thought they were a bit dramatic and unfounded. But after the party last night, Damian, Rallen's chief of security, confronted me. He threatened me with bodily harm if I aided you in any way. He was livid about the fact that I had invited you into the house. I could not sleep at all last night, as I considered why Rallen and Damian were so upset about your presence there. Then Sarah and I started to recall other incidents that seemed out of character for members of One Humanity. I had also seen some documents recently that showed substantial funds being transferred to off shore accounts. The magnitude of response to your attendance at the open house could only mean that they are hiding something. Now I know what it is. My faith in the OH is shattered. I am questioning my very foundations."

I breathed a prayer, *"Father, give me the right words. This could be a turning point for Julian and Sarah."* I looked at Sarah and saw the same confusion on her face.

"God is not closing that door and leaving you abandoned," I said with all the compassion I could muster. "You are at a crossroad. You have an opportunity to embrace truth. *THE* truth of who God is. He has a perfect plan for your lives and has brought you to this point of decision, so that you can experience Him in all His fullness. You have been settling for a counterfeit. You would never be satisfied with the OH in the long term. Jesus is right here extending His hand to you. He loves you so much that He died to give you freedom in this life, and eternal life in the next. I know that you can feel His presence. All you have to do is say yes."

The atmosphere was electric. Time stood still as eternity surrounded us. Both Julian and Sarah began to break down. Tears flowed. Julian reached out and took Sarah's hand. They both looked at David and me and said together, "YES!" Then the glory cascaded into the room. Even David was misty. I was sobbing as I witnessed another miracle of salvation.

"I feel so good and yet so sorrowful for all the years I have wasted on the lies of the OH and the new-age religion. Will God forgive me for my rebellion?" Julian asked through his tears.

"He already has," I answered. Jesus died to give you freedom from all the wrongs you have ever done. Just keep releasing them all to Him. The blood of Jesus is powerful and it was shed for your redemption."

Julian and Sarah stood up and fell into each other's arms. They embraced and let out all their pain. It was all absorbed into the atmosphere of forgiveness that surrounded us. David and I left the room for a few minutes to give them some time to sort out their overwhelming feelings. We took a seat at one of the tables in the coffee shop. We were unable to articulate our own feelings, so we just sat in joyful silence.

Sarah came out of the meeting room. Her eyes and nose were red, but she had such a look of pure delight on her face, it lit up the whole room. One of her employees stared at her with a look of confusion. Sarah caught her look and sent back a radiant smile that answered some of the concern. She asked us to come back to the meeting room.

"Julian and I have so many questions. I never knew that I could feel like this. I feel like a huge weight has been lifted from my body. My spirit is jumping for joy. I am so hungry to know more about Jesus and what He just did for me. What do I do now?" Sarah said as she grabbed my hand and pulled me back to the table where Julian was sitting with his head in his hands. He had covered his eyes, but when he pulled his hands away the look on his face was one of delight.

David and I spent the next hour answering questions. We told them the importance of the Word of God. It would be their food now, and their guide book. We asked them if they had heard of any lively churches in the area. If not, we would help them find a place to go to worship with other lovers of Jesus. We cautioned against religious spirits that would try to steal their joy and freedom. It was a wonderful explosion of brotherly love. We knew that angels were celebrating all around us as two more lost lambs found their way back to the sheep fold.

chapter 14

I felt like I was walking on clouds as David and I left Julian and Sarah, newly minted Christians, at the shop. The bright sunshine and blue sky mirrored our mood as we stepped out into the Ashland square.

"Let's stop by the post office and see if the videotape has arrived," David said. That brought reality racing back. We still had our mission.

We walked to the post office with a sense of anticipation. I was hopeful that the video would be the key to unlocking the mystery of Jacob's location. Our sights were now aimed at the farm. We needed the local authorities behind us if we were going to penetrate Rallen's defenses, but would they comply? Even the video evidence might not be enough to force the legal system to issue a search warrant. We knew that Rallen had friends in high places in Ashland.

I hung back as David approached the counter at the post office. He asked if there was a package there for him. The counter attendant left and was gone for what seemed like forever, but when he returned, he had a padded envelope. David showed his ID and the package was delivered into his hands. I breathed a sigh of relief. As we left the post office, I turned back to look at the attendant. He had quickly picked up the phone. As he spoke into it, he stared right at me with a look of pure hatred. It shocked me to see someone I had never met, give me a look like that.

"David, we need to get this to the police department right away," I warned.

"Okay, but I thought we would take it back to the hotel and view it first," David replied.

"I have a feeling that the OH has its tentacles in every aspect of the Ashland government. I saw the desk attendant make a call as soon as we turned to leave the post office." I hoped that my serious misgivings would come through my voice.

"All right, let's go back to the square and get the car," David conceded.

We entered the square. By this time of the day, the streets were filled with tourists and shoppers. As we approached the car, a young man appeared out of the crowd and ran full speed at us. He smashed into David and ripped the package from his hand. David regained his balance and turned to pursue the attacker. He was nowhere to be seen. David ran a short distance and looked everywhere for the man. He came back to me as I stood in shock on the sidewalk. I could tell by the look of disbelief on David's face that this was the last straw.

"I can't believe this! The OH has won again. This whole town is in Rallen's pocket." David was out of breath and his face was bright red. I could see that he was about to blow, but just as quickly, he regained his composure. He was a professional. He knew that losing his temper would not get us any closer to our goal.

We walked to the park and found a bench. It took a few minutes to overcome the shock and disappointment of this recent set back. I was praying under my breath. "Father, please guide us. Give us some hope that all our efforts are not in vain."

Just then, we saw a familiar face emerge from the crowd. Ashley, from the Berkeley center was walking right toward us.

I couldn't believe my eyes. I jumped up to greet her, but she just winked and walked past us.

With a slight tilt of her head, I knew that she wanted us to follow her. I grabbed David's arm, and we followed Ashley from a safe distance. She went into the coffee shop that David and I had discovered near the park. As we entered, I just saw her disappear around the corner in the back of the shop. We went to the counter and ordered coffee. We casually walked to the back and entered a small meeting room. There was Ashley.

"What are you doing here?" I asked.

"And why all the cloak and dagger?" David interjected.

"Claire and I were praying and we felt that you could use some back up," Ashley explained. "I know some of the OH members here in Ashland. I thought I could be your under cover person. I also know that they have eyes all over this town. I don't want to blow my cover right off the bat."

"Do you know Julian and Sarah Edgers?" I asked.

"As a matter of fact, I do. But they are very dedicated OH members. You probably won't get much help from them," Ashley frowned.

"The good news is that they have turned their lives over to Jesus, just this morning as a matter of fact. We left them a little while ago sitting on cloud nine." I was not sure of Ashley's relationship with the Lord, but I hoped she would be happy for our friends.

"Fantastic! You might not know that I am a believer too. I was raised in church and then wandered away in my teen years. I was just exploring the OH when you met me. Then when I started working with Claire, she took me to one of the meetings at Rock Church. I renewed my relationship with the Lord, and I have been growing in God every day since." Ashley was glowing as she expressed her new-found love. I put my arms around her and we hugged for a minute, two sisters in the Lord.

David cleared his throat and we brought our focus back to the tasks at hand. "Do you have some ideas on how to penetrate the resistance here in Ashland? We have been blocked at every turn."

"I don't have access to the hierarchy here, but your friends, Julian and Sarah, do. I think we should meet with them and do some brain storming. If we pool all our information and experience, plus some targeted prayer, I am sure the Lord will give us revelation and direction," Ashley suggested. I was impressed with her grasp of the ways of the Spirit. Then again, I realized that people who are rescued from the new-age religion and brought into the Kingdom of God, had an advantage. They had experience with the kingdom realms. All they had to do was transition from the dark kingdom to the Light. They thought that they had been living in the light, until they experienced the true light of Jesus and the Gospel. Everything else was a pale imitation.

The three of us settled on a plan to regroup at Julian and Sarah's shop, Moonstone. David and I would walk out the front of the coffee shop. We would just look like we were headed back to revisit their shop. Ashley slipped out the back and made her way through the alley to the rear entrance of Moonstone. Sarah and Julian were excited to see Ashley and learn of her recent commitment to the Lord. They had met Ashley in Berkeley at a conference earlier in the year. Once we were all settled at the table in the meeting room of the shop, we held hands and asked for the Lord's direction and favor.

"Since you left us a while ago, Sarah and I have been discussing our next move. I would love to go out into the street and announce our newfound faith. However, our involvement in the OH would give your search for Jacob a big advantage," Julian expressed his conflicting feelings.

"I am repulsed by the thought of having to even be in the same room with Rallen Mandu," Julian continued. "Now that I see how he has manipulated and used us for his own gain, I want to confront him. On the other hand, if I can be of assistance in bringing him to account for his deeds, I know that will bring the greater reward."

"We feel that Jacob is being held at the farm outside town. Do you have access to that property?" David asked.

"I have been there, and I've been in meetings when we discussed the security measures for the farm. I don't have keys, and I would have to find a good excuse for visiting. There has to be a way to get you on to the property for a proper search," Julian replied.

"How many security personnel are there? Also there is the problem of the dogs." David was getting us all into the problem-solving mode.

"There are actually only two full-time guards. The dogs are another problem, but I am sure we can find a solution to their threat," Julian added.

Ashley interrupted the discussion. "I know how to neutralize the dogs. We lure them out with food laced with a sedative. I used to work in an animal clinic. We administered sedatives for all kinds of procedures. I could calculate the right dose to put them down but not harm them."

"We could also create a diversion to get the security guys distracted while you searched for Jacob," Sarah suggested.

Julian brought in some sandwiches and coffee for us as we continued to put the pieces of the plan together. When we had worked out all the details, we decided to implement our plan sooner than later. We would reconvene in the meeting room in two hours. If we had all the pieces together, we would head out to the farm that afternoon.

David and I went back to our hotel to gather our resources and change into some more rugged clothing. When I knocked at David's door to let him know I was ready, I felt a rush as I admired his worn Levi's and flannel shirt. He looked like he was going on a camping trip. I really wished that was the case. I could imagine us together out in nature, but I had to catch myself. The mission. Keep your eyes on the prize, I kept saying in my mind. I noticed his approving glances as he saw me in jeans and T-shirt for the first time.

chapter 15

David pulled into the alley behind Moonstone. We entered the rear entrance and slipped into the meeting room. Everyone was already there. Ashley had a backpack. Julian and Sarah were dressed in street clothes.

"I was able to speak to Damien a few minutes ago. I let him know that I needed to check on a few things at the retreat center. We have an upcoming event. He said fine and that he would let the staff know when to expect me. Sarah and I will drive our Range Rover, and we can hide David in the back. Ashley, you and Joy will be in charge of the dogs and the distraction. You know what to do," Julian said with confidence.

Ashley and I headed out first in her VW bug. We needed to be in place before Julian and Sarah drove into the compound at the farm. I tried to match Ashley's confidence, but I was fighting my fears. So many things could go wrong. Then again, we knew that God was backing us up. How could we fail?

"I am amazed at how easy it was for me to find the sedatives I needed for the dogs. That just boosts my faith. I know that God is leading us every step of the way," Ashley stated.

"David and I found the firecrackers in the first store we went to. I see what you mean about divine assistance. Now we just have to pray for perfect timing." I was still a little unsure of the details of our distraction plan.

"No problem," Ashley stated. "I have a cell phone with Julian on speed dial. We will know when he arrives and when he finds Jacob."

Ashley drove into the track beside the fence that surrounded the farm. We checked our watches and saw that we were right on time. We grabbed our bags containing the items to implement our plan. Ashley was in charge of the dogs. I was tasked with the distraction for the security guards. We would lure the dogs first, and then the guards to the fence line of the property and vanish before they knew what had happened. We hoped that they would think that the dogs had been shot. As they dealt with the dogs, the team at the compound would be searching and finding Jacob. Fortunately, Julian was familiar with the layout of the retreat center. He knew of some likely hiding places.

We had just taken our places in the trees by the fence, when Ashley's phone began to vibrate. She answered and received the message that the team was just arriving at the compound. We were to wait five minutes and then attract the dogs to the fence area. Ashley pulled the hood up on her black sweatshirt. She opened the bag of beef strips laced with sedative. She began to walk out into the field, just as David and I had done on our first visit to the farm. It wasn't long before the dogs came running across the field to intercept the intruder. As they neared, Ashley started to throw the lure toward them. When the dogs smelled the meat, they immediately stopped and sniffed then devoured the scraps of meat. Ashley retreated to the fence line tossing meat along the way.

Ashley burst through the trees. "It's all yours," she said as she passed me headed for the fence and the safety of the car. I quickly lit the fuse on the firecrackers. We had cut the string to only include seven or eight individual crackers. We wanted them to sound like gun shots. They were sounding very convincing as I also jumped over the fence and headed to the car. Ashley already had the engine going. Against all instinct, we slowly left the track and made it to the highway. As we cruised by a break in the tree line, we caught a glimpse of the two guards running across the field. Two big black lumps were visible in the grass. The dogs had been neutralized.

We drove about a quarter mile past the entrance road to the compound and waited for further instructions from Julian and

David. We had been parked under a tree only a couple of minutes before the phone vibrated again.

"We heard the firecrackers. Good work. When the guards took off, we were able to get David out of the car. We are searching now. So far no sign. I'll call if we need you." Julian's voice over the speaker phone sounded tense.

Every time a car passed our position, we ducked down. The tree afforded some camouflage, but we did not want anyone to take notice of us. The minutes were creeping by as we waited for another call. Just then, I saw a familiar car approaching from the direction of town. I had seen that car in the driveway of the OH house in Ashland. As it passed, I recognized Damian. Ashley saw him too and quickly grabbed the phone and dialed Julian. There was no answer. What should we do? We looked at each other and made a decision.

"Duck down. I am still known in Ashland as an OH member. I will drive into the retreat center. Maybe we can divert Damian before he sees David."

I found a blanket in the backseat of the VW. I pulled it over my head as I wiggled into the tight space in front of the passenger's seat. Ashley took off her sweatshirt and threw it in the back. Then she turned around and headed toward the farm. She had the presence of mind to drive slowly up the drive. She did not want to alert the guards.

"I can see the guards out in the field. They're searching around the dogs. Now one of them is headed into the tree line." Ashley was narrating the scene. "Damien is just getting out of his car. He started out into the field, and then he saw me driving up the road."

Ashley parked the car and quickly got out. She had cracked the window so that I could hear what was going on.

"What are you doing here?" Damien's voice boomed.

"Julian wanted me to help with the conference logistics. I was supposed to meet him here," Ashley answered with a confidence that I could hardly believe.

"I must attend to a problem with security. I will deal with you and Julian shortly," Damien replied.

Ashley opened the passenger's side door and acted like she was getting something out of the car. "If you crouch down and use the cars as cover, you can make it to the main building safely."

"What then?" I whispered.

"Just do it. We will make it up as we go. God will protect us," she replied.

I slipped out of the car and scurried past the parked cars and into the big house of the retreat center. Once inside, she led me to a back hallway. Ashley called out to see if any of the team was in the house. No answer. She stopped and took a minute to call Julian again. Still no answer. We went to the back of the house and peeked outside. There was a maze of smaller buildings, cabins that would house the retreat participants.

"I attended a retreat here once. I think I can find my way around." Ashley sounded so confident I was able to set aside my rising fears.

"Lead on, I'll be right behind you," I told her.

We explored the compound, stopping at each cabin to see if the team was there. All the cabins were deserted and locked. We finally came to a large out building. Ashley peeked into the door and saw a flashlight sweeping the space inside.

"Julian!" Ashley called out.

"What are you doing here?" Three pairs of questioning eyes looked back at us from the gloom.

"Damien just arrived," Ashley informed us. "We couldn't get you on the phone, so we drove in. I talked to Damien briefly before he went out to help the guards with the dogs. He said that he would 'deal' with us when he was through. We have to get back to the main house right away."

"Of course, he did not know that I was in the car. I hid and made it to the house without being seen," I added. "Have you found anything to indicate Jacob has been held here?"

David stepped forward, "Not yet. The whole compound seems to be deserted. One of the cabins looks like it's being used for the guard's quarters. Otherwise, nothing."

"We are running out of time if we are going to maintain our cover," Ashley said. "I think Julian, Sarah, and I should go back to the house and meet with Damien."

"Joy and I can make our way back to the fence road and meet you there," David announced.

"Okay, good luck. We will have our hands full keeping Damien and the guards busy. We will have a lot of explaining to do," Julian said.

The three former OH members left the out building. David and I waited a few minutes before we slipped out and rounded the building. The tree line of the property bordered the back. Once in the trees, we began to breathe a little easier. There was a path through the underbrush. We followed it toward the fence road where we would meet up with one of the cars. As we followed the path, we kept an eye out for any breaks in the trees that would expose our position. We almost missed the small shack nestled into the trees on the right side of the pathway. We approached the shack and saw that the door was secured with a big padlock. There were no windows. I went to the door and called out cautiously. "Jacob, Jacob, are you in there?"

"Who is it?" a voice replied from within.

"Jacob, its Joy, Joy Morgan. Your mom sent me here to find you."

"Thank God! I knew someone would come." Jacob's voice was familiar, and I could hear all the relief he expressed.

"We will find some way to open the door. Detective David Kramer is with me. We will get you out very soon," I reassured him.

As we looked around the shack for something to use to pry the door open, we heard voices from down the path. They were deep and rough. It had to be the guards.

"It's time to make a stand," David said with conviction. We stood in front of the door to the shack, ready to confront the guards.

"Who are you and what are you doing here?" the tallest man of the two bellowed.

David took out his badge and flashed it for them to see. "I am Detective David Kramer from the Berkeley Police Department, and you are under arrest for kidnapping."

The tall man's look of surprise turned to rage. Despite his bulk, his next move was lightning quick. He covered the distance between himself and David in three giant steps. Lashing out, he punched David in the temple, sending him down and out. The other man grabbed me to keep me from responding or running. The big man took out a set of keys from his pocket and unlocked the shed. Jacob came out of the door squinting in the sunlight. He was disoriented but realized immediately that his would-be rescuers were neutralized. Even though he was out of his makeshift cell, he was still a captive.

I was quickly tossed into the shed, and the man holding me took hold of Jacob. Big man scooped David up in his massive arms and set him in the shed as though he were a rag doll. The door was slammed and the lock clanged into place. David and I were now at the mercy of the One Humanity security team.

I felt around in the dark and found David. I picked up his head and placed it carefully in my lap. Tears were starting to stream down my face. How could this happen? Where was God's protection? I was tempted to give in to despair. The man that I had trusted to protect me was lying incapacitated before me. I was reminded of the Bible verse that I had quoted to others who were going through a crisis. "God did not give me a spirit of fear but of power and love and a sound mind." Second Timothy 1:7 was a powerful reminder of who we are and who God is. I reached out to the Lord and asked for His Peace. I asked for wisdom and strength. I asked for angelic assistance. I felt so helpless, but I knew that I could not rely on my own resources. This situation required divine intervention.

David moaned and moved his head. He was coming back to consciousness. It took a few minutes for him to realize where he was. The darkness must have been frightening, opening his eyes to nothing that would orient him to his situation.

"David, I'm here." I kept my voice low and comforting. "We are in the shed that Jacob was being held in. The guards are gone and they took Jacob."

David slowly sat up. He reached over to find me in the dark. I took his hand. I was filled with relief that he was able to move.

"My head really hurts. That guard was so big and so quick. I didn't see it coming."

"We are in a bit of a serious situation, but I have been praying and I know the Lord will lead us out of this," I reassured David and myself.

"I'm sorry for getting you into this mess. I was not prepared for the capabilities and commitment of the OH."

"I could say that I got *you* into this mess."

"Well, whoever's mess this is, we have to find a way out of it," David said as he tried to stand up. He didn't get too far before I felt his weight sink back down to the floor of the shed. "Oh, man, that blow took the stuffing out of me. It might take a while for me to get back up to 100 percent."

"Take your time. I don't think the guards will be back. They have to deal with Jacob and if their past behavior is any indication. They will be covering their tracks and heading for another location to hide in. There is no telling how many OH houses Rallen has."

David and I settled back against the back wall of the shed. There was a thin mattress and blankets that were Jacob's bed. It was some cushion against the hard wood floor. We were sitting close together and David reached over and took my hand. Warmth spread through me. His closeness and his need for my reassuring touch filled me with joy even in the midst of this crisis.

We sat that way for some time. We could not see anything, and somehow that fact made it easy for us to open up to each other. We shared stories of our childhood. We delved deeper into our faith, and the details of our surrender to God. Our hearts were being knit together. I was reminded of a verse somewhere in the Bible about God turning what was meant for evil to good. I knew that I would look back on this time in the shed not with fear, but with thanksgiving. How else would we have allowed ourselves to be so transparent? The foundations of an enduring friendship were being built.

"Jacob? Joy? David?" Voices penetrated our prison.

I jumped up. "In here!" I recognized those voices.

We heard the padlock rattle. "Are you all right? Is Jacob with you?" I heard Julian through the door.

"David and I are fine. The guards took Jacob away and then locked us in here," I replied.

"We'll get you out of there. Look for something to break the lock." Julian was directing the other rescuers.

A moment later, there was a loud clanging noise as Julian attacked the padlock.

I feared that the loud noises would draw the guards. David called out to our friends outside. "Stand back. Let me try to break the door open from this angle."

Three explosive kicks later, the door burst open. David and I were blinded by the light from outside. When our vision adjusted, we were relieved to see Julian, Sarah, and Ashley making their way toward us. We embraced and praised the Lord.

"How did you get locked in this shed?" Sarah asked.

"Let's get going and we will tell you when we are safely away from here." I was still afraid for the return of the guards.

The trip back to Ashland was nerve wracking as we kept looking out for pursuers. When we were back at Moonstone, we met up in the conference room with coffee and scones. David and I told the story of finding Jacob and then the attack by the guards.

"Why didn't you call us? We could have come sooner," Julian asked.

"I left my phone in your car. I knew you had yours. In fact, I need to get it before I forget," David explained. "I don't know what happened to my pen light. It must have fallen when I was knocked out. By the way, how did you get past Damien and the guards?"

"We just walked right by them as they were carrying the dogs back to the main house. They didn't try to stop us. I don't think they had put all the pieces together yet," Julian explained.

"I can't believe we were so close to rescuing Jacob. It's like we're back to square one."

Ashley was expressing all of our combined frustration.

"Not entirely," David said. "We now know for sure that the OH is responsible for Jacob's disappearance, and we have them on charges of assaulting an officer. I am going to bypass the local police department and go straight to the state police and the FBI to get help with our investigation. They will have the authority to search both OH locations. We will build a case and follow as many trails as it takes to find Jacob."

"How can we help?" Julian asked.

"Check in with some of the OH members here in Ashland and see what they are saying. Someone has to know that a major threat is brewing," David suggested.

We confirmed our assignments and parted. David retrieved his phone and we went back to the hotel. It seemed like we had been gone for days. David went to his room to make phone calls and I went to mine to shower and change my clothes. I also wanted to check in with Claire. She needed to know that we had seen Jacob. Although he was still being held by the OH guards, he seemed to be unharmed. I would not tell her about what the guards had done to David. I didn't want to cause her more pain. Before I called, I prayed for guidance in what to say.

"Claire, it's Joy," I declared after she picked up on the third ring.

"Thank God! I got your message. I have been waiting on pins and needles ever since," Claire replied.

"There has been a major break in the investigation."

"You found him?" Claire's voice rose up in anticipation.

"Yes, but he is still being held by One Humanity security." I hated to burst her bubble.

"What do you mean? Why hasn't David arrested the guys?" she demanded.

"It's not that easy." I took a few minutes to explain our visit to the farm and how we were overwhelmed by the guards. We had seen Jacob but could not get him to safety. "Don't despair. David is getting help from the FBI and state police. Now that we know for sure that the OH has Jacob, the legal process will move quickly."

"What if they take him out of state? They could take him anywhere now." Claire was desperate for answers.

"I believe that God will protect Jacob, just as he has been doing. He did not bring us all this way to fail. Please hold on to hope." I wished I could be there to comfort her. "Let me pray with you before I have to go."

My prayer for strength and renewed hope helped me as much as Claire. I felt the Lord's presence bringing calm. Claire said she felt better but hoped that the good news would come very soon. We signed off with I love yous.

chapter 16

There was a knock on my door. It was David. He asked if we could meet for a few minutes. I said I would come to his room. I joined him at the familiar small table. As I sat down, I was reminded of the other times we had met there. We had shared meals and strategies. Something in David's mood told me this would be different.

"I have notified the FBI and state police. They are setting up a joint task force. Neither agency has a headquarters in Ashland. I suggested that we set up our base right here in the hotel. There is a meeting room that would accommodate the team. I have already reserved the room for the week. I don't know how long it will take to wrap this investigation, but I wanted to be sure we could use the space for a while." David was using his official voice. "Things could start moving pretty fast. I will be very involved with the task force. The time for our work together may be at an end, but I would like you to stay here as long as you can. I will need your moral support and prayer."

"I will help any way I can, but I want to be involved when Jacob is found. He needs to see me. I want to be there to comfort him and help him heal," I pleaded.

"I will make every effort to make that happen. While I am working with the agents, you could continue to coordinate with Julian, Sarah, and Ashley. I will try to make room for a daily briefing with you all. I believe that their help will be essential to our success."

David reached out and took my hand; his voice softened. "No matter how things go from here, I want you to know that this time with you has meant a lot to me. I think we have become good friends and I hope we can always keep our connection."

I tried not to get choked up, but I could feel the emotions welling up in me. I looked into David's eyes. It seemed like time stood still. There was so much I wanted to say. Then his cell phone rang.

David reluctantly pulled his phone out of his pocket. He flipped it open and gave me a sheepish look as if to say, "Yes, I'm keeping this with me all the time now. Hello, this is Detective David Kramer. Okay, I will be there momentarily." He closed the phone and gave me an apologetic look. "The first of the task force members are here. I have to go."

I went back to my room and gave Julian a call. I told him about the task force. He said that he and Sarah and Ashley would like to meet with me that evening. He invited me to dinner at their home. He said Ashley could pick me up in about a half hour if I was ready. I said, of course. When we hung up, I tidied up my room and headed out to the lobby. I said hi to Ben at the desk and he waved me over.

"Big doings!" he said. "I heard about all the big guns coming into town and to think they are going to be staying right here. I helped the manager get the conference room ready. They have a closed-circuit TV and everything." Ben was excited and talking so fast I could hardly keep up.

"It will be pretty busy for a while, but remember, you still have a job to do. Keep your eyes peeled for any suspicious activity, okay?" I replied with an air of mystery in my voice.

"Yes, ma'am. You can count on me," Ben replied with eyes as round as saucers.

"Thank you for all you have done for Detective Kramer and me. You have been a great help," I said with a warm smile.

"Really? Wow! I was just doing my job, but I'm glad I could be of service," he replied as he threw back his shoulders and stood a little taller.

"Oh, here is my ride. I will see you later," I said as I saw Ashley's little blue bug drive up.

Ashley was her usual bubbly, talkative self. She rattled on, but I couldn't really follow her narrative. I was thinking about David. I felt a part of me was left behind in the hotel. A feeling of loss overwhelmed me. Would this be the end our partnership? Would we lose the connection that we had built?

"Don't you think?" Ashley's voice rose a couple of octaves.

"About what?" I asked as I came out of my reverie.

"I knew you weren't listening. What's going on?" Ashley gave me a quick questioning look.

"David is getting swept up in the FBI investigation. I don't think he will be working with us as he has been. I just miss him being part of our team," I explained.

"You mean you miss *him*. I've seen the way you two look at each other. There is a lot of chemistry there," Ashley said with a sly grin.

I didn't know what to say. In my heart I knew she was right, but my brain just couldn't admit the truth. I had tried very hard to keep my relationship with David on a professional level. There was too much at stake to let personal feelings cloud our mission, but now that the scope of the search for Jacob had changed, I was grieving.

"It's okay. I know you are having a hard time admitting you have feelings for David. From what I have seen, no matter what happens, you two will find a way to keep your special relationship," Ashley said with her signature confidence.

I couldn't reply to her statement. Luckily, we were pulling into the parking space behind Moonstone. As we entered the conference room, Julian and Sarah were already there, and had a stack of paperwork laid out on the table in front of them.

"I hope it's all right if we have our dinner here. We want to run some things by you," Sarah explained.

"What's all this?" Ashley asked.

"Documents, I have been collecting them over the last few months; they paint a very shady picture of the OH financial dealings. Taken one at a time, they are not too damaging, but when you start to see the pattern, they become very unsettling. Rallen has been systematically funneling funds from the foundation into his private off shore accounts. He has some very creative ways to disguise his movement of thousands of dollars. I can't wait to meet with the FBI and show them the serious misuse of funds that the OH has perpetrated in the name of peace and light. I feel like such a fool to have been a part of it all. If I had not just found my new life in Jesus, I would be having a serious crisis of faith right now." Julian was pouring out his soul.

"David is just now getting the task force organized. I think their first order of business is to find Jacob. Then, I know they will be looking into One Humanity and their questionable practices. After all, that is what got Jacob kidnapped in the first place," I replied.

For the next hour, we fueled our brain storming session with coffee, sandwiches and some amazing strudel that Sarah had baked that morning. I didn't know how they both found the time to run their business and deal with the crisis we all faced. Julian had reached out to some of the local OH members and felt them out carefully. He found that they were all aware of a serious problem. They would not divulge the details, but said there was a hasty meeting of the leadership that very afternoon. They were surprised that Julian and Sarah had not attended. The wagons were being circled. They were going to close the public center in Ashland just as they had done in Berkeley. According to Rallen, the authorities were planning a systematic persecution of all OH branches. He said there were some disloyal members who were trying to destroy all that they had worked for. Of course we knew who he was talking about. It had not taken long for Damien and Rallen to put two and two together. I felt that we needed to call David and let him know that the leadership team was probably at this very minute covering their bases and making plans to leave town.

We were just getting ready to call David when Julian's phone rang. It was David. He asked if I was there; he needed to talk to me right away.

"David, what's wrong?" I asked.

"The task force has assembled. They want to talk to us to get the background on what has been going on. Can you be here in the next fifteen minutes?" The edge in his voice let me know that there may be some complications.

"Of course, I will get Ashley to bring me to the hotel immediately."

As I entered the hotel lobby, there was tension in the air, and even Ben looked nervous as he stood behind his desk. He gave me a wide-eyed look as I passed him heading toward the meeting room. When I entered the room, I could see what had caused all the concern. The room was packed with men in suits and ties. A few state police officers were sprinkled in the mix. Serious was an understatement. I saw David wave me over to a seat next to him at the head table.

"Let's begin. I don't have to remind you that in a kidnapping case, time is a critical factor. We also know that the perpetrators may be in the process of destroying evidence and moving our victim to parts unknown." The man at the head of the table was obviously in charge. I had not been introduced to any of the men in the room, but I assumed that he was a senior FBI agent.

He pointed to David and I and said, "This is Detective David Kramer from the Berkeley Police Department and his civilian consultant, Joy Morgan. They will be filling us in on the background. I hope you have all read the brief that we faxed out. Detective Kramer can help fill in the details for us."

For the next forty minutes, David and I explained the disappearance of Jacob Cohen. I gave some information about the new-age group One Humanity. There were a few questions that interrupted our story from time to time. When we finished, the head FBI agent, who had finally identified himself as Special Agent Dennis Hall, asked a question of his own.

"Detective Kramer, when you went to the OH compound to search for Jacob Cohen, where was your gun? And why did you leave your phone in the car?" Morgan asked.

David tensed as he realized that he was being criticized for his actions. "Since I was working with civilians, I felt it would be best not to involve any weapons. Besides that, the OH personnel had not posed a threat to us during any of our other encounters. As far as the phone goes, we had one phone in our party and I didn't want to add any confusion or chance for interruptions."

"I see." But Agent Hall's tone of voice did not convey the same message. "We will shelve those concerns for now. Our focus needs to be on finding Jacob Cohen and capturing his kidnappers. Now, are there any more questions? If not, we will proceed with our plan. You have all been assigned to your various duties. We have search warrants for all the OH properties in the area. Let's get going. Keep me posted on your progress."

As the groups of officers and agents formed up and left the room, David asked what his assignment was. Agent Hall just gave him a chilly stare and said, "I think you have done enough." I could see David's color flood his face, but he kept quiet and just nodded to me and we left the room. We went to David's room and sat at the small table.

"I was afraid of this," David began. "The FBI has expertise in kidnapping cases, but sometimes they take their authority to extremes. They are questioning my decisions to bolster their ability to take command of the investigation. They are overlooking the fact that the kidnapping took place in my jurisdiction. I should be leading the team. Instead I have been sidelined. I believe that they will come to regret that decision. You and I have the background and understanding of the OH. We are valuable assets that they are choosing to ignore." David's frustration was bordering on anger.

"We have a resource that they aren't even considering. We have unseen allies. Let's take a few minutes to focus on God's agenda. Let's ask for *His* guidance." I reached out and took David's hand.

We took turns praying and then praised God for all that he had done. We set our intension on following His lead. A blanket of peace descended over us and all fear and frustration evaporated. David looked at his watch, and we both agreed that we would sleep on our next move. We were not going to be sidelined. We knew we had a task to do and the Lord would provide the means.

chapter 17

I went back to my room and took a long soaking bath. I felt the peace of God that I had experienced with David linger. I got ready for bed and read a chapter from Psalms just before I drifted off to sleep. Somewhere in the night, I began to see a picture in my dreams. *I saw a river. A large log building was partly obscured in the trees above the river. I saw the word* Applegate *over the scene.* When I awoke the next morning, that picture was still fresh in my mind. I knew that it was a message from the Lord. I quickly got dressed. I called David on the room phone.

"David!" I said excitedly. "I think the Lord has given me a dream as a clue to where Jacob is being held. He is in a log house on the Applegate River."

"I know where the river is located outside Jacksonville, but the house could be anywhere," David expressed his misgivings.

"Let's call Julian and Sarah and see if they know of any places the OH may have out there," I suggested.

"Okay, come on over to my room," David said. As soon as I entered, he made the call and then put the phone on speaker.

"Julian, its David Kramer."

"What's going on? I understand there are FBI agents and state police officers swarming all over the OH properties." Julian sounded concerned.

"They have taken over the investigation. However, Joy and I are exploring other options. Do you know of any OH properties on the Applegate River?" David asked.

"There is a house out there that some members have used for individual retreats, but it's not an OH property really. It belongs to one of the members," Julian explained.

"Do you have an address?" I could tell that David was getting excited.

"I don't know the exact address, but it is on Quail Run Road just off Highway 238 outside of Jacksonville. I could help you find it," Julian suggested.

David gave me a questioning look and we both came to the same decision. "No, we can find it. Thank you for the info. I will let you know if this leads us anywhere."

David closed his phone and I said, "Good call. We should keep this as quiet and simple as possible. Are we going to tell Hall about our lead?"

"Somehow I don't think that a dream from God is going to instill much confidence in Special Agent Hall. Let's keep this to ourselves," David declared. "I will have my phone handy in case he wants to get in touch and I will be taking my gun. Are you comfortable with that?"

"I will trust your judgment and the Lord to protect us," I answered.

"I guess being shut out of the investigation has its advantages after all. Let's grab some coffee and pastries from the breakfast room on our way out," David suggested.

Our journey from Ashland to the Applegate region outside Jacksonville was very solemn. David and I were both lost in thought as we traveled through the beauty of these back roads. We had been thwarted so many times in our quest to find Jacob that I was cautious. I did not want to get my hopes up too high. I felt certain that God had given me the direction we were following, but here we were on our own again. The teams of FBI and state police officers were combing the One Humanity properties and we were off on what would seem to them a wild goose chase.

As we neared the turn off to Quail Run Road, I broke the silence. "What are we going to do about the guards? I'm pretty sure they will still be in charge of hiding Jacob."

"That is what I have been mulling over all the way here. I don't want to use my fire arm if at all possible. I'm really not prepared to shoot them. If Big Man sees me hesitate, he could easily disarm me. There has to be another way," David replied.

"This is where we could really use some angelic assistance. I don't think the Lord has brought us out here for a joy ride. This mission has to come to a conclusion at some point. Why not today?" I was ready to yield to God's plan. If only I knew what it was.

"Keep your eyes open. That house should be on this road somewhere," David said.

We could see the sun glinting off the river ahead when we spotted a log house off the right side of the road. "That's it!" I cried out. David drove past the property as we both tried to get a good look at the lay of the land. We passed the house by about a quarter mile and stopped where there was an access road on the same side as the house. We found a place to park the car in the trees out of sight. We sat for a couple of minutes. I grabbed David's hand and prayed for God to give us divine strategies and angelic assistance for the task ahead.

We found a path that seemed to head in the direction of the log house. We quietly and slowly proceeded; every step was taken in faith. We made it to the clearing around the house and stopped. Observation of the house yielded very little information. It was quiet until we saw one of the big black dogs from the retreat center jump up from the front porch and start barking. Oh no! Not the dogs again! There only seemed to be one of the dogs on duty. I was ready to run back to the car when we realized that the dog was not barking at us. He was headed to the opposite side of the property barking wildly.

"Do you see them?" David asked.

"I only see one of the dogs," I answered.

"Not the dog, the angels. Two very large warrior angels are standing in the trees over there." David pointed in the direction that was holding the dog's attention.

Big man came rushing out on the porch of the log house, yelling at the dog. When he could not get the dog to stop barking, he ran across the clearing to see what was wrong. When he reached the dog, it took off into the woods. Big man followed the dog. We didn't see the other guard anywhere. Stepping out in faith, we rushed to the house and entered the front door. The front room was unoccupied. David quickly searched the rest of the house. He found a door that was locked. I immediately joined him. Taking a deep breath, David turned the lock and opened the door. There in the darkened room was Jacob. He was on his knees in front of a small bed.

"Jacob," I gently called out his name. He turned around and squinted to try to see who it was in the doorway.

"Joy?" Jacob said cautiously.

I crossed the room and pulled him up from the floor. I gave him the biggest bear hug I could manage, and we both started to cry. Relief and gratitude flooded my soul.

"Hey, guys, I hate to break this up, but we need to get out of here," David interrupted our reunion.

I grabbed Jacob's hand, and we made our way back to the front door. David peeked out. The coast must have been clear because he waved us forward. We ran across the clearing and were just entering the woods when we heard the dog. He came charging toward the path that we were using for our escape. Jacob was having a hard time keeping up. The many days that he had been kept in isolation must have weakened him.

"David! We have to slow down or Jacob won't make it!" I called out. Just then, the dog caught up with us. David jumped in front of Jacob and me. He had his gun at the ready, but the dog stopped only a few paces from us. He crouched down and whimpered pitifully. David looked back at us and said, "It's not the gun. Those two big angels are hovering over us." I looked all around but could only see trees.

We heard crashing from down the pathway. Big Man was coming. David stood his ground. When the guard saw us, he lurched forward, but then he saw the dog at his feet. A puzzled look crossed his face. As he looked up above our heads, his face froze with fear. He dropped to his knees.

That was our cue to leave. We made it back to the car. I sat in the back with Jacob. Neither one of us could speak. There was a holy awe that surrounded us.

"You asked for angelic assistance and God answered big time!" David exclaimed.

On the drive back to Ashland, there was not much spoken. Everyone in the car was processing the events of the day and the last week. For Jacob, the challenge was much greater. He was faced with adapting back to some kind of normalcy. The trauma he experienced would take some time to heal. I didn't want to add to his discomfort by tossing questions at him, so I just sat with him in the back seat of David's car holding his hand and praying silently for peace.

As we neared Ashland, David broke the solemn silence. "We need a plan. As soon as we let the authorities know that Jacob has been found, things are going to get very hectic. They will want interviews with all of us. We will be thrust into their timeline and could even face a barrage of media coverage. Do you have any ideas on how to approach this? Jacob, are you prepared for all the pressure?"

"Through all that has happened, I have had a profound sense of peace and protection. I know that God will guide us all past the coming wave of activity." Jacob's voice conveyed the truth of his words.

"I think we should let the FBI know right away that our objective has been accomplished, but I don't think that is the end of the investigation. We have to be involved with the resolution of who is guilty and why they targeted Jacob in the first place. Finding Jacob is just the tip of the iceberg in the OH inquiry," I added.

Jacob looked at me and nodded. "I was taken to keep me quiet. I know too much about the true motives of the group and especially Rallen's selfish ambitions. I don't know what their ultimate solution was supposed to be. I was never in fear for my life. I knew that God was with me every step of the way. I could see even from my imprisonment that their whole organization was beginning to unravel. My disappearance was the catalyst that led to the closure of the Berkeley Center and now the dismantling of the main headquarters in Ashland. It's just like the devil to overplay his hand. The move to cover up their dirty deeds has led to their downfall."

I was encouraged by Jacob's insightful assessment. He was a remarkable young man. I could see that he would emerge from this experience a stronger person.

"I have to call your mom. She wants to be here for you, and I promised that I would let her know the minute you were safe."

David handed his phone back to me. I called Claire and was so gratified that I could finally give her some good news. I gave the phone to Jacob and he and his mom had a tearful reunion. When he hung up, he let us know that she would be on her way to Ashland immediately.

The closer we got to the hotel, the more tension I felt. I had no idea what Special Agent Hall's reaction would be to our bold initiative. Although the results were fantastic, the methods would certainly come under scrutiny. Based on the way he handled our initial involvement, I knew that he would take exception to what he would view as interference. Would the outcome outweigh the method? How were we going to explain the direction we got from the Lord and the intervention of angelic beings?

We pulled into the parking lot and I put a hand on David's shoulder. "Let's get our stories straight. The tip we got about the log house came from Julian and we created a distraction for the guard and the dog."

"What kind of distraction?" David asked.

"Pastries!" I blurted out. "You circled around the house and laid out our left over pastries in the woods. Then you made a noise by beating a piece of dead wood on one of the trees. The dog took off to see what the noise was and helped himself to the food. Then the guard came out to see what the dog was doing and followed him into the woods. As soon as they were out of sight, I entered the house and you doubled back. We could hear the guard yelling at the dog as we ran back to the car."

"That's quite a creative explanation. I hope it works," David said.

"I just hope the Lord forgives me for substituting pastries for angels."

"Sounds good to me," Jacob replied.

We walked into the lobby of the hotel; a few guests there gave Jacob a second look. He was disheveled and a bit dirty. I realized that we needed to get him a room of his own so he could clean up. I hoped Claire would think to bring some clothes for him or perhaps David would have something that would do. I was sure that he probably would appreciate some food and water sooner rather than later.

"I will talk to Ben and see if we can get Jacob a room," I suggested to David. "You should probably check in with Hall."

"Thanks a lot! I get the worst job, but it's okay. I can handle it," David said as he turned to head down to the task force room. "Time to face the music."

Ben found a room for Jacob just a couple of doors down from mine. We headed in that direction. As we passed the conference room, we heard a heated discussion and raised voices filtering into the hallway. I grabbed Jacob's hand and walked a little faster. We went to my room first.

"Are you hungry? Thirsty?" I asked as I invited him to sit at the table in the corner.

"Yes, the room service at the OH prison left a lot to be desired," Jacob answered.

"I can imagine. Here's some water and a few snacks. As soon as David comes back, I will ask him about some fresh clothes for you, and then we will get you a proper meal."

"This is great! Junk food was definitely not on the menu where I was being held." Jacob gave me a broad smile that broke my heart. I wanted to scoop him up in a big hug. I couldn't believe that he was sitting right there in my room. I had to steel myself against a fear that something would happen and he would be snatched out of our hands just like the two video tapes.

There was a knock on the door. When I opened it, I was relieved to see David was alone. He came in and told us that Special Agent Hall had not been happy about the way we went behind his back, but he was glad that Jacob was safe. He would let his agents know the investigation would move into the phase to find Jacob's captors. He said some progress had already been made in that area.

"I had to lobby pretty hard for you, Jacob. To give you time to adjust and get your bearings before the interviews begin," David told him.

150

"Thank you, Detective Kramer, I appreciate everything you have done for me," Jacob answered with such sincerity that I almost got choked up again.

"David, do you think you might have some clothes that Jacob could use until we can get him some of his own? I would say that what he has on is history."

"Sure, they may not fit so well, but I've got some sweats that should work," David replied. "I'll be right back."

David returned with some clothes and I gave him Jacob's room key. They left and I was alone. I was still in a state of shock. Time seemed to be standing still. I realized that I needed to give God a large helping of thanksgiving. So I began to praise him. As my voice ascended to Him I was enveloped in a cloud of glory. Time was engulfed by eternity.

A knock on my door brought me back to earth. I felt like I had spent hours in His presence. I went to the door, and David asked if I could come to his room.

"How long were you with Jacob? How long has it been since you left here?" I asked.

"Only about fifteen minutes. Why?"

"I was praising the Lord, and I think I stepped into a portal. I felt like a few hours had passed."

"That would account for the look on your face and the tingle I felt when you opened the door," David replied with a beaming countenance. "We need to talk about out next move."

"What do you mean? Jacob is safe now," I questioned.

"That is not the end of this. I vowed that I would expose Rallen Mandu, and I was hoping you would want to be a part of that effort."

"You're right, I definitely want to see him get what is coming to him, not only for what he did to Jacob, but what he has done to all the gullible members of One Humanity. I will meet you in your room in ten minutes."

chapter 18

When I arrived at David's room, he had a pot of coffee waiting. We sat at his table and he reached out and took my hand. "Let's pray for guidance. I want justice for Jacob, but I don't want my personal feelings to cloud my judgment. I am angry with Rallen and his crew for their tactics. They preach love and acceptance, but their motives are far from pure. They manipulate and mislead their followers for profit and power. I want to make sure that they are not free to continue their disgusting scam."

"I'll start," I offered. "Father, thank you so very much for bringing Jacob back to us. You were there for us at every turn. We acknowledge that we could not have succeeded without you. Now we ask that you would once again lend your supernatural help to the task ahead. We believe that you have put inside us a burning desire to see the OH brought down. No one else should suffer under their devious plans. Expose them to your light and help us to bring the truth for all to see."

David and I drank coffee and brainstormed for an hour. We came up with a plan that seemed practical and logical. Then I realized how time had flown by. I asked David to check on Jacob. He returned a few minutes later and let me know that Jacob was resting, but said he could really use a good meal. David suggested we go to the Thai restaurant and get some take out. We jumped in David's car and were on our way to get our meals when we passed the OH center in the Ashland Square. It was empty. It looked like there had never been a center occupying the building.

"That was quick," I observed.

"Yea, but it doesn't look good for our plan. If the center is gone, maybe all the properties have been vacated. Hall said that they had raided the OH house and were sifting through evidence. He also said they would be sending a team out to the log house on the Applegate. I really want to know if they bagged any of the major players yet, like Rallen, Damien, and even Big Man and his side kick."

"After our lunch, maybe you can check in with him," I suggested.

We ordered our takeout food and waited while it was being prepared. We saw some familiar faces at one of the tables in the restaurant. They were looking at us, and not in a friendly way.

"I think those are some of the people we saw at the OH house the night of the party," I said.

"From the looks we are getting, I'd say they are none too happy with us. They know that we were involved in the shake down."

"Their reaction could make it harder for our plan to work," I speculated.

Our food was ready, and we paid and left the restaurant. Back at the hotel, David and I went to Jacob's room. On the way, we took one of the chairs from my room and showed up with all the ingredients for a friendly lunch. Jacob was in a good mood. He was clean and dressed in David's comfy sweats. As we settled in for our meal, Jacob said he wanted to say grace.

"Heavenly Father, thank you for this food and these friends. Thank you for protecting me all these days. I know that your hand was over me all the way. I could feel you right beside me. I know now what Pastor Ben said is really true. You will never leave me or forsake me. I know now that I can do anything as long as I keep my connection with you wide open. Bless us and this food. Amen."

Our meal was a delight. Jacob ate like he hadn't had any good food for a month, which was pretty much true. We chatted and laughed and David got to see what an amazing young man he had helped to bring back from the clutches of the OH.

As we finished up, the discussion turned serious. Jacob started to get emotional as he shared with us some of the more frightening moments of his recent journey—a journey that he had not wanted, but one that had strengthened his newfound faith.

"If I had not had the Lord with me all the way, I would not have been able to endure the treatment that I received from Damien and his men. It was all the more upsetting that these were the people that were supposed to be 'enlightened.' I had bought into Rallen's message of a new age of brotherhood and peace. I wanted it to be true. There was a part of me that saw the kernels of truth in his spiel. It wasn't until I found the true source of peace that I recognized the counterfeit. The night that I went to the Rock Church and met Jesus, that empty place inside of me got filled to the brim. When I thought about what One Humanity was selling, I was outraged by their deception. Rallen was capitalizing on people's need for a Savior by disguising himself as a messiah—a new-age messiah that could not deliver the goods." Jacob's conviction and zeal was compelling.

"So how did you wind up being kidnapped by the OH?" David asked.

"After my encounter with Jesus, I took a few days to get my bearings and figure out what to do. I couldn't just go back to the OH. My life was totally rearranged. I had been working for them. I called and quit my job. Luckily I had a friend that had been bugging me to join him at a nonprofit organization. Two days later I was working there, but I just couldn't shake the feeling that I had a responsibility to confront Rallen. I wanted him to know that his new-age shtick was totally bogus. I thought my testimony might just bring him to the Lord. Boy was I wrong. I finally got up the nerve to call and set up a meeting with him. That was the last day of freedom for me, until today."

Before he could continue with his story, there was a knock on the door. David went to answer it, and in came Claire. She ran to her son and took him up in a big hug. Tears flowed, kisses were lavished. Then she turned to me, and we embraced. She kept saying, "Thank you! Thank you! Thank you!" She realized that there was one other person she needed to thank. She approached David and he held out his hand. She ignored it and grabbed him in a bear hug. David returned her gesture.

"I cannot thank you both enough. You have put your lives on the line to save my son. I will always be grateful. If there is ever anything I can do for you, you know you have it."

David smiled graciously and said, "I was doing my job, but I must say that this case has been one that I will never forget. I met an amazing woman and learned that I am not alone in my work. God has supernatural resources that were essential to the success of our mission."

I could not help but blush at David's statement and Claire noticed that the bond between David and I had certainly grown.

"You two make a great team," Claire stated. "I am so fortunate to have you both on my side. I agree with you on the importance of God's involvement with this journey. Even though my faith in Him is very new, I can see His hand in everything that has happened. He has given me peace throughout these last few days, and now that Jacob and I are both believers, I am so excited to see what God has for us. With Jesus in our lives, the future looks so much more interesting."

"You and Jacob have some catching up to do. David and I can go back to his room and spend some time before the task force calls us all to give our statements." I was happy to give mother and son time to reconnect.

Jacob and Claire stood hand in hand with big smiles on their faces. The joy they felt radiated throughout the room as we left.

"I am going to check in with Hall and see how much time we have before he needs us. If there is time, we need to get together with Julian, Sara, and Ashley. They are an integral part of the next phase of our mission," David declared.

"Okay, I will be in my room just come and get me."

Back in my room, I took some time to soak in all the relief and joy that we all had been experiencing. I lay on my bed and closed my eyes. I felt like a big warm quilt was being wrapped around me. I could sense the Holy Spirit recharging my batteries. There was still work to do. He was preparing me for the challenges ahead.

I must have drifted off because the knock on my door startled me. It took a minute to get my bearings. The knock came again and I managed to make it to the door. It was David.

"Special Agent Hall wants you to come to the command center. I have already given my statement and answered his questions. You are next. They are leaving Jacob and Claire for last. He agreed to interview them together," he announced.

"How did it go for you?"

"Discounting Hall's attitude, I think it went pretty well. Just don't let his gruff style throw you off."

It took an hour for me to give a statement and answer all of Hall's questions. I managed to stay calm and overlook his accusatory approach. He seemed to accept the pastry story that we had agreed upon to explain how we distracted the dog and guard at the Applegate property. He said that I should stay in Ashland for the next few days in case he needed me to help with the ongoing investigation. I agreed and let him know that I wanted to cooperate in any way possible.

"How was it?" David asked with concern as soon as I knocked at the door of his room.

"Not bad, I just had to keep fighting the feeling that I was in the principle's office facing detention."

"Good, now let's connect with Julian and see if we can meet. Maybe we can invite ourselves over for dinner tonight. They would probably love to meet Jacob and see Claire again. Of course we need to see if Jacob is up to it." David looked to me to see if that was a possibility.

"I will go and check on them. You can call Julian and hopefully the plan will come together," I said.

I went to Jacob's room and saw that the hotel staff had installed another bed. Claire was not going to let her son out of her sight for a while. I asked them about meeting up with Julian and the gang. They were more than excited to connect with them. Jacob had not met them, but the idea of talking to people who had been OH members and had made the choice to follow Jesus was compelling. Claire wanted to thank them for their part in bringing Jacob back to her. I let them know that I still needed to check with David and would be back to give them the plan for the evening.

As I knocked and entered David's room, he was just putting down his phone. He gave me the okay sign and a big smile. We were on for a dinner with Julian, Sarah, and Ashley.

"I also checked in with Hall and he is going to wait until tomorrow morning to interview Jacob and Claire. He also said that there would be a task force meeting around ten in the morning and wanted us to attend. He has some updates on the progress in finding Jacob's kidnappers," David said confidently.

"Let's go get Claire and Jacob and head on over."

"They want to meet at the Moonstone conference room. They are having a local restaurant cater our meal. I was a little disappointed since I was anticipating Sarah's amazing cuisine, but it's not about the food. It's about us all getting on board with the plan."

We packed into David's car and headed to the Ashland Square and we parked behind the shop. Using the back entrance had become a standard procedure since it made less impact on the business and fewer eyes to take notice of our movements. Experience had taught us that the OH had eyes everywhere. We knew that Julian and Sarah had been identified as adversaries. Though we didn't feel particularly threatened, it was better safe than sorry.

The greeting for Jacob and Claire was joyful and extravagant. There were lots of hugs and kisses. Jacob was beaming and Claire was overwhelmed with emotion. The melding of kindred hearts was beautiful. They could identify with the grateful expression of their faith. They had been rescued from the delusions of the enemy. They were forgiven and free.

Once we were all seated around the table, Julian offered an amazing prayer of thanksgiving and blessing for the meeting and food. We dug into the salad and lasagna. I looked at David and winked. He nodded with agreement that the food was not a disappointment.

David opened the discussion when the meal was almost done and the small talk had run its course. "We are so grateful that Jacob is here with us tonight. The most important part of our task had been accomplished, but there is another aspect we need to address. I'm glad that we have so many of One Humanity's former elite here to help with the next phase. God has given us a mission to not only expose the kidnapping, but to bring the OH down. Joy and I have seen the hand of the Lord at every turn and He did not bring out his angelic hosts without putting His seal of approval on our efforts.

I believe it's His will to expose Rallen Mandu and destroy the false religion that he has created. To do that, we need as many voices as we can gather to weed out this abomination. So I propose that we bring all the OH members together. I am sure that they have many questions about what is going on with the FBI investigation. We can use that curiosity to our advantage. When we have them all together, we will use your testimonies and Jacob's kidnapping to open the door for God to minister and bring the truth. We can take the ground that the enemy thought was his."

I could see from the looks on all the faces around the table that this plan was going to get support from everyone. Smiles were growing and Jacob began to laugh. His laugher was contagious. We all joined in and released much of the pressure that we had been under. It was a Holy Ghost party. As we let out our laughter, I saw visions of demons fleeing and the enemy's plans going up in smoke. One of the shop employee's came to the door to see what was happening. The look of concern changed to a big smile as she felt the presence in the room. She just waved at Sarah and went back to her job.

As the laughter died down, Jacob began to speak. "I needed that! I feel so good right now. God is showing me the trauma that I had experienced had a purpose. It wasn't pleasant at the time, but we are reaping the rewards now. And there are more to come. My disappearance has brought many souls into the kingdom, and I can see that this plan is going to bring many more. Oh, there will be some hard hearted characters who will never surrender to God, but many more are ripe for the picking. This is a great set up to bring Glory to Jesus. I am over the moon to have my Mom on the same page with me. Just these few hours that we have had together today have been like heaven. We have a whole new life and relationship ahead. Thank you, Lord!"

"I want to add an amen to Jacob's words," Julian began to pour his heart out to us. "If not for Jacob, Sarah and I would not have heard the true gospel. We would not have met David and reconnected with Joy. They brought the good news right at the moment that we were in a crisis of faith. We are both learning so much, and our future has opened up to unlimited possibilities. I know that we will have a great impact on this town for Jesus. Heaven knows, they need it."

Ashley spoke up next, "I'm with you, Julian. I knew the Lord as a child but had wandered far away. Being part of this team to bring Jacob back has changed my life. I have experienced Jesus in a whole new way. There is so much more to the Christian life than I ever imagined. I'm excited to see how God is going to use me to help build His Kingdom here on Earth. Being here in Ashland, I have seen firsthand the clash of the kingdom realms. We really are in a battle for the souls of those around us. The devil is so sneaky. He put his lies in a package that even I thought was enticing. I should have known better because of my roots. My parents tried to ground me in the truth, but I let myself be sucked into a big fat lie."

It was my turn to add my voice. "This journey has given me a new zeal for using my knowledge of the new-age mirage to help people see how flimsy it really is. Just coming up against Rallen and his whole bundle of lies has made me see how I can use my background as a weapon in this fight. I am announcing to you and to God that I want to use all my talents to bring God's light into the deception of new age beliefs."

We all reached out across the table and grabbed hands. We were in it all the way. The plan before us, and the plan as God would unfold it in the future. I looked at all the faces around me and felt a current of eternity course through me and move on around the circle. "Wow, did you feel that?" Jacob exclaimed.

"That is what you call Holly Ghost and fire," Ashley proclaimed. "I remembered that from my Pentecostal past. I didn't realize how much I missed it."

"I can see we have a lot to learn from each other. What an exciting adventure I see ahead," Sarah said with eyes shinny with tears.

"That is the thing about living in Christ. There is an unlimited supply of hope. The world is devoid of hope. That is why there are so many suicides and drug deaths," Julian interjected. "I know that sounds like a downer right now, but it gives me perspective. This is a life-and-death proposition. If we don't hold out hope to people, the devil can easily destroy their very lives."

"Well said, Julian. That does give us some understanding about the importance of our mission right now. We have a great opportunity to rescue some very vulnerable people. They have seen their hopes in One Humanity dashed. What will replace that devastating reality? I say we tell them about Jesus," David responded to the challenge.

Sarah brought in coffee and cheesecake from the shop. We settled in for some brain storming about how best to get the OH members together, and where we could hold a meeting for a large number of people. Julian and Sarah were an invaluable resource. They knew the area and the people. Time was of the essence, so we had to come up with a way of getting the word out immediately.

We put our plan together and delegated the work needed to accomplish it. Sarah said that the OH had an existing phone tree. She would initiate the message about the meeting for members to share their concerns about the recent closure of the One Humanity Center in Ashland. Julian knew the owner of the OH center building. He would contact him and see if we could use the space for our meeting. As soon as he had a place secured, the word would go out. We tentatively set the meeting for the evening of the next day.

With plans in place, we relaxed and once again began to share our recent experiences, especially the newfound faith of many in the group.

I wanted to bring up a subject that I felt compelled to share with these baby Christians. "Most of you are in the blissful first stages of your love affair with Jesus. I am enjoying just being around you as you realize how much love and hope you now have in Him. As wonderful as salvation is, there is more. God has a second work that He wants you to experience. It is called the baptism of the Holy Spirit."

"I knew all about that when I was a kid," Ashley interrupted. "It always seemed so lofty and unattainable. I saw people pray for hours trying to get it. Isn't it reserved for very special people like pastors and stuff?"

Before I could answer Ashley's question, Jacob intervened. "Not really. I received the baptism all on my own in the middle of OH persecution. I'm not that special, but God knew I needed the power

I got from that experience. I also needed to be able to pray in my new language so that the devil didn't know what I was saying. When I pray that way, I know I am lined up with God's will."

"How did you know about the baptism? You were so new to your faith when they stole you away from us," Claire asked.

"I had this." Jacob reached into his pocket and brought out a small New Testament. "I read and reread this all the time they had me locked up. The gospels were so amazing and helped me get to know Jesus, but the book of Acts. Wow! That's where it really got exciting. The day of Pentecost jumped right off the page for me. As I was reading it, my cell became alive and electric. I fell to my knees and surrendered to the presence of the Lord. So many feelings rushed through me that I just had to express my love and thankfulness to God. When I opened my mouth, a language that I did not know came out and as I just kept on praying that way, I knew that I had received the gift of the Holy Spirit."

Everyone at the table felt the reality of Jacob's words. Those of us who had already received the baptism relived their own experience, and those who had not yet been gifted knew that they too could have a heavenly language and the impartation of the Holy Spirit's power.

Eternity touched down. The door was open and faith for receiving the Baptism of the Holy Spirit was released. I gave an invitation. "Anyone who wants this second work, just say yes to the Holy Spirit right now and start to speak as you feel His presence erupt inside of you. I am going to start praying in my language and anyone else who wants to, please join me."

"*Eyasha pelentas coriando…*" The words flowed out of me and I heard others expressing their praises and prayers in their own unique languages. I became consumed by the Spirit of the Living God and time stood still. I was released for a moment and opened my eyes. I looked around the table and everyone was praying in a language from heaven. The glory in the room and on each face was overwhelming.

As the prayers receded, Ashley spoke first. "That was so easy! Why did I let myself be so intimidated? I feel so full, and I know that I have a resource that I never thought possible."

"Ashley," I said. "The enemy would love for people to be skeptical and fearful of this amazing gift. People even make fun of our languages. But this gift is for all Jesus lovers. My mother spent many years in a powerless religion, and when she received the baptism, she put it this way. 'When you become a Christian, you still have to live in a fallen world. You feel like you are paddling upstream. The culture and world around you are going one way and you have to work really hard to go against the current. But when you receive the Baptism of the Holy Spirit, it's as if He puts a motor on your boat and you have all the power you need to go upstream.'"

Everyone clapped their hands and affirmed the truth of my mom's observation. Joy broke out and we all started giggling, there was a glorious recognition that we were all united in our faith and experience.

Then all of a sudden, we were startled by a loud noise as the back door to the shop was thrown open. We felt a foreign presence enter the room and looked at the entrance to the conference room to see who would be interrupting our intimate gathering.

It was Damien!

chapter 19

All eyes were on Damien. His face was contorted in hatred and intimidation. His dark eyes were like daggers. The old adage "if looks could kill" took on new meaning. Then I realized he was holding a gun. David stood up to confront him.

"Sit down. Don't give me an excuse for using this." Damien waved his gun and his voice became a low-pitched growl. "Julian, I know you stole documents from the OH Center office. I want them NOW."

Julian was frozen and took what seemed like forever to move. He gathered up the files that he had shared with us. "Take them, just don't hurt anyone."

Damien tossed a back pack on the table. "Put them in there and hurry. I should shoot you for your betrayal, but lucky for you Rallen has urged me to be merciful."

"Where is Rallen?" David asked. His voice was calm and confident.

"Somewhere you will never find him. I am sworn to protect him. I'm gathering all his documents to keep them out of your hands," Damien replied. He motioned for David to hand him the bag of files. Then his eyes narrowed. "You! You're the cause of all this!" He had suddenly realized that Jacob was sitting at the table. "Mercy or not, you deserve to die!"

A shot rang out. David leaped to his feet and body slammed Damien to the floor. The gun flew out of his hand and slid across the room. Julian jumped up and kicked it away from the two men struggling at his feet. David planted a massive punch into Damien's face and the man went still, knocked out.

"No! No! No!" Claire wailed. The sound sent shivers up my spine. I looked and saw Jacob lying on the floor. Sarah immediately began checking him for wounds. He had been knocked out of his chair and seemed to be unconscious. As we all watched, he slowly came around.

"What happened?" Jacob asked.

"Damien shot you," Claire said with tears streaming down her face.

"I don't think so. My head hurts, but I know that the bullet missed me."

"What do you mean?" Sarah asked.

Jacob sat up and rubbed the back of his head. He stood and picked up the chair that had tumbled over with him. "When Damien fired his gun, it was like watching a movie in slow motion. I could see the bullet coming toward me. The next thing I knew I was on the floor with Mom and Sarah hovering over me." He looked at David, and they had a moment of acknowledgment. I knew what that look meant. Jacob's guardian angel was on the job.

"Julian, do you have anything we can use to restrain Damien? I think he's coming around," David asked.

Julian left the room and came right back with a length of rope. He also used a napkin to pick up the gun. As soon as Damien was tied up, David took out his phone and called Special Agent Hall. "Buckle up, guys. Things could get crazy for the next little while," David said as he looked each one of us in the eye. "We should all stay right here so that the FBI can interview us."

"I think this calls for another round of coffee," Sarah said as she left the conference room.

Claire gave Jacob a big hug and then started patting him around his head and shoulders. She needed to have physical proof that her son was unharmed. We all sat down at the table again.

Despite the presence of Damien squirming in the corner of the room, we all expressed our thankfulness to God. I looked at what had been such a threat just a few minutes ago and saw a pitiful, toothless lion. I couldn't help see the representation of the devil. He was no match for the forces of heaven.

We had barely gotten our feet back on the ground when Hall and his crew arrived. They took Damien out of the room with plans to transport him to the local police department for detention and interrogation. Hall stayed behind with one of his agents to get our statements. David took the lead and explained the events that had just occurred. We all agreed with his story. The only part we left out was Jacob's miraculous escape from being shot. David said that Damien tried to kill Jacob and showed him the bullet hole in the wall of the conference room. He said that when he knocked Damien to the floor it threw off his aim. He emphasized that the charges against Damien should include attempted murder.

The next couple of hours ground by as the FBI agents took each of our statements. It was getting late, and we all needed rest and quiet after all that had taken place that day. David took Claire, Jacob, and I back to the hotel. An agent was stationed in our hallway to guard against any other surprise attacks from OH members. I gladly retreated to my room and took a long, soaking bath. I had trouble unwinding from the stress of the day. I also knew that there was a possibility that we had not ended the threat from One Humanity with Damien's arrest. I wondered what had happened to the two guards we had first encountered at the compound. Finally, I forcibly pulled my thoughts away from those concerns and focused on what God had done that day. Jacob was safe. He and his mother had been reunited. Damien was in custody and Rallen was long gone. We had put a serious dent in his organization. I hoped that our meeting with the OH members tomorrow would kill it all together.

chapter 20

I t was a brand-new day. I awoke with praises on my lips. Hope was filling me up. We had a mission to accomplish and I knew that God was going to bless our efforts. David called and wanted to meet with me in the breakfast room. I quickly dressed and headed toward the lobby of the hotel. Sam was in his usual place. He was smiling ear to ear when I approached him.

"Looks like there is a happy ending to all your hard work, I saw Jacob Cohen and his mom."

"Yes, we are all very thankful for his safe return, and I want to thank you for all your help these last few days." I returned his smile and patted his hand as he beamed.

"Detective Kramer is in the breakfast room," Sam said.

"Thanks, I'll be joining him."

"How was your night?" David asked as soon as I was seated at his table.

"I had a hard time unwinding, but finally got some good rest. I couldn't help feeling that we are far from finished with this saga," I answered as I sipped my coffee.

"We have the meeting tonight. That should be our focus for today. A lot hinges on the way we approach the people who are reeling from all the changes," David observed. "We also have a meeting with Hall this morning. He wants to go over some issues and give us updates on his part of the investigation."

"Oh boy, issues? I am sure he has plenty of them," I stated while I tried to remain charitable.

"We can weather this. I trust God to straighten out all the details and satisfy the authorities," David reassured.

"Look, lady, the breakfast room is for guests only!" We heard Sam's voice bellowing from the lobby.

We recognized the woman as soon as she entered the room. It was the "spy" from the lobby. We suspected that she was the one who had stolen our first copy of the incriminating video. She searched the room. When she saw us in at the corner table, she rushed toward us.

"Who do you think you are? You come into our town and turn everything upside-down. You have no right to persecute us. This is religious discrimination, and we intend to fight it all the way."

We were so taken aback that no reply was readily available. Then Sam came into the room with one of the FBI agents at his heels.

"Ma'am, I am going to have to ask you to leave. This is private property and I have an agent right here to see you off the premises." Sam's voice was bold and confident.

The woman turned and saw the suited agent with his air of authority. She conceded to Sam's demand. As she headed back out of the room, she turned and shouted, "You have not heard the last of me!" The agent took her by the arm and led her to the front door.

David and I sat in stunned silence for a couple of minutes. We had been blindsided by the woman's vehemence and not a little surprised by Sam's boldness.

"That doesn't bode well for our meeting tonight. How will we be able to present our case with people like that in the crowd?" I asked.

"Only God knows, because He is in charge. I know that this is an important part of why we came here. This town and these people need to hear the truth of the Gospel of Jesus Christ. It is our mission to plant the seeds that the Holy Spirit will water in days and years to come. Who knows, we could be setting the stage for a revival in this area," David said with conviction. "By the way, Julian reached the owner of the building that the OH center was housed in. He said we could use it tonight at no charge. Using the center as our venue will lend continuity, and having Jacob give his testimony will be key.

Also, Julian and Sarah's story will open doors for others to pursue the truth. Sarah has already activated the phone tree."

"We should get everyone together early at the center to pray and prepare the atmosphere," I suggested.

"I will let you know the time for our meeting with Agent Hall. I've got some phone calls to make to the Berkeley station. See you later," David added as he rose to leave the table.

I entered my room and immediately felt the weight of intercession come over me. I dropped to my knees at the bedside and began to pray. I started out with a prayer for mercy and peace over the woman who had accosted us at breakfast. I knew that she was being controlled by the enemy. I asked the Lord to send angelic hosts to surround her and guide her to the truth. I prayed for every OH member in Ashland that they would be compelled to attend the meeting we had planned for that evening. I asked for divine protection for each one of us as we prepared for the confrontation. I asked that the atmosphere in the center would be one of love.

As soon as I finished my prayers, I called Sarah and asked that she and Julian and Ashley come at least an hour early so we could join in prayer and unity. She said that she had started to bake cookies for the meeting. She would also supply coffee, tea, and punch for the OH members. I had not even thought about refreshments, but of course, that was Sarah's expertise.

A knock at my door alerted me to the arrival of the meeting time with Special Agent Hall. I answered the door and David just gave me a look that said volumes. We would both need to rely on the Holy Spirit to guide our words.

Hall and two other agents were seated around the conference table in the meeting room when we entered. The feeling in the room was one of serious skepticism.

I knew that their radar was blaring that we were not telling them the whole truth about what we had experienced in our search for Jacob. How could we tell them about angels and visions? Not only would they think we were crazy, it could ruin David's career. We needed all the creative power of the Spirit to guide us through this next ordeal.

"First, some updates." Hall began the meeting without ceremony. "You know that we have Damien Kushnir in custody. He has not given us any information on the location of Rallen Mandu, or should I say, Milo Ripley. One of our investigators has done some digging into Ripley's background. This is not the first scam that he has been evolved in. He has a rap sheet that is pretty interesting. How he was able to set up this hokey Humanity scheme beats me. What we figure is that he allowed his underlings to put their names on all the permits, leases, and transactions. He had a woman named Naomi Bell that did a lot of his dirty work. She has disappeared right along with him. I don't think we will get a location from Mr. Kushnir. We will probably end up pinning the kidnapping on him. Even with Jacob Cohen's testimony, there is no direct evidence of Ripley's involvement."

"What about the videotapes? Did you find them? They have verbal references to Mandu's, Ripley's involvement," David interrupted.

"Yes, we were able to recover the two tapes. I understand you have the original in Berkeley," Hall replied.

"Yes, but don't they prove that the OH had something to hide and took Jacob to keep him quiet?" David countered. "I also have a memo directing the Ashland center to keep Jacob hidden."

"How did you come by that memo?" Hall asked.

David looked down and answered slowly. "Well, we kept getting blocked by the Ashland Police. So we did do some snooping in the OH house."

Hall frowned and sent a look of disapproval at David. "I can see that you have been conducting your investigation in a very loose and unconventional manner. There are quite a few discrepancies that I have noticed. You probably rendered that evidence inadmissible."

I felt compelled to add my voice in support of David. "You could say that this whole situation, both here and in Berkeley, is very unconventional. We are dealing with a cult. The OH was a fantasy built up by a very slick charlatan. Don't forget all his financial misdeeds."

"We are well aware of the financial aspects of Ripley's crimes. He will be indicted and charged if we can track him down. I am just not sure if we can link him to the kidnapping. He was very well insulated by his associates. Besides Kushnir, we also have in custody the two guards that were directly tasked with Jacob's imprisonment. The big one, Luke Candle, has a pretty colorful past. He was a pro wrestler for a while and then turned bodyguard to Mr. Ripley. We have figured out that he doesn't know much about the operations of the OH. He just followed orders. When we question him about Jacob Cohen, he just keeps babbling on about big golden soldiers in the woods. What do you think that means?" Hall looked at us with a smirk.

David and I looked at each other and knew that this was a trap. We both gave Hall a look of complete innocence and puzzlement. No words were necessary.

Our interview with Special Agent Hall began to fizzle out when he realized we were not going to play his game. We told him about the meeting that we planned for that evening. He was not very happy about it, but did not protest too loudly. David assured him that the security aspects of the gathering were minimal. Hall offered to send a couple of his agents to infiltrate the crowd. We both let him know that would not be necessary. The presence of strangers might negate the effectiveness of the meeting. We told him that our objective was to answer the concerns of the OH members and steer them in a positive direction.

As we left the command center, David asked if I would like to take a ride. I looked at him with curiosity. He just smiled and said he would like to get out of Ashland for a little while. I was more than happy to accompany him on his little excursion. My unfounded fear that we would be separated by the task force was proved by the fact that we had been working together nonstop for the last two days. Though we had been together, the pace had kept us focused on other people. I was thrilled that David wanted to spend some down time with me.

"Let's wander over to Jacksonville. I would like to go back to that Bistro we found there. A quiet lunch would be a welcome break," David said.

"Sounds wonderful to me," I replied.

chapter

21

The drive to Jacksonville was pleasant. We chatted about everything but the investigation and the upcoming meeting. I found out that David was an only child. He was raised in a secular Jewish home. His family played down their roots and did their best to fit into the typical American stereotype. They had taken a trip to Israel to visit family there. Something about being in the Jewish homeland had stirred David to dig deeper into his heritage. That is what had led him to Ben Danielson and Rock church. He had met Ben at a fundraiser for Jewish student scholarships. Ben had intrigued David with his knowledge of the Jewish faith and history, but as the friendship deepened, David learned of the progression of Ben's faith. Ben had followed the avid study of the profits to its ultimate conclusion. Yeshua, Jesus, was the long-awaited Messiah. Ben had an encounter with Jesus and gave his life to the Savior. Through teachings and writings from other Messianic Jews, Ben, and then David, had fulfilled God's plan for them and the Jewish people.

We walked into the bistro and felt immediately relaxed. It was cozy and warm. The aromas from the kitchen were inviting. We found a booth near the back of the room and settled in for a good meal and conversation. It seemed like we never lacked for topics. It was so easy to talk to David. I felt like we had always been friends. We ordered iced tea and looked at the menus. We ordered different dishes from the last visit. David asked for the Ruben sandwich and coleslaw, and I ordered the soup and salad combo.

"What will happen after the meeting tonight? From what Hall was saying, the investigation here in this area has wound down," I asked David with a hint of apprehension in my voice.

David reached across the table and took my hands. "No matter what happens, you and I will always be friends. I know we live in separate states, but there are lots of ways to overcome distance. These days with you have been the best thing that's happened to me in a long time."

I felt myself melting at his touch and his words were piercing my heart. I know I was blushing. Words were hard to find. Just when I thought I could reply to his precious words, the waitress arrived with our meals.

The moment had passed, and I felt like I had failed David. I wanted to tell him how I felt. How he had become a part of me. How I missed his presence when we were apart. There were a couple of awkward moments as we began to eat our food. Then it was back to our friendly chatter.

"I was thinking about the meeting at Moonstone last night," I steered our conversation to deeper matters. "I was taking a risk presenting the baptism of the Holy Spirit to the group. I know there are some Christian churches that don't think that the baptism is valid for today. Did you feel uncomfortable?"

David looked down. It took him a while to find his words. I was hoping his silence wasn't his answer. "Pastor Ben has taught on the subject a few times and given invitations to the congregation. So I knew about it, but I have to confess, last night was the first time that I released myself to experience it."

I was surprised by his confession, but as I looked in his eyes I could see that there was a boldness that I had not seen before. "Wow! That is so wonderful. Tell me how you are feeling now. Have you been praying in your new language?"

"Excited, and yes. I have had a hard time keeping the joy bubbles from bursting out. Dealing with Hall this morning was so jarring. I had hoped we would get a chance to discuss this today. That's one reason why I asked you to take this drive with me. I was up half the night praising and praying in my new language. It was so powerful, just like you said. I feel like I have a greater level of understanding of the spiritual world. I am soaring, even though I know I have to keep my feet on the ground."

"I had thought since you are so sensitive to angelic presence that you were already spirit filled," I replied

"I don't think the one is exclusive of the other, but I am excited to see what other gifts have been lying dormant. Tell me about the time you received the baptism."

"Oh boy, this is kind of silly." I had a confession of my own. "When I was born again, again on my Christmas visit from Maui, my mom gave me a book on the Holy Spirit. I flew back to Hawaii and started reading it. One day I was reading, and I began to shake. I could hardly keep the book in my hands. I felt the Spirit overwhelming me, but I kept thinking, 'But I have to finish the book first!' I just couldn't keep reading so I ran into the bathroom. This was a place that I knew I would find the most privacy. I stood there in the middle of the bathroom and began to speak in my heavenly language. The Spirit would not wait for me to be ready. He knew that with what I was facing I needed the power right then and there."

David commented with a big smile. "I have to admit that is a pretty cute story."

We finished our meal and decided to take a walk to get some fresh air. We walked down the street and passed the same new age shop that we had seen on our last visit. I stopped by the window and turned to David. "Let's go in and check to see if that same girl is working. I want to see if the Holy Spirit would like us to plant some seeds."

David was excited by the idea. Since we were in agreement, I felt we truly were being led to minister to Parvati. As we entered the shop with its signature incense-laden atmosphere, we did not see anyone. Then we heard voices from the back of the shop. I hesitated, but David moved ahead to see who was there. Parvati was talking to a woman who had her back to us. When Parvati saw us, she was physically taken aback. Her companion turned to see why she had had that reaction and we saw that it was Naomi. I didn't know what to do, but David sprung into action and went toward her immediately.

Naomi quickly and smoothly disappeared into the back room of the shop. Parvati tried to block our pursuit, but David just pushed by her, and we were through the doorway. As we entered the darkened back room, Naomi was nowhere to be seen. There were not many places to hide, so we concluded that she had left by the back door. When we stepped out of the door into the bright sunlight, we were momentarily blinded. We looked around and just barely saw the sweep of Naomi's purple skirt disappear around the corner. David took my hand and we ran down the alley. At the corner we scanned the street.

Naomi was gone. We made our way down the street looking in shop windows and opening doors. At the third doorway, we encountered a small deli. As soon as we entered, we saw the shop owner with eyes wide scrambling to close the door to the kitchen. David boldly approached the owner and only had to give him a look. The man stepped aside, and we were into the kitchen. A worker was just recovering from the shock when we entered. He saw the look on David's face and turned to look back through the kitchen. It was a signal to us that Naomi had gone that way. We quickly made it to the back door, and as we opened it, we heard a cry of distress. There was Naomi on the ground holding her ankle. She obviously had slipped on the way out and fell down the couple of steps and twisted her ankle.

"Naomi! What are you doing here? We thought you had escaped with Rallen," I exclaimed. She just sealed her lips and continued to grimace at the pain in her ankle.

David could tell that we would not get much out of her. Her loyalty to Rallen Mandu was iron clad. David took out his phone and called Hall. David read her rights to her and we settled in to wait for the FBI team to make good on the arrest.

"What about Parvati?" I asked David.

Naomi looked at me with anger. "She has nothing to do with this. Leave her alone!"

"Oh, you *can* talk," David observed. "We will have to ask her some questions. It looks like she may have been harboring a fugitive. Who knows what other services she has performed for the OH hierarchy."

"Who do you think you are? You can't harass us. We are a religious group. We have rights!" Naomi proclaimed with all the vengeance she could muster.

"You forfeited your rights when you abducted Jacob Cohen. I just wonder what was so important that you felt you had to silence him. I believe we are just looking at the tip of a very sinister ice berg," David returned.

Naomi was just about to answer when Special Agent Hall and a couple of his men arrived. They took command of the situation and took Naomi into custody. The two agents escorted Naomi to their car, but Hall hesitated. He turned and gave us both a wary look.

"I am not sure how you do it, but you are always a step ahead of us. How is it that you always seem to be in the right place at the right time?"

David gave Hall an innocent look and answered, "Just luck, I guess."

We could tell that David's answer did not satisfy the special agent, but he did not challenge it.

"Let's go back to Parvati's shop and see what she has to say for herself," David suggested.

We went back through the deli and smiled at the cook and the owner as if to say, "No big deal. We do this all the time."

On our way back to the shop, David and I strategized on how to approach Parvati. We wanted to glean as much information from her as possible. We agreed that she had not been very helpful on our other encounter. She might be a tough nut to crack. David knew that a threat of taking her into the police station for questioning could be the key. He said to follow his lead as we approached her.

When we reached the shop, the door was locked and the closed sign was in the door. We walked around the block and came down the alley to the back door. As we came up to the door, Parvati burst through carrying an armload of files. When she saw us, she reacted with surprise and dropped most of her burden. She stood there in the alley, frozen in place.

"I have some questions for you. We can go inside the shop and discuss this quietly or we can take you down to the police station, if you like," David announced in his most authoritarian voice.

Parvati started to protest and then thought better of it. Suddenly her surely attitude melted away. "Okay, help me with these files and then we can go and talk, but I am telling you right now that I don't have a lot of the answers you are looking for."

We cleaned up the papers from the alley and as we shuffled them together, we caught glimpses of One Humanity letterhead.

"So what do you want to know?" Parvati started as we sat in her office.

"Why were you protecting Naomi? You must know that she was implicated in the kidnapping of Jacob Cohen," David asked.

"She is a friend. I just wanted to help her any way I could."

"Is that why you were hiding those documents? Did she ask you to keep them for her?"

"I wasn't hiding anything. Those are just some files that I was taking home to work on for my business."

"Come on, Parvati, I saw the One Humanity logo on many of the pieces of paper we helped you round up."

"Those are private files. You have to have a search warrant to look at them." Parvati was beginning to get her attitude back.

"That can be arranged. Why don't you cooperate? Surely you can see the writing on the wall. The One Humanity organization is history. Both centers are closed and Rallen Mandu has disappeared. He is covering his tracks and you should be doing whatever you can to stay out of the line of fire. If you help us, we can help *you* stay out of the criminal aspects of this case. I have a feeling that you are a pawn in all of this." David was gambling that Parvati would be more valuable as a witness than another arrest.

We could see Parvati calculating her options as we sat and waited for her decision. "All right, you win. I was a member of the OH, and I really am a friend of Naomi's. We knew each other long before Rallen came into the picture. She came to me today to see if I could get rid of some files. I don't know what is in them. I was doing it because of our friendship, a favor you know. You can take the files.

I don't want to get mixed up in all this. I am actually relieved that the OH is busted. I never really trusted Mandu. I couldn't figure out why Naomi was so infatuated. Where is Naomi now? Did you catch her?"

"Yes, we tracked her down and she twisted her ankle. She is in custody now with the FBI," David answered.

A cloud crossed over Parvati's face. "What a mess. I feel so bad for her. She was blinded and now she is taking the fall for that man!"

"Thank you for your help. I would ask that you stick around town so that we can ask you any questions that come up," David cautioned.

"I can do that. I have to keep my shop open anyway. I'm sorry I was such a pain. I really do want to help make sure that Rallen can't dupe anyone else."

David and I gathered up the files and headed back out to the street. We checked the time and felt the pressure of the looming OH member meeting. We had to get back to Ashland and prepare. David also needed to meet with Hall and give him the files. I was amazed again that a simple lunch outing had turned into a cat-and-mouse adventure. I prayed that our meeting that evening would not hold as many surprises. I hoped we could create a safe atmosphere for the OH members to open themselves up to the truth.

chapter 22

David and I returned to the hotel in Ashland. He headed off to see Special Agent Hall. I went to my room to take a few minutes to check in with the Lord and get my instructions for the meeting. I took a quick shower and wrapped up in my robe then stretched out on the bed and centered my mind on the goodness of God. I began to see all the ways that He had protected and guided us in the last few days. I felt His presence reassuring me that He would do the same during the meeting with the One Humanity members. I got the impression that we needed to cleanse the meeting room. It had been the domain of the opposition forces for some time and we needed to open it up to be invaded by heavenly battalions. I could see the Hosts of Heaven descending and preparing to meet the enemy head on. The meeting was not just about opening minds. It was about defeating the strategies of Satan that had ruled over that building and the town for many years.

There was a knock on my door. Wrapping my robe around me, I jumped up and answered it. David said he would be ready in fifteen minutes to go to the meeting site and hoped I would be ready as well. I assured him that I was not only ready but equipped. He left and I dressed quickly. I also located a bottle of anointing oil that I had in my suitcase and stuck it in my purse. Within the allotted fifteen minutes, I was armed and ready.

The owner of the building that used to house the OH center met us at the door. We had a good two hours before the meeting. He showed us where the light switches were, the bathrooms and tables and chairs that we could use. David thanked him for his generosity.

David had learned that Lester Main, the owner, was a member of a local church community.

"It's the least I could do. I never really liked renting to that crew. I am glad to see them go. That Rallen fella was spooky if you ask me, and I won't even get into that other one, Damn-y-on. I feel a lot better now, and I know that God will get me a new renter real soon," Lester declared.

I could have hugged him right there if I hadn't picked up that he was not the hugging sort. "We are going to reverse the atmosphere in this building. I believe the next time you come in here you will feel a difference," I assured him.

"Well, anything is better than what went on here before. You folks have a good evening and don't forget to turn out the lights and lock the door when you leave," Lester reminded.

"Should we set up the chairs and the tables for the food first?" David asked.

"Maybe we should wait for the others to help with that. I want to anoint the building before we get into a lot of busy work," I answered.

"Okay, but how do we do that?" David looked a little uncomfortable.

"It's not difficult. It's just a way to seal the atmosphere so unwanted spirits do not invade. It is a way to declare that this space now belongs to the Lord for His purposes."

"That sounds like a great idea to me," David agreed.

I took my bottle of oil from my purse. We went to the entrance to the building and I put some oil on my fingers. I handed the oil to David and he followed my lead.

As I applied the oil to the door posts, I said, "In the name of Jesus, I consecrate this building to the uses of the Most High God, Yahweh. All other spirits must flee. Any unclean spirits will not be able to enter this doorway. Every demonic force will be neutralized on entering this building."

David's eyes were round as I looked at him. "Woah! I didn't know you could do that. I've got to learn how. I could really use that in some of the creepy places I have to go into."

"Any believer can take authority over the demonic realm. I want you to do the next doorway. We can take turns on the doors *and* windows," I assured him.

It took David a couple of tries to get the wording down, but I could tell that the authority that he wielded in the natural world was very well suited to the task at hand. When we had finished anointing every area we could think of, David was very comfortable with anointing an environment. I was amazed again at how God was using this experience to teach us more about the spirit realms and how to use our gifts to make a difference.

"Now I want to do one final declaration in the meeting room. I want the enemy to know that we have the authority here, and we will not tolerate any disruptions or outbursts," I stated as we entered the area where we would hold the meeting.

I took David's hand and began to declare, "In the name of Jesus, I bind and arrest any defilement and cast it into the dry places, never to return again. I shut and seal the door from the spiritual to the physical with the Word, the Blood and the Anointing. I release a fresh application of the Blood of Jesus over this room, over us and over every person that enters this room. I release the Spirit of the Living God over this room and over this meeting tonight."

We were both speechless as we felt the Presence of God descend into the room. Time stood still as eternity invaded.

David squeezed my hand and I opened my eyes. "Can you see them?" he said.

I looked around. I did not see the angels, but I could feel their presence. For a moment, I envied David's gift until I remembered that I had many gifts of my own, and we were both part of the one Body of Christ.

"This room is filled with angels. Big ones and smaller ones are busy cleaning the room. There were some cobwebs in the corners. Little mouse like critters were scurrying under foot, but they have been sent packing. The angelics are decorating the room for a party. This is so exciting. I have never seen so many in one place. Something big is going to happen tonight," David explained what he was seeing in the spirit.

The front door opened and our team began to arrive. Julian and Sarah came in carrying bags of goodies. Ashley had the coffee pot and could barely see her way into the room from behind it. There would be no shortage of hot drinks. They knew their way around the center kitchen, so we let them get settled before we asked for their help in setting up the room for the meeting. As we began lining up the chairs, Claire and Jacob entered and were greeted warmly. Jacob was to be our star for the evening and we were all so thankful that God had rescued him and given us all a chance to use his trials to the glory of God.

Jacob was more than happy to pitch in with the chairs. Physical activity was a joy after being cooped up in small spaces for so long. The guys took over the room set up, and the girls went to the kitchen to prepare the refreshments. We were delighted to hear male laughter coming from the meeting room.

"Jacob is in high spirits tonight," I announced to Claire.

"Yes, he is so resilient. He's just happy to be back into life. We have had such a wonderful time sharing our new faith and our joy at his return. The last few hours have been like heaven," Claire explained.

"I feel so positive about this evening," Sarah spoke up. "Julian, Ashley, and I were praying this afternoon and we felt the Lord's presence so profoundly. We all got confirmation on the productive nature of our meeting."

Ashley piped in. "I even got a vision. Wow! That was really trippy. I saw Jesus with his shepherd's staff in a field of goats and sheep. He was walking through them and separating them into two different herds. He gently nudged the goats away with his staff. He was so kind, but also very deliberate. He welcomed the sheep into His fold. There was no way to escape His authority to separate the two herds. I believe he will be at our meeting tonight doing the same thing to the OH members."

"Ashley, that's remarkable. You are growing in your gifts. When we have everything set up, I want us all to meet and pray together. We have some things to share with you as well. I hope we will have time for you to recount your vision to David and Jacob. It is a real faith builder," I said as I basked in Ashley's radiant expression.

It was a half hour to the meeting time. We all gathered in the main room and stood in a circle with hands clasped. David gave his testimony about seeing the angelic forces in the room. Ashley described her vision. We were all overcome with praise for God's faithfulness. We were saturated in God's presence as we praised and sang. We became quiet and reverent. David began with a prayer for favor and a fulfillment of all that God wanted to do that night. We each took our turns praying. Each prayer seemed more powerful than the last. Jacob's humble prayer of thanksgiving and request for divine direction as he was about to give his testimony to his former OH brothers and sisters, was the last, and left tears in all our eyes.

As if on cue, the front door opened and the first attendees entered the center. We all scrambled to our places. Ashley and Sarah were the greeters. Julian manned the refreshment table. David, Jacob, and I took our places on the front row of the seating. We wanted to keep a low profile. Some of the members would be looking for a confrontation. We wanted to keep the atmosphere as calm as possible.

We were amazed at how quiet it was. We could hear the greetings from the front door, but as soon as the members entered the meeting hall, they became silent. They nodded at Julian and quietly took some coffee and cookies and just found a seat to wait for the meeting to start. I turned and saw the "spy" lady at the refreshment table. My heart skipped a beat as I recalled our last run in with her. She could be our challenge. She certainly had strong feelings about what had taken place in Ashland during our quest for Jacob. I was surprised to see her look around the ceiling of the room with a look of apprehension. She slowly found a seat and sat quietly munching her cookie. I gave David a look, and we communicated our relief at her seemingly uncharacteristic behavior.

By seven o'clock, the meeting hall was packed. We had to bring in a few more chairs. Julian moved to the front of the room and welcomed everyone. "Thank you all for being here tonight. I know that you are in varying states of distress and disbelief at the events of the last few days. We wanted you to come together tonight, so we could share with you our perspective. A lot has changed for us. I am hoping we can come together now to make sense of it and make a way forward for our community. We are sitting here tonight in what was once the One Humanity center. We all heard about the closure of the Berkeley Center and did not think that it could happen here, but the problems that led to that closure followed us."

"The event that precipitated all of this is centered on one person, Jacob Cohen. Some of you have met him through OH conferences. He was very active in the Berkeley center. However, actions by the leadership of our organization put us in jeopardy. I want Jacob to speak to that. He has a story to tell that will clear up a lot of the confusion."

Jacob reluctantly took his place before the group. "This is really hard for me. I have had some dark days recently. I don't take this responsibility lightly, but I have to tell my story and set the record straight. They were not my actions that brought about the demise of the One Humanity centers. I was a victim in the plans of the leadership to cover up their true motives and practices. Rallen Mandu is not who you think he is."

Right then, the "spy" lady jumped to her feet. She opened her mouth to shout something at Jacob, but when nothing would come out, she clapped her hand over her mouth and turned and ran from the room. She was out the door of the center before anyone could make sense of what had just happened.

Of course, our team knew what was going on. The reigning Spirit in the room would not allow the enemy to speak through anyone. There was an eternal destiny being forged in the meeting and nothing would be allowed to hinder it.

Jacob regained his composure quickly. "I believe that was some kind of protest. I am sorry that she would not wait to hear my whole message. Each of you will have to make a decision about whether you believe me or not, but I do hope you will hear me out.

"I was part of the leadership team in Berkeley. I was privy to the inner workings of the organization. Some of the more, let's say, creative accounting, did not bother me. I saw it as a means to our important end, but something happened to change my point of view.

I met a man named Ben at a Jewish scholarship fundraiser. We struck up a conversation. I was intrigued by his confident and joyful personality. We met for coffee a week later, and he began to share with me his life story. It turns out that he is a Messianic Jew. That means he is Jewish but has also become a disciple of Jesus. He believes Jesus is the Messiah that our forefathers have been waiting for. I was skeptical but couldn't shake the feeling that there was something special about the man. He invited me to his church. He is the pastor of Rock Church in Berkeley. I went to an evening meeting with a couple of hundred other young people. The music drew me in. Then the message that Ben brought made me question everything about my life and my choices. He asked if anyone wanted to meet Jesus. I couldn't believe it when I found myself at the front of the church. I was being drawn by a presence that I had never experienced before. Ben prayed for me and led me through a simple prayer for forgiveness and surrender. I wanted Jesus more than anything I had ever desired. I gave Him my life in exchange for His infilling presence and eternal life to boot."

Jacob paused here to take the temperature of the room. I looked around and saw more than a few tears flowing. Along with those with softened faces, I also saw hardened glares. Sheep and goats.

"Needless to say, my life took a radical turn that night. I went home and dug out an old dusty Bible I had gotten somewhere. I began to read about Jesus. He was a subject that was never brought up in my secular Jewish home. I was meeting Him for the first time. I couldn't get enough of His words and deeds as He ministered to my people. Sometime in the night I fell asleep, and when I awoke, I knew that I had to make a life change. The thought of going back to the OH center sickened me. I called in and let Naomi know that I was resigning. She asked me to come in and explain myself. I let her know I could not do that. One week later I was working for a nonprofit organization and attending services at Rock Church whenever the doors were open. As I became more grounded in my new faith, I began to feel unsettled by what I had done for the OH leadership. Their practices were sketchy at best and illegal for sure. I knew that I had to confront Rallen. I didn't want to, but I felt it was my duty.

Maybe he would hear me and clean up his act. I couldn't have been more wrong about that."

Jacob paused in his story. He scanned the faces of the crowd. I looked around too. Every emotion possible was being displayed on their faces. Grief, unbelief, revelation, denial, anger, disappointment, sorrow, and more were playing out in the OH members as they let Jacob's story sink in.

"I went to the OH center in Berkeley to see Rallen. I had not been there for a few weeks. When I entered, I felt like a stranger in a strange land. Nothing seemed the same. My spirit was rising up inside of me. I wanted to turn around and run away, but I was determined to deliver my message. I asked the receptionist if I could see Rallen Mandu. I recognized her, and she certainly recognized me. The look of disapproval was very evident on her face. She said she would have to check to see if he was even in the building. I took a seat and waited. A couple of members came into the waiting area and saw me. There was hatred in their eyes. I was amazed at their blatant reproach.

"Finally, Naomi came out and asked me to follow her into the conference room. Rallen, Damian and two guards were waiting. The guards were standing behind Rallen. It was very intimidating. Rallen began by expressing his disappointment in my abrupt resignation from the OH. He said that he was considering legal action for breach of contract. That was a surprise as I did not remember having a formal contract with the OH. He produced a document that I had never seen before with my signature on it. I didn't know what to say. It was an obvious preemptive strike at intimidation. I gathered my courage and launched into my testimony about my recent conversion to Christianity and my crisis of conscience. I hoped that I could bring some balance to the One Humanity's financial practices.

"Rallen's countenance darkened. I could see his anger rising. He pounded the table and jumped to his feet. 'How dare you!' he bellowed. Then he turned to his guards, and with a wave of his hand, they moved toward me and grabbed me by the arms. I was taken to a small room and tossed inside and the door was locked. It was dark and I couldn't believe that I was being treated like that.

"That was just the first of many small dark rooms I endured over a period of weeks. When they needed to transport me, I was injected with a sedative. They fed me very little. No one ever told me why I was being detained. Fortunately, I had a small, pocket-sized New Testament with me. When there was enough light, I would devour the Word of God. It sustained me. I never gave up hope that the Lord would deliver me from my captivity. I really didn't know what the end game was going to be. I hoped I would never find out.

"Yesterday Detective Kramer and my mother's friend, Joy Morgan, rescued me from a cabin on the Applegate River. I am reunited with my mom. I praise God for His goodness and for his faithfulness. I also want to thank the people who never gave up looking for me.

"Now I would like to introduce Detective David Kramer who can give you his perspective, and also an update on the state of the OH."

Jacob turned and motioned for David to take his place at the front of the room. I scanned the faces in the crowd, and everyone looked eager to hear what David had to say.

"Thank you all for coming here tonight. I know that what you have heard is difficult to absorb. I am David Kramer, a detective with the Berkeley Police Department. I have been on the case to find Jacob Cohen from the beginning. Joy Morgan has been an invaluable resource and consultant throughout the course of the investigation. Joy would you stand."

I stood and faced the group briefly, but even in that short exposure I was overwhelmed by the negativity being directed at David and me.

"Thank you, Joy. We followed the trail of Jacob's disappearance here to Ashland. We were thwarted in our efforts by the local authorities. However, we had faith that we would find Jacob. We never gave up hope. As Jacob has said, we found him yesterday at a cabin outside of town that is owned by an OH member. He was being held there by one of Rallen's security guards. We were able to distract the guard long enough to release Jacob and bring him back to Ashland. The FBI has set up a command post at one of the hotels in town. They have apprehended some of the major players in Jacob's kidnapping. Naomi Bell, Damian Kushnir and Luke Candle are now in FBI custody. Rallen Mandu has escaped the area. There will be an ongoing search for him. As you can see, the Ashland center is closed and the OH house has been confiscated. So for all intents and purposes, One Humanity is out of business. Your leader has been exposed as a fraud and a thief. His real name is Milo Ripley, and this is not the first scam he has perpetrated. His disguise as a benevolent peace maker has been ripped away."

A man in the crowd jumped to his feet and yelled, "I don't want to hear this blasphemy. You are lying, and I refuse to give you any more time to defame our precious leader. I will always be an OH member." He turned and started to walk out of the room and a few others followed suit.

The majority of the people just watched them go with a few sad shakes of their heads. They turned back to David and waited to hear more.

"We are here tonight because we understand how disappointed you are. Your faith has been shattered. I believe you have been searching for spiritual significance in the wrong place. I would like Julian to come forward now and give you his testimony. He was an OH member, but he has found a new way to express his longing for connection to God."

Julian took David's place at the front of the room and took a minute to scan the group and look each one of them in the eye. He knew these people and he really cared about what would happen to them.

"You know that I was part of the OH leadership team," he began. "I was very involved and have had loving relationships with many of you. I think you also know that I am a man of integrity. Even before the Jacob investigation, I was having problems lining up the philosophy of the OH and its fiscal practices. I was in charge of the financials here at the Ashland center. Some things just didn't add up. I am a business man and I know how to balance the books. Large amounts of money were being siphoned off and sent out of the country into holding accounts. When I asked about this, I was given some very evasive answers and then just ordered to do my job without asking questions. Many of my encounters with Rallen were uncomfortable. I was beginning to see through his façade. When I heard that he was being investigated for kidnapping, I was not surprised. I thought that his misdeeds had finally caught up with him."

Julian paused, and I knew what was coming next. I breathed a prayer for him. He was about to relate his conversion experience, and this was crucial to the importance of the evening.

"David Kramer and Joy Morgan came to our shop and questioned us about the Ashland OH. At first I was defensive, but as I got to know them, I saw in them something that stirred my spirit. They had a level of peace and confidence that radiated out from them. Through interactions with them, I began to see they had an answer that I had been searching for. They introduced me to Jesus. The real Jesus. Not just another ascended master. Jesus is God's son, and he came to earth to show us the way to live in harmony with God. He died so that we could be free from the burden of sin we carry. I let Jesus into my heart, and I have been feeling a peace I never knew existed. You can have it too. Just believe that Jesus is the son of God that He died for you, and that His blood can wash you clean. Accept Him into your heart and you will know the truth, and it *will* set you free."

One of the members raised her hand. "I let Jesus into my heart when I was a little girl, but then I walked away. I want him back. Help me get him back in my life!" Her tears began to flow.

Julian looked at David and me. David gave me a nod and I rose from my seat and took Julian's place before the group. "That is very easy. Just tell Him that you are sorry for walking away. Tell him you want Him back in your life. He has never left you. He can't wait to resume your relationship and put you on a new path. He wants you to fulfill your destiny that He designed for you since before you were born."

Another member raised their hand. "What if I never knew Jesus that way? What do I do?"

"That is not hard either. Are there others who want to meet Jesus and accept Him into your heart?" Most of the people raised their hands.

"Okay, let's pray together. I will say a part, and you will say it out loud after me."

Heads were nodding and tears were flowing.

"Jesus, I am sorry for ignoring you. I am sorry that I never listened to the voice inside of me that said you were real. I am sorry for all the wrong things I have done. Please forgive me. Wash me clean with your precious blood. I know that you died for me. If I was the only person on Earth, you would have come down to rescue me. I know you love me, and I want to love you back. I give you my heart. Come and live in me now. I want all that you have for me. Teach me how to live for you."

Now there were sobs and even a few giggles erupting from the group. I was amazed to see quite a few beaming faces shining back at me. The power of the Holy Spirit fell and we all began to praise God for his goodness. Some of the people jumped to their feet and held their hands up to the Lord. The surrender was evident. A few sank to their knees and began to pour out their hearts and hurts. I looked to our team and we knew what we needed to do. We began to circulate throughout the group and pray individually for each one. Some needed more support to let go of their doubts and programming, but no one left the room. The presence of the Lord was so strong that none of us wanted to leave the heavenly atmosphere.

After almost an hour, Julian stood before the group and brought every ones attention to his words. "I believe we have the beginnings of a wonderful move of God. We all have met in this room many times. I would like to propose that we keep doing that. We will need each other as we start on this journey with God. Let's pool our resources and rent this facility. Let's make this our home church. We will be just the first of many to respond to the Holy Spirit in this space. It has been blessed and anointed. David tells me that there are hosts of angels in attendance. Let's keep this going. Let's share our newfound faith with our families and friends. The OH led us down a dark path. We will use this space to establish truth and revival in Ashland. Are you with me?"

Many shouts and affirmations resounded from the group. I could see the joy and hope that was flowing from them. They had a mission and a focus for their new spiritual awareness. David and I looked at each other and knew that what had started out as a frustrating search for Jacob Cohen, would now be turned into a triumph for God. That was what only God could do; turn what the enemy meant for evil into His perfect plan. For me the victory we were experiencing had a small seed of sadness. I could see the end of the amazing path that the Lord had set me on. I could see my days of working with David coming to an end.

chapter 23

My eyes popped open and registered the morning light streaming in through the window of my hotel room. I was flooded with emotion. Joy and sadness were tussling for my attention. "This is the day the Lord has made. I *will* rejoice and be glad in it," I said out loud. I would face the day with gladness because I knew that God's will had been expressed and many miracles had manifested by His faithfulness. The miracle of Jacob's return to his mother, the miracle of salvation for so many One Humanity members, the miracle of a new congregation established in Ashland and the miracle of my connection with David Kramer. We had shared so much and yet said so little about how we felt about each other. There was the time in the Bistro in Jacksonville when David opened up the subject. Why didn't I pursue that conversation? What was I afraid of?

My reverie was interrupted by a phone call. It was David. He said that the FBI team was wrapping up and wanted to meet with us one more time to ask a few final questions. We would meet with them in the conference room in one hour. He asked if I wanted to meet him in the breakfast room shortly before. I said, of course. When I hung up the phone I felt an overwhelming apprehension. I did not know if it was from the prospect of meeting with Agent Hall or with David. Both meetings held some looming questions. Would Hall press for clarification on how we were able to stay ahead of his team throughout the investigation? How about the excuses we had given about the angelic interventions we experienced? Then, there was David. Would I find the courage to tell him about my feelings for him? But where would that lead? We were both committed to our careers and lived in separate states. How practical would it be to pursue a relationship?

With questions swirling around my head, I showered and got ready to go to breakfast. As I walked down the corridor toward the front desk, I felt like I was marching to my doom. I was so conflicted. I couldn't bear to think about saying goodbye to David and never seeing him again. Yet opening that door to a possible relationship was so daunting. I had loved my single life. I loved my career as a teacher and a writer. A wave of relief and disappointment hit me as I entered the breakfast room. David was sitting with Claire and Jacob.

"Good morning!" I greeted them all with as much cheer as I could muster at the moment.

"I am so glad we caught you this morning," Claire exclaimed. "Jacob and I are checked out and we are on our way back to Marin. I thought you might be able to join us, but David says you have some FBI business to attend to. But I will look forward to your return to my home. I hope you can stay for a few days before you go back to Boise."

"I look forward to spending some time with you both in a more secure location," I said with a genuine smile.

Jacob returned my smile and added with a twinkle in his eye. "Thanks to you and David, I will be enjoying that secure location more than you will ever know. I cannot thank you both enough for all you did for me. You never gave up. I have heard about all the setbacks and roadblocks that were put in your way. You guys are amazing, and you make a dynamite team."

David and I shared a look that held a million questions and answers. When I looked at Claire I could tell that look had not escaped her notice. "When do you think you will be done here? Your trip back to the bay area will give you both a chance to *de brief.*" She put an emphasis on those last words that made me blush.

David quickly jumped in and said, "Oh, it should wrap up before noon. Then we will be more than glad to get on the road."

We spent the next few minutes in pleasant chatter as we drank coffee and picked at our breakfast. We were all anxious to be going.

We said goodbye to Claire and Jacob with hugs and blessings. Then David and I walked to the conference room with some trepidation.

As we entered the room, there was a beehive of activity. Files and electronics were being packed up. Agents were hurrying around the room to make sure nothing was left behind.

"There you are." Special Agent Hall approached us as we entered. He acted like we were late for our interview, but according to our watches, we were a couple of minutes early.

"I have set up a table for us in the corner. I hope you don't mind all the activity in the room. We have to get back to our headquarters and process all of this." He pointed to the files and documents being packed up around us.

Before we could respond to his statement, he launched into his inquiry. "I still don't know how you managed to know exactly where the perpetrators would be at any given moment. Did you have some inside source that you failed to share with us?"

David and I shared a look and I nodded for him to attempt to answer the rather sticky question. "I assure you, Agent Hall, we never withheld any information from you or your team. Because of our involvement from the beginning of the investigation, and thanks to the expertise of my consultant Joy Morgan, we made some very good calculations that turned out to be right on the money."

Hall gave us both a skeptical look. Then, addressing me he said, "With all of your 'expertise,' do you have any idea where we can find Mandu, or should I say, Ripley?"

His question was dripping with sarcasm, but I chose to answer him without matching his tone. "No, you would be more equipped to track him down. I would say follow the money."

After a pause, Hall replied, "Okay, if you don't have anything else to add, we will consider your participation completed. However, if we need you later, you may be called upon to answer some additional questions."

We were dismissed without a courteous hand shake or thank-you. Agent Hall rose from the table and turned to one of his team members to help him sort a stack of files. David looked at me and shrugged. As we left the room, David had one word of commentary. "Turf."

We discussed our next move and decided we would check out of the hotel and visit Sarah and Julian one more time before we left town. We needed to say a proper goodbye. As we drove toward the square, I had a flood of memories wash over me. We had only been in Ashland a few days and yet it seemed like much longer. After all the events that were packed into those days, I could not help but feel like I would miss all of the excitement.

I think that David was having similar thoughts because he was so quiet. We parked in front of Moonstone and walked slowly into the shop. Ashley was at the counter and greeted us warmly. She even came around and gave us hugs. "Julian and Sarah are waiting for you in the conference room."

I gave her a questioning look and said, "How did you know we were coming?"

With a big smile, she said, "Sam called me when you were checking out. He and I have become friends. He will miss you guys. He said that he has never been so appreciated by any guests and he will miss all the excitement."

"Next time you see him, tell him that we will miss him too," I said.

"I will see him tonight. He is part of our new congregation. Turns out he is a devoted Christian. What a guy!" Ashley gushed.

We entered the conference room and greeted our friends. They jumped to their feet and embraced us in turn. They had coffee and goodies waiting for us.

"Ashley is working for you now?" I asked.

"Yes, she is so great. She has decided to stay in Ashland and help with the church. She has a background in the Word and church organization that will be valuable," Sarah replied.

"Do you have a name for your new congregation?" David asked.

"We were thinking about something similar to the OH and calling ourselves HR, Heaven Revealed," Julian proclaimed. "It is a declaration that God can take what the devil meant for evil and turn it to good."

"Not to mention that it is a symbol of the work we have ahead of us. Tilling this soil, planting seeds for salvation and bringing heaven to earth," Sarah added.

"Your excitement is contagious! I wish we could stay and help you," I proclaimed.

"So do we, but we know that you have already done so much for us here in Ashland. I think your mission is complete. That is not to say the Lord doesn't have a new one for you," Julian returned.

I felt emotion welling up. We had bonded with these precious people. I wanted to make sure that they were going to find favor and blessings as they established their church in that rich soil. "I want to caution you. Don't allow a religious spirit to invade your congregation. Always keep your worship fresh and real. Remember your first love, Jesus. Keep Him front and center of all you do. I will be praying for you and feel free to call me anytime if you have questions or prayer needs."

"We are rooting for you. You may want to come to Berkeley some time and visit Rock Church. It would be a great inspiration." David had his council as well.

More hugs and some tears later, we were back in the car and headed out of town. As we entered the freeway and set the cruise for parts south, the silence was filled with a palpable tension.

"You…"

We—" David and I spoke at the same time, abruptly ending the silence.

"You go first," David said.

"Okay," I surrendered. "We did a good thing. I am so amazed at how the Lord led us through that maze to find the prize. Jacob's release was just frosting on the cake. All of the changed lives are the real blessing. I really don't want it to end. The thought of going back to Boise sounds pretty boring." I looked over at David and said with all the sincerity I could find, "I will miss you!"

David cleared his throat. I could tell that he was fighting down his emotions. "Do you remember the lunch we had at the bistro in Jacksonville? I tried to tell you then how much our time together has meant to me. You didn't respond, and I have been in limbo ever since. Now to hear you say you will miss me warms my heart. I hope our connection never gets broken."

I was unsure how to respond. He said *connection*; was that professional or emotional? I wanted it to be more, but I didn't know how to open that door. Where would it lead us? "I hope you mean relationship, because for me, that is what I want us to move toward. I really don't know what that will look like since we are from such different worlds, but I am willing to step into the next level." There, I said it. Now the ball was in his court.

The silence descended again, and I sat frozen waiting for him to break it. I wanted to shout out, "Say something!" but it would be far too awkward. So I just waited, feeling the temperature rise in the cabin of the car.

"There is a rest area up ahead. Let's stop and take a break," David finally said.

As we exited the car and headed to our separate bathrooms, nothing was said and not a glance was exchanged. In the ladies' room I berated myself for being so bold. I had pushed the issue too far. Now I may have ruined everything. I was close to tears, but knew I had to pull it together before I left the bathroom.

When I came out, David was leaning up against the car, looking completely relaxed. I was far from relaxed. I walked back to the car as slowly as I could, wishing every step that I could find a place to hide and let out all the emotions that were boiling up inside of me. As I neared the car, David came forward and met me. He took my hands and looked right into my eyes with perfect confidence and said, "Yes, that is what I want too. I didn't want to respond until I could look you in the eye and give you my complete attention. The thought of you leaving California without acknowledging our relationship and an ongoing commitment would leave me broken hearted. I, too, have many questions about how this is going to work, but let's take it one day at a time."

To say that I was relieved and overjoyed would have been an understatement. I gave him my biggest smile and went in for a hug. We lingered and our bond strengthened. I felt like life was full of promise. Being in David's arms was like coming home.

We released our hug and stood looking into each other's eyes. I thought we might kiss, but we hesitated. We were taking it one step at a time. I thanked God for His goodness and for our maturity. We would savor each step.

Spontaneous laughter erupted as we got back into the car. The tension that had filled the cabin was replaced by indescribable joy. Now the silence was golden. Our hearts were beating in synchronized harmony. David finally broke the spell when he said, "You never told me about Hawaii."

"Really? Are you sure you want to hear about my wild days in the islands?" I replied.

"Sure, we have at least another hour drive to the Bay Area. Let's have a story to fill the time," David urged me on.

"The Cosmic Earth Collective had a center in Lahaina, Maui. We had started a natural foods restaurant and an airbrushed clothing store on Front Street, the main street through town. Back in the late '70s, Lahaina was a sleepy art community. Most of the shops were filled with handmade items, not the cheap trinkets of today. Our commune was housed in two homes a mile or so north of town. They were side by side and were across Front Street from the sea wall. My first day in Hawaii was otherworldly. The atmosphere, the colors, the vegetation was out of a dream. As we drove away from the airport, I saw a vivid rainbow over the mountains. I felt like it was a personal welcome to the islands."

"Wasn't it a special privilege to go to that center?" David asked.

"I guess so, but it also had to do with skills. I had been a part of the production team in Berkeley. I could sew and airbrush with the best of them. I was also friends with the team leader in Lahaina. I had worked closely with Ellen in the sewing school in Berkeley. She actually requested my help as the shop grew in popularity.

"We only had a handful of members in Lahaina, and we had two businesses to run. At first I worked in both places. The 'Garden of Eden' restaurant was in an open air patio on Front Street. You couldn't see it from the street. A wooden fence and a grove of banana trees obscured the view from the public. The tables were tucked into the foliage as you walked on a wooden pathway to the back of the property where the kitchen was housed in a small screened in shack. The 'Cosmic Connection' clothing store was closer to the middle of town in a very old store front. It took a lot of work to make it presentable. We sold airbrushed clothing; much of which was hand-made, exclusive designs. We also sold lots of new age books and a few gifts. There was an airbrush studio in another screen shack in the backyard of my house on Front Street. I could walk outside and work. Ellen lived next door in the other house with her two children. Of course we shared the houses with other members."

David interrupted my narrative again. "It sounds idyllic. Was it really all goodness and light?"

"As is the case with all human endeavors, there is always something that spoils the best laid plans. The principles of the CEC taught us to share everything, but the unregenerated human nature always bleeds through. I suppose I was a little naïve to think that the sharing would extend to relationships between the women and men of the commune. There was Joel. He was the father of Ellen's two children. They weren't married because Joel was unpredictable. He came and went on a whim. He bounced from one center to the next seeking his place in the group. I don't think he ever found it. Ellen and Joel had a tumultuous relationship. Love and hate battled for supremacy. It was Joel that brought my island dream to an end. It would be five years later, but he managed to destroy the Maui commune."

"You know if this is going to get too painful, you don't have to continue." David could tell by the change in my voice that I was dredging up some ghosts from the past.

I took a deep breath and said, "I want you to know about my past. I hope you can see that the life I had in the commune is like a story. I can hardly relate to that person now. Do you want to hear more?"

"Yes, I want to know everything about you." David's words sent a wave of excitement though me. This was a watershed moment. If he could accept my past, I knew that we would have a future.

"The shop grew and prospered. The restaurant, however, lost its lease, and we had to give up that project. That was fine with me since I felt a lot more at home in the studio or behind a sewing machine than waiting tables. We couldn't expand the size of the shop, so we just packed more into it. Pretty soon Ellen and I could not keep up with the airbrushing. We wanted to spend more time creating new designs for the clothing line. I was tasked with finding and managing independent artists all over the island. I would take bundles of clothes to them and exchange them for the newly painted ones they had completed. The clothes had to be heat set. That meant I had to spend some time in a Laundromat watching the clothes tumble in a large industrial-sized dryer. I got to be an expert at folding and smoothing out wrinkles."

"It sounds like you were a hard worker. Where was all this wildness you mentioned?" David asked with a glance that held mischief.

"Just as I worked hard, I also partied hard. You can imagine that in a place like Lahaina there was no shortage of clubs and bars. I really wasn't a big drinker, but I liked to join my friends for the festivities in town. Halloween was a particularly wild night. Downtown was blocked off, and the party spilled out into the street. Everyone dressed up. We enjoyed the show and being part of the show. The town did not calm down until the wee hours of the morning. I remember this one Halloween. Some friends from up country came down to visit and party with us. They were sleeping on the fold out couch in the living room. We had a full house. There was a front deck on the house with a sliding glass door into the living room. I woke up earlier than the other people in the house and wandered into the kitchen. I peeked into the living room to make sure everyone made it to their bed that night. There on the floor, just inside of the sliding glass doors, was a strange young man, fast asleep. I thought maybe he was a friend of someone in the house. It was only after everyone in the house was up that we discovered that the still sleeping man was a complete stranger to us all. He must have been really tired and just crashed in the first convenient spot. That might give you a glimpse into the lifestyle of the islands."

"Weren't you afraid? I mean complete strangers just entering your home?" David asked.

"Not really. We just thought it was funny at the time, but looking back on it, I can see how God's hand of protection was over me throughout those wayward years. There were many times I could have been a victim of foul play. My mother's prayers covered me, and God was saving me so that I could fulfill my destiny."

"Okay, I agree that was a pretty wild story, but I have a hunch there is more to it than that," David urged me on.

"You can probably imagine that the *island lifestyle* also opened the door to relationships with men," I began.

"I would be surprised if you didn't have a whole string of men chasing you," David added.

I blushed a deep shade of red at that comment. I hated to bring up the subject with David, but he wanted to hear about my Maui days and that was a part of the story. "You have to understand the times and the culture of the commune to get an accurate view of my love life. I mentioned before the 'love the one you're with' mentality of that time. I enjoyed the attention, but I didn't want to get tied down. My marriage had spoiled any 'happily ever after' dreams I may have had. I just wanted to have fun and when things got too complicated, I was done. I suppose deep down I was always searching for my soul mate, but I never found him even after many tries. Can we move on to other more comfortable territory?"

"Darn, it was just getting good," David said and then we both laughed. The laughter broke the tension, and I felt like I could resume my story of my days in "paradise."

"We had friends that lived up country. That is the island way of saying they lived on the slopes of Haleakala Crater. All the islands are volcanic. Haleakala is a dormant volcano. As you rise in elevation, the weather is more moderate. It is cooler and many people prefer living there. Lahaina actually translates to something like 'relentless sun,' and it is hot much of the year. I remember driving around the island with the air-conditioning on high, just so I could have the pleasure of wearing a sweater. We would visit our friends to get out of the heat. We would go there especially around the Thanksgiving and Christmas holidays to celebrate with our 'family.'" I took a breath and looked over at David. He seemed to be envisioning the scene of a Christmas in Hawaii.

"Yeah, Christmas in Hawaii," I said.

David looked at me with surprise. "Are you reading my mind now?"

"Well, I just know it is a hard one to picture. We had to work overtime to fit the holidays into the tropical setting. Every year, there would be one shipment of fresh pine trees to the harbor at Lahaina. We had to be there right when it arrived or we would not get a tree for the holidays. Just the smell of the pine in the house helped to set the mood," I explained.

"That seems like a very normal snapshot of family life. What made your time in Hawaii so 'wild'?" David asked.

"Okay, how about jumping off a cliff into a waterfall pool, hiking into Haleakala Crater and spending the night in a cabin, taking a last-minute helicopter ride over the island of Maui, nearly drowning in a high surf off the north shore of Oahu, eating mangos in the nude by an up country pool," I challenged.

Now it was David's turn to blush. "All right you've got me there. I have a feeling that the mango eating incident is just the tip of the iceberg. No need to go on."

"You would be right there, and somewhere in my deeply buried archives I have the pictures to prove it." I hoped he would understand that not every island memory was open to discussion; at least not at this stage of our relationship.

We sat in silence for a moment, and I knew that he was thinking about those pictures. I hoped he was wondering when he would get to see them. There would be a lot of steps to go through before that would be appropriate. We had not even had our first kiss. We had come close a few times, but something always interrupted or cautioned us. This was not our first experience with love. We both had some baggage. I hoped that time would allow us to unpack it.

I was ready to change the subject. "Now, what about you? Did you have some wild times you would like to confess?"

Our eyes met, and I gave him a sly smile. He hesitated and then began to tell me about his younger days. "You know, there were the usual escapades involving cars, girls, and alcohol. But my family was pretty traditional. They tried to keep a lid on it. I am thankful now because I could have done some irreparable damage that would have kept me from pursuing my career in law enforcement. When I joined the police force, I had to put all that youthful experimentation away for good."

"A man with your looks and charisma must have had a lot of girls chasing you. Did you ever get caught?" I asked.

David hesitated to answer and was still processing my complements. "Yes, I met Rachel pretty early on. I was ready to settle down. I wanted a family and a home. I wanted the normalcy and predictability. My career was not a place where I would find those things. I needed the balance. This is probably as good a place as any to tell you that I have a son."

David glanced at me quickly to try and read my reaction. I was surprised and yet not shocked to learn that there was a lot more to David than I had learned in the last few days. "Where is he? What's his name? Do you see him often?" All the questions came tumbling out.

"Slow down, Nelly, I guess I have a few stories of my own. Jonathan is twenty-three years old. He just graduated from Cal Tech. He's sort of a computer whiz. He would probably say computer geek if you asked him. In my estimation, there is nothing geeky about him. You might say he is a chip off the old block. I am very proud of him. He has been offered a few jobs in Silicon Valley and he is reviewing his options. He is even looking at a few startups in Seattle. He was twelve years old when his mother and I split. It was the usual scenario of the obsessed workaholic husband and the frustrated, ignored wife. We tried counseling, but we had both outgrown our relationship. When I converted to Christianity, it was the last straw," David paused.

"I know we have talked about your past a little, but you never mentioned your marriage," I stated.

"I suppose it is an area that I just as soon not open up for conversation. There were good times, of course, but the bad times were really bad. Let's just leave it at that for now," David said with finality.

We rode in silence for a while, both caught up in our own thoughts. I could tell by the traffic and terrain that we were nearing the Bay Area. Our trip would soon come to an end. I was hoping and praying that this would not be the end of our friendship. There were so many unknowns. I knew I had to get back to Boise soon. David had to get back to work and wrap up the investigation of Jacob's kidnapping. Would this be the parting of our way? Without the expediency of the quest to find Jacob, would we have enough in common to keep our connection alive?

Preoccupied, I was surprised when we were driving up the street to Claire's home. As we headed into her driveway, I felt an immense weight bearing down on me. I looked at David and he avoided my attempt to make contact. We slowly and reluctantly opened the car doors and started walking to Claire's front porch.

I was getting ready to knock on the door when I saw that the door was slightly open. A feeling of dread came over me. I knew that something was terribly wrong. I looked at David and he gave me a warning look. He immediately stepped in front of me and reached for his gun that was at hand in his shoulder holster under his jacket. We walked into the house and could see that there had been a struggle. A chair was tipped over and a rug was rumpled. The hand-blown glass vase from the coffee table was shattered on the floor. I called out for Claire. No one answered.

chapter 24

"Claire!" I cried out. David gave me a warning look. I couldn't help myself. The shock and grief was overwhelming me. I stood, frozen in the living room as David searched the house.

"Nothing," David said as he returned to the front room. "No other signs of struggle or invasion. They must have let the intruders into the house. Perhaps they knew them."

"I know who it was," I finally found my voice. "The Berkeley One Humanity members, they are extracting their revenge."

"You may very well be right, but we need to get a forensic team in here to inspect the scene. I can't believe it. I thought we were done with all this. Obviously, Rallen was not done with Jacob. Claire is just collateral damage. Not that I think they have come to harm," David quickly back tracked his words, but we were both working hard not to envision the worst case scenario.

David called the Berkeley Police Station and gave a brief account of his whereabouts and the scene we had walked into. He asked them to notify the Marin PD and have a team sent out to secure the crime scene. We walked out to the car and sat, waiting for the team from the police department to arrive. There was a heavy atmosphere of disappointment clinging to us both. We had worked so hard to find Jacob. Now he AND Claire were in jeopardy. I looked at David and said, "What now?"

David surprised me when he held my eyes and said with authority. "I will not let the enemy win! I refuse to allow his tactics of discouragement and intimidation take me off the mission that God has given us. What now? We fight!"

"Thank you for that," I replied. "I am with you all the way. We overcame the powers of darkness in Ashland, and we can do it here. Let's call Julian and have the group intercede for us and for Jacob and Claire's protection."

"I'll also call Ben at Rock Church. They have a prayer chain that will activate a covering for us," David said as he reached out and took my hand. He began to pray and immediately the heavy atmosphere was lifted. Our faith was renewed. There was a good reason for this set back. We were willing to let the Holy Spirit reveal that reason to us in due season.

By the time the crime scene team arrived, we had made all of our support calls. David met with the detective from Marin PD and passed on as much information as was necessary to aid their investigation. He let him know the case was an ongoing one and they should keep David up to date with their findings.

When David returned to the car, I had a question for him. "Now that Claire's home is a crime scene, where am I going to stay?"

"I see what you mean. Let me call Ben back and see if he has any ideas. At the least you could stay in a hotel in Berkeley, but let's see if there may be another option. I really would hate for you to be on your own. The unpredictable nature of the OH members should not be underestimated. We already did that and you can see where we are now." David gave me a knowing look that was also an apology.

I sat in silence as David made his call to Pastor Ben. "Pastor Ben and his wife Rachel want you to stay with them," David announced. He is going to call a few of the Rock Church intercessors and have them meet with us this evening."

"That sounds good," I replied with as much enthusiasm as I could muster. The weight of the task ahead was again settling over me.

"We have to trust that the Lord will lead us just as he has all along this journey. He will not leave us now!" David countered my mood with his determined declaration.

It was a quiet ride to Berkeley. I was clinging to hope. From the look on David's face, he was brooding over his disgust with

Rallen Mandu and the tactics of the One Humanity group members. The only reason that I could see for abducting Claire and Jacob was revenge. All the secrets the OH were trying to hide had been exposed, unless there were deeper layers of deception that we had not uncovered yet.

I was surprised when we pulled up to Ben and Rachel's house. I had been so absorbed in thought that the time had flown by. David and I approached the cozy home tucked into a bank of trees and azalea bushes. As soon as we rang the doorbell, a group of people met us at the door and engulfed us with hugs and welcomes. I couldn't hold back my tears as I felt relief and comfort from those precious people.

"Come in! *Mi casa es su casa.*" Pastor Ben led us to the living room. The seating had been expanded with dining room chairs filling all the nooks and crannies. David and I took a seat on the overstuffed couch. A large coffee table was filled with cups and carafes, glasses and pitchers of lemonade, and plates stacked with homemade cookies. Rachel filled a glass and handed it to me. I didn't realize how thirsty I was. I drank the whole thing in nearly one gulp. David settled for a cup of coffee.

Pastor Ben broke the awkward silence. "We are here to do warfare. The enemy has done enough damage to our family. We will not tolerate his destructive interference any longer. I know that we will be the victors in this battle. God has promised that we are more than conquerors. We have already begun storming heaven with our requests for assistance. We will continue until we get peace and the answer to our question. 'Where are Claire and Jacob?' While we continue, Rachel would you please show Joy where she will be staying. And, Joy, you are welcome to stay with us as long as you need to."

"I'll get your luggage," David said as he stood and headed to the door.

"Thank you so much for letting me stay here." I wanted to let Rachel know how much their offer meant to me. I would feel safe and protected in their home.

"Not a problem at all. We are looking forward to helping you in any way possible. I know you have been through a lot. The least we can do is give you a safe haven now."

Rachel was so gracious and loving, I wanted to just fall into her arms.

"Here you go," David announced as he brought my bags into the room.

"I had better get back to the prayer group," Rachel said. "You have your own bathroom right here. Please take all the time you need to get settled." She gave David a big smile as she left the room.

The room was beautiful. The bed looked so inviting. I was tired. Not just physically. I looked at David, and he was standing in the middle of the room waiting for me to say or do something. I just walked up to him and put my arms around his neck. I laid my head on his chest. He wrapped his arms around me and we stood there that way for what seemed like forever. I didn't want to let him go.

I finally looked up at him and he said, "We can do this. We just need a good night's rest. Tomorrow we will find a way to end this quest once and for all." His confidence was medicine for my emotions. I felt that anything was possible if David Kramer was with me.

"I will let you get settled, and then let's join the group for prayer," David suggested. I just nodded my head and let go of him. He quietly left the room.

As soon as David was gone, I dropped to my knees beside the bed. I began to pray in the Spirit. The words felt like they were connecting directly to heaven. I felt the Lord's presence, and it was like electricity that was recharging my batteries. The peace of the Lord washed over me and I knew that I knew that God had Jacob and Claire in His hand. There had to be a very good reason why this journey was continuing. There was another stronghold of the enemy that He wanted us to destroy. I got up with a renewed determination to fulfill God's will. The mission was not over.

I entered the living room amidst the powerful torrent of prayers, praise, and petitions from the Body of Christ. It was a war room. I could feel the tide turning. Suddenly one of the members of the Rock congregation stood and began to give a word of prophesy. The boldness and authority was undeniable.

"The victory is mine says the Lord. I will perform it. Watch and see what I will do. There are many more souls that will be rescued. My name will become a praise in the land. My servants will be rescued and the testimony of their mouth shall bring forth breakthrough in the lives of many that have wandered in darkness. David and Joy, I have anointed you for this battle. You shall find success; trust in me at every turn. You will not be defeated. When the way seems the darkest, I will go before you. Look to the light. Take your first steps in faith and go to the Devil's Mountain."

The group was silent for some minutes as we all absorbed the message that we had received from the Lord. The last line was a curious statement. How would we interpret the direction the Lord gave us? I opened my eyes, and David was looking at me with questions in his eyes. We did not know what the Lord meant by Devil's Mountain.

"I know what the first step is," Pastor Ben spoke and broke the silence. We were all relieved to know that he had revelation on the puzzling direction. "Mount Diablo is a recreational area just east of here. There are many vacation homes there. I am willing to wager that Rallen or one of his members has a home there. That would be a very good hiding place. What I don't understand is what do they gain by kidnapping Jacob and Claire? Is it just intimidation? Is it an act of revenge?"

Those questions hung in the air as we all waited for clarification from the Holy Spirit.

"Rallen Mandu is a toothless lion. He feels like his power has been stolen. He will do anything to gain an advantage over the believers who have disrupted his little kingdom. Taking Claire and Jacob is a desperate effort to take back some control. He is not really thinking about the outcome. He just wants to strike back." Rachel's voice of reason was welcomed and reassuring.

Pastor Ben stood and announced that the meeting was a success. He thanked everyone for coming and asked them to continue to praise the Lord for His answer and for continued guidance. The group began to embrace one another and say their goodbyes. Little by little they left, leaving just the four of us, Ben and Rachel, David and me. Rachel asked if she could fix us something to eat, but no one was hungry. We were so full of the presence of the Lord that food seemed trivial. Ben and Rachel said good night and slipped off to their bedroom. David and I were left in the front room to say our goodbye.

"Tomorrow is another day," David announced. "I have to go into the office for a couple of hours to check in and compile some reports. I will also do some digging to see if we can come up with a connection between Mount Diablo and the OH. We may be on our own again. I don't know how I will be able to convince my boss that we got a lead from a prayer meeting."

"I can call Ashley and see if she knows anything. As soon as we get some information, we have to go and find them," I said with determination.

"Information or not, we will go to the mountain and follow whatever leads we can find. Now we both need to get some rest. Lord, give us perfect peace and sweet sleep," David prayed.

I walked David to his car and gave him a quick hug before he got in. As he drove away I felt a rending in my heart. We had been so close for so many days. He was going back to his apartment—back to his normal life, without me.

chapter 25

I was asleep as soon as my head hit the pillow. My eyes didn't pop open until nine the next morning. I just lay in bed feeling God's presence as soon as I was aware of my surroundings. Sunshine was streaming through the window. I felt rejuvenated. My hope level was very high. I took a shower and dressed slowly. I did not feel the same pressure that I had felt when we were looking for Jacob in Ashland. The word from the Lord the night before still resonated within me. My confidence was in the Lord. I wandered out into the kitchen and found some coffee and a note from Rachel. They had gone to the church to attend to some business, and they had let me know that I should make myself at home. I also found some fresh baked muffins on a plate on the counter. I was pretty hungry, and I helped myself to two delicious carrot raisin muffins.

After my muffin and coffee break, I took the kitchen phone into the living room and sat on the couch. I found Ashley's phone number in my notebook and called her. She answered right away. I brought her up to date on the surprising turn of events in Berkeley. She was very concerned until I told her about the prayer meeting and the awesome word we got from the Lord.

"Do you know anyone from the Berkeley OH center that may have a vacation home in the Mount Diablo area?" I finally asked the burning question.

"You know as soon as you mentioned it, I made a connection. I have actually been to a place near the recreation area. It was on the outskirts of a small town. Clayton is on the north side of the park. We had a retreat there a couple of years ago. There are some challenging trail hikes. We went on one that took us to one of the peaks. It was like an initiation. I made it, but it was a hard climb." Ashley was off on one of her tangents. I had to rein her in.

"Do you have an address for the house?" I asked.

"No, but I could give you directions."

"Who owns the house?" I had to pry information out of her.

"I am not sure. Just let me give you the directions."

It took some time to get the directions straight. Ashley is a dear, but she has a hard time sticking to the task at hand. I had to steer her back to the directions as she kept wanting to tell me stories along the way. As we wrapped up our call she said that she would get the Ashland group together and pray for us. I was glad to have the extra prayer covering.

A knock on the front door got my attention; when I opened it, a very agitated Detective David Kramer whisked into the house.

"I can't believe this!" David nearly shouted. I had never seen him so upset. "I called Agent Morgan just a few minutes ago and he said that there was some misunderstanding with the Ashland Police Department. They released Damien on bail before the FBI could take custody. Who knows where he could be right now. He may be the mastermind behind Claire and Jacob's abduction. I am so angry! That man should never see the light of day, let alone be free to continue his evil deeds."

"David, remember the prayer meeting last night. God is in control," I tried to calm him down with a soothing voice.

"And bad things happen to good people. Damien is not going to stop until he has extracted his revenge on Jacob and us, for that matter." David was not going to be denied his righteous anger.

I offered David some coffee and a muffin. He drank a few sips of coffee and completely ignored the food. He was pacing the floor. He needed to do something. I told him about Ashley and the house in Clayton.

"Let's go!" David said as he rushed for the door.

"Wait. We don't know what the situation will be at that house. We should have some back up," I pleaded.

"I don't want to have to wade through red tape. I will let my commander know where we are going. We are just following a lead," David countered.

A quick phone call later and we were in David's car headed east to the Mount Diablo Recreation Area. It took less than an hour to travel past the town of Walnut Creek and on to Clayton. As we approached the town, the dark outline of the mountain loomed ahead of us. The town itself was picturesque. The sun was shining, and the trees were in full beauty, but it was hard to ignore the presence of the mountain in the distance. I took out the directions that Ashley had given me and began to recite them to David. A few wrong turns later, we found the right road. It was a dirt track that wound through the trees. There were a few other vacation cabins along the way. When we approached the area where the OH member had his home, we saw a number of cars parked outside. It looked like there was a meeting going on, or maybe another retreat. Under the circumstances, I was leaning toward the meeting scenario. With all the setbacks the group had endured, there would be a lot to sort out.

"What's the plan? It looks like we are outnumbered here," I asked David. I could see his wheels turning. He was calculating the risks. Thankfully his anger had subsided, and he had a cool calculating look on his face.

"Let's park the car back at that last cabin. It looks like it hasn't been occupied in a while. Then I will approach the meeting house and see if I can tell what is going on," David proposed.

"Oh no, you don't. I am going with you. We are a team, and you may need help or at least moral support," I replied.

"It could be dangerous, especially if Damien is there. Remember, he was not above using a weapon last time we saw him," David countered.

"We have to know if Claire and Jacob are being held in that house. I can't wait around and let you take all the credit for finding them." I gave him a wry smile.

"Okay, but you stay behind me at all times," David relented.

Using the parked cars for cover, we inched our way toward the back porch of the house. We kept low and approached the set of two small windows. It was obvious that the front of the house faced the Mountain View. As we approached, we hoped that the group would be meeting in the front and facing away from the back of the house. We quickly peeked through one of the windows. The kitchen was part of an open plan and led right into the front room. At least fifteen people were gathered there. Damien was standing in front of the large picture window with its view of Mount Diablo. Next to him were Claire and Jacob. Jacob looked like his hands were tied behind his back. Claire was not restrained. They both were sitting with heads bowed. I was not sure if they were praying or had been drugged.

Our worst fears had just been confirmed. I looked at David and he shook his head. My thoughts exactly. This was a very bad situation with no easy resolution. What would happen if we just burst into the house? David had intentionally left his gun in the car. Using it could make a bad situation deadly. I grabbed David's hand and sent a prayer of desperation to the Lord. When I opened my eyes, David had a look of determination on his face that told me we were going to confront the situation head on. We could only hope that the element of surprise would allow us to gain the advantage.

The back door was not locked. We entered, and just as we approached the group in the front room, a blast of radiant light exploded in the middle of the seated group. Damien, who was standing, was knocked to the floor. A look of awe and fear was evident on every one's face. I looked at Claire and Jacob and they were looking up with radiant expectation. David and I could not see what they were fixed on, but we felt the presence of the Lord so intensely that we were frozen in our tracks. No one in the room seemed to even notice us.

Damien got to his feet and looked right at us with such hatred it was like a weapon piercing the atmosphere. He grabbed Claire and dragged her to the front door. It took us a couple of minutes to wade through the mesmerized people sitting all around the room. We made it to the front porch in time to see Damien force Claire on the back of a four-wheeler. They took off through the woods before we could even get off the porch. David looked around frantically until he spotted a second vehicle parked under a car port. It was a dirt bike. He looked at me, and I gave him a nod. He started it up, I hopped on the back, and we were off chasing after Damien and Claire.

We had more maneuverability with the bike than Damien had with the four-wheeler, but we were still a few minutes behind him. The dirt track that led into the trees quickly turned into a steep trail. We could see a cloud of dust ahead. The trail split and thanks to the dust cloud, we knew which way Damien had gone. At the trail head, I saw a sign that said, Eagle Peak Loop Trail. From the angle of the trail, I knew we would be heading up to Eagle Peak. A trail like this was not made for motorized vehicles, let alone a four-wheeler. I kept my prayers for protection going as we ascended the trail. I couldn't understand what Damien's plan could possibly be. It was a loop trail. That meant it would come back to the place where it started. What kind of get away was that? Unless he was not trying to get away, but was leading us to a date with disaster.

I tried to remember the word from the Lord that was given to us just last night. God had assured our success, and that souls would be brought into the Kingdom, but that may not mean there would not be some casualties along the way. I was holding on to David for dear life. As we gained more altitude, the trail became more rocky and narrow. The drop offs were becoming more precipitous. As we came around a bend in the trail, I saw a glimpse of Claire's hair streaming behind her. We were gaining on them. A few more twists and turns, and the trail flattened out at what was an over look. We were at the top of Eagle Peak and the cliff and the trail ahead looked like it just dropped off the edge of the Earth. Damien was not slowing down. In fact, he was gunning the motor and headed for the edge of the cliff. Just before they dropped from sight, Claire was tossed off the back of the vehicle and seemed to make a soft landing right on the edge of the cliff. David stopped the bike and we both ran to Claire. She was just getting up and looking over the edge of the cliff when we met her. The explosion of the four wheeler left no doubt that Damien had met his end. His blind devotion to Rallen Mandu and his hatred for God's people had driven him to take his own life. He thought that he had done damage to us by taking Claire with him, but now it was evident that God had thwarted his plan.

"Claire, are you all right?" I asked as soon as I could peel my eyes away from the flames and wreckage below the cliff.

"Yes, thanks to the angel that was stationed at the edge of the cliff. He plucked me off the four-wheeler and placed me gently on the ground. I have never seen an angel before. I am so blessed, and now David and I have something in common," Claire proclaimed with a beaming smile directed at David. "Did you see the angel?"

"Yes, he appeared just as we came into the overlook. His timing was perfect," David replied.

"Jacob!" Claire exclaimed like someone who had just woken up from a dream.

"We have to get back to the house and rescue him from that group of Rallen fanatics."

I looked at David and said, "You and Claire take the dirt bike down. I can walk. Rescue Jacob and I will meet you at the house as soon as I can get off the trail."

David reluctantly turned and headed with Claire to the dirt bike, and they were gone.

I started to walk down the trail and the shock began to wear off. Damien. He had sacrificed his life for a lie. He was so deluded that he would rather end his life than face the truth. He almost took Claire with him. I shivered, even though the air around me was warm. Tears began to flow down my cheeks for the senseless loss of life. Even though Damien had been our nemesis, he was still a person that could have made different choices. I was crying for the loss and to release the tension that had built up over the last couple of days. I thought of the old saying, "There but for fortune go I." I had been led astray by the enemy and sucked into a delusion with the Cosmic Earth Collective all those years ago. Thanks to God's grace and my family's prayers, I had been rescued. I knew I had to tell this story. If my experiences with the CEC, and now One Humanity, could warn just one person from following this New Age lie, my life would have a greater purpose. I had written one book on alternative cults, but now I wanted to use my gift to bring a more personal story that could make a difference. I thought about all the salvations that had come from this journey to find Jacob. His story could have an even wider influence if more people learned about his transformation.

I was so lost in my reverie that I was startled when I saw David appear on the trail ahead. "What's happening? Is Jacob okay? Where is the dirt bike?"

"Whoa, I have all your answers if you will just give me a minute to explain," David assured as he raised both hands in a hold on gesture. "Jacob is fine. I decided to walk up to meet you. There is no emergency at the house below. In fact, everything is pretty wonderful down there."

"What do you mean?" I asked.

"When we arrived at the house, everyone was either lying on the floor or kneeling. Jacob was praying with one of the members and leading her in the prayer for salvation. As Claire and I walked in the room, the *glory* was so heavy that we had to sit down immediately. When that burst of light hit the room, God invaded. I guess a couple of the members fled, but most of the members went down in the Presence. Some were crying, some were repenting, some were praising. Jacob was making his way to each one of them to minister and lead them to the Lord." David's countenance revealed the beauty of the scene he was describing.

All I could do was step forward and embrace David. As I did I felt an electric jolt. The *glory* was still all over him. We stood like that in the trail for what seemed like an hour. I could hear birds singing, the whisper of the wind in the trees around us, and the beating of our heart in unison. We finally parted, and the exchange we had as we gazed into each other's eyes was timeless. David finally took my hand and we began our walk back to the house.

chapter 26

When we entered the One Humanity house, I was surprised to see people in every possible position around the room. Some were lying flat and I could tell that they were under the power of the Holy Spirit by their ecstatic countenance. Some were kneeling and weeping in repentance. One was lying prone with his face to the floor, prostrate before the Lord. A couple members were seated, and Jacob was ministering to them, helping them understand what had just happened. The glory was still heavy in the room, and I had a hard time standing even at the threshold of the door. I gave David a look and he answered back with a look that said, "See what I mean." David and I moved to chairs close by and sat. I closed my eyes and soaked in The Presence. The peace was pervasive. Time seemed to stand still.

After a while, I heard stirring, as each member came back to the present moment. Someone went into the kitchen and put on a tea kettle. Another member went about helping people back into chairs and couches. When everyone was back into a group formation, we all looked at Jacob.

"I don't have to tell you that what happened here today is miraculous. God in his sovereign will has chosen this group to receive an outpouring of grace beyond explanation. I do know, from my recent experiences, that the Lord is bringing together an army of warriors who are aware of the deceptions of new age doctrines. A major campaign has begun to bring truth and light into our culture. We are fortunate to be a witness to his *power* and *purpose*. We have been brought out of the darkness into His marvelous light. Literally!"

At this, there was a corporate affirmation of yes, amen, giggles and whoops. We had all witnessed the light explosion in that very room. "We cannot take this experience for granted," Jacob went on. "We have a mandate and a mission. I know that you all have contacts and connections to many One Humanity members. God is going to give you supernatural wisdom on how to approach them, and offer them an invitation to the Kingdom Realm. Some of you have a church background. It will just be a matter of resurrecting your knowledge of the Word and the truths of God. Others will need mentoring. I want you to know that I am offering myself as a resource to you. You will also want to start attending a Kingdom believing church. If you need guidance in that, just ask. Now, I believe that David and Joy have a sad bit of news to share with you."

I looked at David and gave him the go ahead. "You may have seen Damien grab Claire and rush out of the room just as the burst of Light occurred. He commandeered a four wheeler and raced up the path to Eagle Peak. Joy and I took the dirt bike that was in the shed and followed them. We made it up to the overlook just in time to see Damien gun the motor of his vehicle and fly over the cliff. Miraculously, Claire was spared by divine intervention. One of God's warrior angels was stationed at the cliff edge and scooped her off the four-wheeler just before it went over. There was a terrible impact and a fire. I'm sorry to say, Damien did not survive."

There were gasps and expressions of grief all around the room. David allowed a few minutes for everyone to absorb the dreadful news. Their recent salvation and suddenly shifted point of view, brought home the full meaning of Damien's desperate act.

I looked at Claire. The toll of the last few hours was evident on her face and her posture. I addressed the group, "Today will be a red letter day for all of you. I am glad that you all have this support group for the way ahead. You also have the Holy Spirit to guide you. I hate to leave the site of such an amazing encounter with the Lord, but Claire and Jacob have been through a lot. We need to get them back to familiar surroundings, so they can regain their equilibrium."

The former OH members were more than understanding. Although they hated to see Jacob go, they knew that they could not rely on him completely for their faith. With hugs and kisses, tears and laughter, the group released Claire, Jacob, David, and me. We filed out of the house and down the road where David's car was parked. The ride back to Berkeley was quiet. Claire and Jacob were huddled in the back seat. I think Jacob even fell asleep for a while. There was a satisfying peace that pervaded the cabin of the car. We all felt that the One Humanity threat was neutralized. With Damien's death and the conversion of the Berkeley and Ashland core groups, the air had gone out of the movement. Only Rallen Mandu remained to face the consequences of his falsehoods and lies. He had built a house of cards and seemed to be the only one who escaped its fall and destruction.

Our first stop was Pastor Ben's home. I had called ahead and given him and his wife, Rachel, the good news. David had updated his boss on the kidnapping. Of course, Claire and Jacob would have to be interviewed and statements given to wrap up the incident. David would write his reports. This whole convoluted case would be neatly tied with a bow. What would not appear on any paperwork would be the battles and victories that had occurred in the spirit world.

Rachel fixed a comforting dinner of mac and cheese, broccoli and salad. As we visited around the table, we let Jacob tell the whole story of the amazing God invasion at the OH house at Mount Diablo. Pastor Ben observed Jacob with an appraising eye.

"You know, Jacob, your testimony would have a great impact on the Body. It will also be an awesome evangelistic tool for youth and many who have been duped by the new age movement. Would you consider working with Rock Church staff to put together a plan to get that message out?"

Jacob was stunned, but as soon as he recovered from the surprising offer, a giant grin broke out on his face. We all took that as a yes.

"Take some time to get your feet back under you, then we can set up a meeting to talk about financials and logistics. I see great potential in you as an evangelist," Pastor Ben explained.

David received a phone call just after dinner, letting us know that Claire's home had been released from the investigation. She was free to return. Jacob could have gone to his apartment, but chose to stay with Claire and me. He needed a supportive environment to recuperate in. David also learned that a search and rescue team had retrieved Damien's body from the ravine. Who would they find to notify? Who would claim the body?

We all said goodbye and thanks to Ben and Rachel. I retrieved my bag from the wonderful guest room. David took us back to Marin. The atmosphere in the car on this ride was quite different. The time spent with Ben and Rachel's delicious food had revived us all. The prospect of a new career for Jacob was a topic of much speculation. How would it all work?

All too soon, we were pulling up into Claire's driveway. Claire and Jacob led the way back into the house. David carried my bag for me. He dropped it off at the entrance and said he had to get back to Berkeley to check in at the station.

"How soon will you be going back to Boise?" he asked the loaded question.

"I will be here for a few days to make sure everyone is settled. I hope I will be able to see you," I answered.

"I am not sure what my schedule will be for the next week. Let's tentatively set a date for tomorrow night. I mean a real date. I want to take you out to one of my favorite restaurants in San Francisco. I will call and confirm tomorrow as soon as I can. Then I will pick you up around six?" He asked with pleading in his eyes.

"Yes, six it is," I said. I felt like a teenager being asked out on her first date. I am sure that my flushed complexion was giving me away.

David gave me a quick hug and then turned and walked to his car. I stood in the doorway and watched him go. I was overcome with emotions. Loss and hope, apprehension, and excitement were warring for predominance. Tomorrow night would not come quickly enough.

Back in the house, Jacob and Claire were busy in the kitchen. Jacob was making tea, and Claire was organizing the hastily-vacated room. I knew she needed to restore order to get her balance. The turmoil in the front room had been erased by the investigative team. Much of the destruction was taken into evidence. While the water was working up to a boil, I announced, "Your home has been violated. You have been invaded by the kingdom of darkness. Let's join in a cleansing prayer. We need to establish authority over any hindering spirits."

To my surprise, Jacob took the lead, "Father, we first want to thank you for rescuing us. You are so faithful. Once again, you took what the enemy meant for evil and turned it into good. All the souls that have been ushered into the Kingdom today are a small price to pay for the few hours of discomfort that Mom and I had to endure. Thank you for David and Joy. They have never wavered in their commitment to see justice done. Now we request that your angelic hosts would come and inhabit our home. Clean out any defilement that may remain from the works of Damien and his demons. I take authority over any unclean spirits and I loose peace and safety over our home in Jesus name. Amen."

"Awesome prayer, Jacob, I can see that you have grown mightily in the few weeks that you have known the Lord. Your trials have put you in an accelerated learning curve. I also can see why Ben is recruiting you to work with him at Rock Church," I said.

The three of us took our teacups and headed for the comfort of the living room. I didn't feel any residual fear or demonic activity. The room was once again a sanctuary.

"I saw you lingering with David on the front porch. What were you guys planning?" Claire asked with that familiar twinkle of mischief in her eye.

"What makes you think we were planning anything?" I countered.

"Well, I am sure that this is not the end of the Joy and David story. I have seen the way he looks at you. That man is smitten."

Once again, my blush gave me away, "I think we have a mutual appreciation for each other. We have been through a lot. We made a great team. I'm sad to see it end. I mean, I am glad that you and Jacob are safe and sound. I didn't mean…"

"I know exactly what you are saying. Don't get all flustered. I also know that we have not seen the end of the Joy and David team. God brought you together for a reason, and I don't see that changing at all," Claire said.

Jacob jumped into the conversation, "You guys are meant to be. We all could see that."

"I am glad that you're so sure. I just don't know how it will work out. There are a lot of miles between Boise and Berkeley. I don't want to jump to conclusions. We haven't made any commitments and we haven't even kissed." I blurted out that last line without thinking and really wished I could take it back.

Claire couldn't let that last bit of information pass by. "What! All that time spent in close quarters and no kiss. What is the world coming to?"

"We were trying to keep it all professional, you know. Now that the case is resolved, maybe we can find our footing on a more personal level. He asked me out to dinner for tomorrow night," I confessed.

"Now you're talking," Claire said. "Let me help. This has got to be the first date, right? We can go to my favorite salon tomorrow. You need the works after what you have been through, and a new outfit is also in order."

I tried to protest but was excited to see that I would have support from Claire. I did want to look my best for our "first date."

We all sat in companionable silence for a while. Each one of us trying to assimilate all that had occurred in the last couple of weeks. This had been far from a vacation, but it certainly did take us all out of our normal lives. I was sure that we would never be able to go back to our old ways. I knew that Claire and Jacob were definitely on a path of exploration. Their newfound faith was going to give them a strong bond, even beyond that of mother and son. I also knew that I would want to be more involved with their lives. I wanted to mentor Claire, and monitor Jacob's new career. The future looked so exciting for them, but when I tried to envision my own future, all I could see was question marks. How would I be able to go back to my sedate existence as a grade school teacher in Boise, Idaho? How would I be able to let David go?

The phone rang, and Claire jumped up to get it. She returned to the front room with a scowl on her face. "That was Tom," she addressed Jacob. "Your father is on his way here. Of course, he wants to see you and make sure you are okay, but he is also on one of his crusades."

"What do you mean by *crusade*?" I asked.

Claire just gave Jacob a knowing look and responded, "He always has to feel like he is in control. He wants to know how we let Rallen get away."

"Give him some slack, Mom. He had to watch everything from a distance. I can just imagine how powerless he would feel." Jacob took his familiar position as peace maker between his parents.

"You're right, but I don't want him second guessing our actions. He has no idea what we went through and how difficult it was for David and Claire to find the truth."

Just then, we heard Tom's car drive up to the front of the house. Jacob rushed to the door and out the front walk to greet his dad. They both came back into the house with smiles and playful jostling. That was the male equivalent of hugs and kisses.

Tom approached Claire and gave her a quick hug. "Good to have you two back where you belong. I was really worried about you. You know, I did everything I could from a distance to aid the investigation. I've got to hand it to Kramer. He did a hell of a job. I just wish he had gotten a hold of that creep Mandu. He should rot in jail for what he did to you guys. Oh, and, Joy, thanks for sticking to it and finding my family. You are a good friend."

I looked at Claire and we both were shocked by Tom's praise. He usually didn't want to share the lime light with anyone. I was about to say, you're welcome, when he took center stage again.

"I still have my sources looking for Rallen Mandu, but I guess I should say Milo Ripley. Good name for that faker; I can't believe he got away with his scams and then just disappeared. I'd wager that he'll mess up somewhere along the way and his crimes will catch up with him."

Tom took a breath and continued for the benefit of his captive audience. "Look, Jacob, you should come and stay with me for a while. You know, just till you get back on your feet. I have some job opportunities that you might be interested in. We'll get you back up and running before you know it."

"No, Dad, I have plans of my own. Alex is waiting for me to move back in with him. The apartment is all repaired now, and it is centrally located for my next career plan. I will stay with mom for a few more days, and then move back to Berkeley," Jacob declared with unexpected confidence and conviction.

Tom could not hide his disappointment and skepticism. "Son, I wouldn't want to tell you what to do, but isn't it about time you get your head out of the clouds and get a real job? Wasn't it those *nonprofit* people who got you into this mess in the first place?" Tom said "nonprofit" like it was a dirty word. To him if you weren't making a profit you were out of touch with reality.

"I am not going back to those jobs. I am going to be joining the leadership team at Rock Church. I will also be working toward my ministerial license," Jacob announced.

Tom's look of unbelief was classic. His mouth was open and his eyes wide. It took a minute for him to even register Jacob's words. "You've got to be kidding me! Talk about nonprofit. Working for a church has got to be a step down from what you were doing. How do you expect to ever build your portfolio working for a bunch of preachers?"

"Dad, I am not working to build an earthly kingdom. I am working for God now. He is directing my life, and I have complete confidence in His ability to take care of me and my future." Jacob came back with such power that all protest was eliminated.

"Okay, I am not sure I get your meaning, but it is perfectly clear that you don't need my help. I had better be going. *I* have some earthly kingdom business to attend to." Tom was visibly shaken.

"Dad, let me walk you out to your car. I really do appreciate all that you have done. You will come to see that this path is right for me." Jacob moved toward his dad and put his arm around him as they walked to the door.

"Whoa, that was intense," Claire whispered. I can't believe that is my son. He has matured beyond belief through his trial. I am so proud of him. He would never have been able to stand up to his dad that way before."

Jacob came back into the room and just gave us a big smile as if to say "all is well." None of us wanted to dwell on the scene we had just witnessed, so we sat back and took sips of our cold tea.

"Let's do one of our cooking frenzies," Claire spoke up. "Remember all those times we would get together with friends and we would all make our special dishes at once?"

Jacob perked up and said, "That sounds like fun. What could we make?"

"What is your favorite?" I asked.

"Humm, it's got to be peanut butter cookies," Jacob answered.

"Okay, that sounds good for desert, but we need something a little more savory for the main dish," Claire announced. "I want to make jambalaya."

"Yum! I love that," I said enthusiastically. "I will make a Cesar salad."

"No fair! That's too easy," Claire protested.

"Sorry, boss, that's all I can muster right now. Besides it *is* delicious," I declared.

Even though we were all physically tired, the idea of making some good food for each other motivated us to move to the kitchen. We all began our projects and did the kitchen dance as we maneuvered around each other. Before long, the aroma of cookies and sautéed peppers and sausage mingled in the air. As we sat down to enjoy our feast, a feeling of peace and safety settled over us. We laughed and teased; three souls in tune with each other and with God. It was a beautiful thing.

When the dishes were rinsed and in the dishwasher, we all retired to our rooms. By unspoken consent, we knew we each needed time alone with our Lord. I was too tired to read, so I just got ready for bed and lay back on the bed and focused on Jesus. I thought about that old song, "What a Friend We Have in Jesus." It was running through my mind. I was comforted by the thought that He was bearing all my cares. What a wonderful life to have a friend like that.

I woke up with the first light. I thought I had just dozed off, but it was morning. A new day. A very special new day.

I wandered into the kitchen to look for some coffee, and Claire was dressed for action. She was a girl on a mission. "Don't linger over that coffee, Joy. We have work to do today. I have everything planned out. You have an appointment at my favorite salon in one hour."

"I thought you were kidding about the makeover," I said.

"No way! Today is the first day of the rest of your life. It's a turning point. I just feel it," Claire shot back.

I could tell by the look on her face that she meant business. Without any more protest, I headed into the bathroom with my coffee in hand. One hour later, I was walking into a very exclusive looking spa/salon near Claire's home in Marin. Claire conferred with the coordinator at the front desk, and I just let myself be ushered into the depths of the atmospheric, all-purpose salon. For three hours, I was pampered. I had a massage, facial, manicure, pedicure and a shampoo, cut, and style. The stylist seemed to know just what hair style to create, with very little input from me. Claire had disappeared early on and came back carrying shopping bags as I was released from the styling station.

"I want to see the full effect," she said as she ushered me into a dressing room and laid out a beautiful blue dress, tan pumps and accessories.

"Claire, this is too much! These items must have cost a fortune, not to mention the spa day. I can't believe you are spending all this on me."

"Nonsense, you are the reason I have my son with me today. You and David saved him, not once, but twice. You also saved *me*, if you will recall," Claire argued.

"You're giving me too much credit. God was the orchestrator and director of all that David and I did. The Lord deserves all the credit," I reminded.

When I emerged from the dressing room and stood before the large mirror in the sitting area, I was overwhelmed. Claire radiated pride and clapped her hands. The transformation was impressive. The dress made my blue eyes stand out. The hair style perfectly framed my face. The dress was demure yet clung in all the right places to emphasize my best curves. The effort was worth it and I couldn't wait to be presented to David later on. I was sure that he would approve.

The rest of the day flew by. I changed back into my street clothes and Claire and I had lunch at a small deli. We walked around town and did some window shopping. We chatted and enjoyed each other's company as we had done so many times before, but now there seemed to be an even deeper bond. Our shared traumatic experiences had brought us closer.

When we made it back to the house, Jacob was sitting on the couch in the living room reading. He looked up and saw me, and his eyes widened.

"Wow! You look great! I guess you got ready for your date tonight. David is going to go bananas."

"Bananas? I hope that is a good thing," I asked.

"More than good, spectacular," Jacob proclaimed.

"Thanks, Jacob. Your seal of approval means a lot," I returned.

"Oh, David called by the way. He said everything is all set for tonight," Jacob added.

My relief was palpable. I was glad I had not endured three hours of intense attention for nothing.

After I hung up my new dress and put my shoes and things in my room, Claire and I settled in the kitchen around the large island and had a cup of tea. We talked as only good friends can do with ease and depth. I couldn't help but glance at the wall clock above the refrigerator now and then as the excitement built with every minute that passed. I finally excused myself and went to my room for a few minutes of quiet. I wanted to check in with the Lord. I had to agree with Claire. This night could be a turning point for me. Just thinking about David made butterflies swarm in my stomach. To be at last given the space to enjoy each other's company without threat or a compelling assignment, would be such a blessing. I wanted this evening to be our chance to just be a man and a woman on a date, but my spirit also knew that my future was being written in the process.

I prayed for clarity. I asked for discernment. I wanted to be sure that God was in every detail of our relationship. I prayed in the Spirit for a few minutes and felt the presence of the Holy Spirit. I also felt that His blessing was on this time with David. We were mature, and would not let our emotions override the will of the Father for both of our lives.

As the time neared for David's arrival, I carefully applied my makeup, fluffed my hair, and dressed in my new outfit. I was glad for the warm evening so that I would not have to wear anything over the stunning dress Claire had bought for me. The earrings and necklace were gorgeous. I felt like a princess. Now, I just needed my prince charming to arrive. Oh boy, was I setting myself up here. Calm down girl. I began talking to myself to get under control.

I heard the doorbell ring, and my adrenaline spiked off the charts. Staying calm was a real challenge. I heard Claire call from the front room. It was time for the big reveal.

When I walked into the room, I saw David standing in front of the big picture window. He had flowers in his hand. He was dressed in a suit and tie. He looked so handsome, I stopped short. His eyes grew very big and his mouth dropped open when he saw me. We stood like that for a few beats, when Jacob broke the spell.

"David Kramer, I would like to introduce you to Joy Morgan. You will be accompanying her to dinner tonight, and I expect that you both will have a wonderful time."

"Thanks, Jacob, I have great expectations myself. Although I will have a hard time fighting off all the other men we may encounter. Joy, you look amazing. I don't know what you did, but I highly approve," David finally found his voice.

"Claire treated me to a spa day." I had trouble coming up with an answer.

"Well, I would say that it was time well spent. Thank you, Claire," David said.

"You are welcome. Now are you two just going to stand there all night? You have places to go and food to eat. Let me take those flowers and put them in some water. Can I ask where you are going?" Claire asked.

"Fog Harbor, on the pier," David answered.

"Oh, good choice. Very romantic," Jacob piped up. David and I both blushed and moved toward the door quickly.

chapter 27

s we left Claire's home, David walked ahead and opened the door to his car for me. It was awkward. It was like we were characters in a new play. These roles felt very uncomfortable. Gone was the close camaraderie. I wanted to call foul but didn't want to embarrass David. I know that he was trying to make our night special.

We chatted about the weather and the traffic as we made our way to the Warf; amazingly enough, we found a place to park not far from the Fog Harbor restaurant. I put my arm in his as we strolled to the front door. It was a balmy evening. The smell of the sea was refreshing. The atmosphere of the Warf and the lights on the buildings created a welcoming invitation. We had reservations, and were right on time so, we were seated quickly. The table was perfect. The soft glow of the candles reflected in the window. Though the scene was dark, we still saw some lights shining on the water. It really was very romantic, but I couldn't shake the feeling that we were out of our element. This was not the role I could relate to. I was very nervous and could tell that David was too. I was searching for a way to break the ice.

Fortunately, the waiter arrived to take our drink orders. I asked for ice water with lemon and David his usual iced tea.

"You..." I started.

"This..." David started at the same time.

We both laughed, and I could feel the tension lessen. We had played these parts before.

"Look, I know that this is awkward. After all the time we spent together, here we are acting like strangers. I say we skip the formalities and just get back to being us."

"Yes, I thought you'd never ask. We really have a lot to talk about. Let's get back to common ground, the investigation," David said.

From that moment on, we were talking and relating like old times; we were just two friends out for a dinner with a chance to review the events that had brought us together. David brought me up to date on the official side of things: arrests, court proceedings, ongoing search for Rallen Mandu, and the final arrangements for Damien.

We were so involved with our conversation, the time flew by. Dinner was delicious but it really was not the main course. We were back in sync. David suggested a walk along the Warf, and we felt much more comfortable walking together than when we had first arrived. At one point, we stopped to watch a passing boat with lights and a party aboard. After it was out of sight, David turned to me and looked into my eyes.

"You must know how much I think of you. Our time together through thick and thin has been such a blessing. You have filled a big hole in my life. I can't think about you going back to Boise. We have to come up with a plan."

"I have been avoiding that reality myself. I want to let our relationship grow and see where it leads. I am so connected to you, that the minute I get on that plane, I'll feel like part of my heart is being torn out," I replied with a tear trying to spill on to my cheek.

"Oh, Joy! I feel the same way." David bent down and kissed me full on the lips.

A lightning bolt shot through my body. I thought that if I looked, there would be fireworks exploding over the bay. All the times that we had been so close and avoided getting too intimate, were fulfilled in that one kiss. Our spirits and souls melded. We kissed again and then embraced. I never wanted to let go.

When David left me at the door to Claire's home, I felt like I was walking on air as I crossed the living room floor. I was headed to my room, when I heard Claire's voice coming from the corner of the room. She was sitting in the dark, curled up in one of the big leather chairs. "You look positively dreamy. It must have been a good one."

"The best!" I answered *without* hesitation.

"So give me all the juicy details," Claire declared with her usual hint of mischief.

"We kissed," I replied, so much information in those two words.

"I knew it! He couldn't resist the new and improved Joy."

I gave an exasperated exhale as I sat down next to her in the other comfy chair. "He is not that shallow. That kiss was a long time coming."

"*That* kiss? Only one?" Claire was not through grilling me.

"That's all it took for me to know that David Kramer is everything I have ever wanted in a man."

"I mean, you didn't like make out in the car?" Claire was relentless.

"No! We held each other, and I really hated to let go. As dreamy as I feel right now, I can't help thinking that reality will be knocking on my door very soon."

"What do you mean?" Claire came back.

"We live in separate states. He has his career, I have mine. If we commit to the relationship, who is going to have to change? No doubt, it would be me, since the woman is always the one who gives in. You know me, Claire, I am pretty independent. Could I really give up my life to fit into David's?" My mood was quickly changing to one of doubt and despair.

"Uh-oh! Trouble in paradise already?" Claire stated the obvious.

"I just don't see a way forward. I don't see how two people like David and I can blend our lives and still be who we are."

"Stop looking at it from a win/lose perspective. Stand outside the box. What do you see?" Claire was challenging my assumptions.

We sat in silence for a while. I was trying to step outside of my gloomy assessment of my situation. As hard as I tried, I couldn't see the alternative that Claire was hinting at. I finally said good night and took myself to my bedroom. The air had gone out of my steps. My feet felt like lead weights. I just couldn't process my need for

David, and my need for my former life. All the scenes from those romantic movies played in my mind. The people find each other. They fall in love. Nothing can keep them apart. Happily ever after. Fade to black. The end. Why couldn't I abandon myself to these feelings I had for David? Why did I have to analyze it all? I tried to imagine my life in California. It really couldn't be like the last few weeks with David. We would have to settle into a new normal. Would that be enough after we had lived through such excitement and peril? Too many questions! I needed to sleep on it. If I could sleep at all.

I awoke feeling tired and groggy. I had finally gotten to sleep around two. I looked at the bed side clock and saw that it was seven. Five hours wasn't bad, but the quality of my sleep was questionable. In my dreams, I was constantly being challenged by evil forces, frustration at every turn. I wanted to go back to sleep and rewrite those dreams, but I knew that a new day was ahead; a day that could change my life forever.

When I entered the kitchen, Claire was pouring a cup of coffee. "Here, you look like you could use this."

"That bad?"

"I'm not surprised after the way you were trying to figure everything out last night. You know, some things are better left to unfold naturally rather than forcing the issue." Claire's targeted comment was exasperating. She always could read me.

"I guess being a planner has its draw backs."

"So what's the next *plan*?" Her emphasis on the key word was dripping with sarcasm.

"I've got to get back to Boise. There are so many things I need to attend to."

"That's a good way to sidestep a decision. Blame it on duty." Claire kept the pressure on.

"I need time and space to weigh all the options."

All I got from Claire was an eye roll, and I let it go. I felt too vulnerable to get into the deeper reasons for my hesitation to make a bold move.

I called and made a reservation for a flight home the next day. Home? What did that mean to me now? I was hardpressed to envision my life in Idaho without David or in California without my job, friends, and family. Did one outweigh the other? I had not even gotten a commitment from David. Maybe this whole dilemma was unwarranted.

I would just go back home and see if the bond we had would span the miles. Yes, that was the right thing to do. It would be a test. Suddenly, I felt relieved that I had made a decision. Maybe this is what it meant to let things unfold naturally. I only hoped that David would feel the same way.

"There's someone here to see you," Jacob called from the front room.

I put down the paring knife and wiped my hands on the dish towel next to the salad bowl I had been filling. I had volunteered to make dinner while Clare worked in her office. When I turned from the kitchen counter, David was standing in the archway.

"I didn't hear from you today. So I just came over. I hope that's okay?" he said as he shifted his weight and tried to look comfortable.

"Oh! I've been busy. I have to pack and help Claire clean. I'll be heading back to Boise tomorrow," I explained.

A combination of surprise and disappointment crossed his face. He quickly recovered with a tight smile. "So soon? I hoped we could have a few more quiet days together. I know we have spent many hours in each other's company, but there were so many demands and distractions."

I stood in silence. I didn't know what to say. Now, I felt like I was rejecting him. All I could think to do was change the subject. "Will you stay for dinner? I am making my very special dish, moussaka. It's really just eggplant lasagna, but the name gives it more class." I was trying to lighten the mood, but the effort fell a bit flat.

"Of course, I wouldn't miss a chance to try your *very special dish*. It sounds exotic," David replied, and his acceptance to dinner was a relief.

"Is there anything I can do to help?" he asked.

"It's almost ready. I'm just finishing off the salad. I guess you could spread this garlic butter on the Italian bread over there." I handed the dish of butter to him.

As he took the dish, our hands touched. We lingered, and the look we shared was warm and loving. David put the dish down on the counter and went to the sink and washed his hands. He took up a position opposite me across the island counter and started to butter the bread. We exchanged a few words of light conversation, but mostly just enjoyed the company.

I called everyone to the table, and when Claire came out of her office, she was visibly surprised to see David. She recovered quickly and gave him a welcoming hug. We sat and enjoyed the aromas coming from the food before us. Jacob said a prayer of thanks and blessing, and we all dove into the meal. The talk at the table was easy and full of meaning that could only come from friends that had endured difficult times together. David shared an update on the arraignment of the guards from the Ashland group. Jacob gave a report on the group of OH members who had just found the Lord. They were planning to attend Rock Church on Sunday. We all celebrated *that* news. It was so exciting to see the fruit of the Lord's intervention in the lives of the people we had seen as enemies not long ago.

"I also have some news about the disposition of Rallen's holdings and assets," David announced. "He was able to disappear with funds from his many bank accounts, but his property will be sold, and the proceeds will be awarded to Jacob and Claire. As the victims of his recent crimes, they are entitled to compensation."

There was a stunned silence at the table. We all looked at David for more information and confirmation of his statement.

It was Jacob that broke the silence first. "That can only be God. I am sure we are not the only ones who were harmed by Mandu's misdeeds, but we are the ones who are in the right position to funnel those funds into the Kingdom. I was wondering how we would help the One Humanity members move on with their lives. I have been talking to Ashley in Ashland," Jacob paused. "Ha! I never really put that one together. It seems that she is where she belongs. Anyway, she has some challenges there as well. The spiritual restorations are amazing among the members there, but with the limited economic opportunities in the area, some of them are struggling financially. I know that God has some creative strategies for them, and now I see how he intends to manifest them."

"It may take time to see the funds released," David explained. "I don't see any reason why you can't start planning for your windfall."

We were all energized by the news from all corners of the old One Humanity domain. We kicked around ideas for new businesses and ministries. When we finished eating, we joyously bustled around the kitchen and made quick work of the cleanup. Jacob and Claire made excuses for their departures from the group. Claire was still working on a project in her office. Jacob wanted to write down some ideas the Lord was giving him about the next phase of his work with the members of the Ashland and Rock Church ministries.

David and I made our way to the cozy couch in the living room. We sat quietly for a time, just looking out the big picture window at the lights. David shifted his position and put his arm around me. A cascade of warmth went through me. I loved his closeness and his gentle comfort. I just wanted to stay that way forever, but I knew we had some important matters to discuss.

I broke the silence first. "I love your company. I only wish our circumstances were different. Living in two distant states makes the next steps difficult."

"Love finds a way." David's statement was short but powerful.

"I guess I am too practical. I keep trying to figure things out. I want our relationship to grow and continue, but I also feel a duty to return to my career and life in Boise." I was laying out my concerns.

"God brought us together. He knows the beginning from the end. If it is His will for us to be together, don't you think He can make it happen?" David left the loaded question hanging between us.

I couldn't answer the question. I was stuck on that word "IF." Did it imply a lack of commitment on David's part?

"You have decided to go back to your life up north. I can't interfere with your will. I can only tell you that I love you and see us together," David said with conviction.

He said it! There was no denying the clarity of his words. Was I selfish for wanting him to change his life for me? Would I have to be the one to make the accommodations that would allow us to pursue a future together?

I turned toward him and looked him in the eye. "David, I love you too. I just can't see a path forward right now. I have to go back to my life and sort things out."

He wrapped his arms around me and enfolded me in an embrace that melted all my resistance. Our lips met and we drank each other in.

I laid my head on his shoulder and we sat in complete rest. I let go of all my questions and just embraced the moments that we still had together.

I watched David walk down the driveway to his car. I kept watching as his car drove out of sight down the street. A profound sense of loss overcame all the feelings I had just shared with him. As we parted, there was no planning for the next day. I didn't know when I would see David again.

I went to my room and prepared for bed. I wasn't sure I could sleep, but I wanted to rest and just lift my feelings up to the Lord. I lay on the bed and envisioned lifting all my questions, worries, and emotions up to heaven. "You take all this, Father. I can't carry it. I give it to you." As I released my burden to the Lord, I felt a blanket of peace. The comfort of the Holy Spirit surrounded me and I drifted off to sleep.

I was walking on a pathway. It was beautiful. Trees, grass and flowers were lining the sides. I was enjoying the breeze and the bird songs. I was happy. Soon the path began to change. It became rocky and steep. I kept climbing, compelled to follow the path. The air was colder the wind was stronger. Soon all I could do was focus on each step as I ascended. I didn't know what lay ahead. Suddenly I heard a voice. It was familiar, but it was not reassuring. I looked up, and I was on a very narrow track up the side of a mountain. There was a sheer cliff on my right hand side. It reminded me of the pathway on Mount Diablo. As that thought passed through my mind, I saw a vision. It was a man floating in the air, level with my position on the track. He was covered in a bright light. He was beckoning me to come to him. At first I was attracted to him and then the reality of what he wanted, startled me. I knew that I would not be able to float like him. If I followed his directions, I would fall to my death on the mountain. I cried out, NO! And as I did, his aspect changed, and dark shadows fell across his face and body. I could make out his features. It was Rallen Mandu. He had come to claim me, but I knew that he had no power to do so. I felt a presence next to me on the path. I looked and there was a large golden warrior angel standing by my side. He took out his sword and advanced toward Rallen. One flash of his sword and Mandu vanished. The angel took me up in his arms and we floated to the top of the mountain. He set me down on a vantage point where I could see for miles. There were many pathways and roads that led off into the distance. The angel pointed to one path and I stepped forward to follow it.

I awoke feeling refreshed. I remembered my dream and took the time to jot it down in my journal. I knew it was significant. God would set my feet on the right path. I had nothing to fear. Even as I made my plans to go back to my old life, I knew in my heart there was a new pathway before me. I also knew David would join me on that journey. We had some unfinished business with Rallen Mandu. Or was it *Milo Ripley*? He probably had a new name and a new scam already. Our mission to put him out of business was not complete. I didn't know where that quest would lead us, but I knew that God had not rescinded his mandate. David and I made a powerful team and God had work for us to do.

I reluctantly headed to the bathroom to shower and begin my preparations for my trip back to Boise. Claire said that she would drive me to the San Francisco airport. My flight left at one. David had not said anything about accompanying me to my flight. In fact, there was nothing said about future plans the night before. I felt a void. It was very difficult for me to let go of expectations. This was new ground for me. I knew that it would challenge me to lean on the Lord more than ever.

"How are you feeling this morning?" Claire asked as she handed me my favorite cup full of coffee, cream, and honey, just the way I liked it.

"There are so many emotions warring inside of me, I couldn't even start to unravel them."

"How did you leave things with David last night?" Claire's concern was evident in her countenance.

"Open ended. He is mature enough not to try to force anything, but I know that he is not happy with my decision to go back home without any plan for our future together."

"Ouch! That's got to hurt. What are you going to do now?" Claire *would* have to ask that particular question.

"I'm doing it. I'm going back to Boise and fulfilling my contract to teach fifth grade at Valley View School. I have built a life in Idaho. I can't just turn my back on all of that. If David and I are meant to be together, the Lord will have to work out the details."

"What do you mean *if?*" Claire's voice increased in both volume and pitch on that last word.

"I mean, that I am leaving it in God's hands. I love David, and I want to be with him, but all the rest just leaves me confused and apprehensive."

"A word to the wise, don't let indecision keep you from acting on something that you have always wanted. David is a prize worth fighting for."

Leave it to Claire to hit the nail on the head. She was a master at stating the obvious. Her last bit of advice jolted me into a new perspective. What price love?

The rest of the morning was a whirlwind of activity. We had to be at the airport two hours early. That did not leave much time to finish packing and loading the car. Jacob had said his good bye the night before. He had a meeting at the church this morning. Claire and I managed to get to the airport in time, and we said our good bye at the curb. How could I thank her for all she had done for me? How could we express the depth of our friendship and the intensity of what we had experienced together? We couldn't, so we just held each other and wept.

My heart was full and heavy as I watched her leave. I rolled my suitcase into the building and was startled when a hand reached out to take my bag. It was David! My tears started up again as I fell into his arms.

We finally parted, and David said, "I couldn't let you spend your last hours in California by yourself."

"Thank you! I am so surprised and delighted that you came to see me off."

"Let's get you checked in, and then go get some coffee," David suggested.

We made our way to the concourse and found a quiet table in the corner of a court yard coffee shop. I was so happy to see David, that I had a hard time finding the words I needed to express my emotions. I finally just said, "Your showing up today means a lot to me. I can see that you are willing to go the extra mile to make us work. Claire said something last night that really shifted my perspective."

"I hope it was in my direction," David smiled.

"Yes, she pointed out that my indecision should not spoil the love we have for each other."

"Good for you, Claire. My feeling exactly. I have every confidence in our ability to overcome any obstacles on the road to our life together."

I let that sink in for a moment. I loved his positive affirmation and his vision of "our life together." All I could do in response was to reach out and take his hand. Our connection was like molten electricity, warm and exciting. How could I just get on a plane and leave that behind?

David finally broke the silence. "I have registered for a forensics conference in Salt Lake City in September. I plan to take a few vacation days after the event and drive up to Boise to see a certain school teacher I know there."

"Oh, David! That is fantastic. I *so* look forward to having you on my stomping grounds. We will have a wonderful time. I am so glad we have something like this to look forward to. You are so amazing. I love you more with every one of your surprises."

"You like surprises? I will have to see what else I can do," he teased.

"Only good ones." We both laughed.

We sat and sipped our coffee and talked for a while. Then I looked at my watch and saw that it was time to go to the gate for my flight. David walked me to the gate area and then stood with me while the boarding was called. Just before I was due to join the line, he took me in his arms and kissed me good. We ignored the OOOs and AHHs around us. I was in heaven and couldn't have cared less that we had made a scene. One last quick kiss and David said, "See you in September."

About the Author

Patricia Carroll is a former member of a new-age communal organization; she has firsthand knowledge of how "even the elect" can be drawn to the realm of alternative spiritual pursuits. For twelve years, she devoted her life to a Berkeley, California, counterfeit religion. But on one destined night in a church in Boise, Idaho, Jesus appeared to her and beckoned her back home. She uses many of her own memorable experiences in her story that give it a solid foundation.

She did return to her home in Idaho and pursued her career in early childhood education. After dedicating years to young children and training adults, she is now pursuing her passion for writing.

CPSIA information can be obtained
at www.ICGtesting.com
Printed in the USA
LVHW092033070721
691954LV00001BA/102